Lenore And The Problem With Love

John Blossom

Published by J.T. Blossom, 2019.

LENORE AND THE PROBLEM WITH LOVE

First edition. December 13, 2019.

Written by John Blossom.

In loving memory of my grandfather, Elmer Byron Hough, who first showed me the awe-inspiring and mysterious power of creativity and music.

"When by mutation a new rose is born in a garden, all the gardeners rejoice. They isolate the rose, tend it, foster it. But there is no gardener for men. This little Mozart will be shaped like the rest by the common stamping machine. This little Mozart will love shoddy music in the stench of night dives. This little Mozart is condemned...

...Only the Spirit, if it breathe upon the clay, can create Man."

Antoine de Saint-Exupéry, Wind, Sand and Stars / A memoir, 1939

tr. Lewis Galantiere

"BLESSED ARE THE MEEK, for they shall inherit the earth."
Mathew 5:5-9

Lenore And The Problem With Love

A Novel by J.T. Blossom
Copyright © 2019 J.T. Blossom All Rights Reserved

CHAPTER ONE

The counselor's door flew open before I even touched the knob, and a large man in a white lab coat stood there smiling eerily. Startled, I jumped back with Brandon, stuffed my hands into the pockets of my jeans, and took a deep breath. The doctor's frizzy white hair made him look a little like Einstein, or the guy with the bogus-looking time machine in that old movie, "Back to the Future." A sweet wave of Enlightenment washed out of the red-lit office and hit our nostrils and mingled pleasantly with the aromas from Comey's Coffee Shop downstairs. The counselor didn't seem to notice at all that he had startled us.

"Oh good, you're both here! Pardon the incense. I can't help myself. Enlightenment doesn't do anything significant for me anymore, but I just really like the smell, you know? It helps me keep my head straight and my memories fresh! I'm Dr. Pendleton. Sorry about the unorthodox greeting. I can't afford a receptionist, but I did hear your footsteps! Come in, please, come in!"

I laughed inwardly at the coincidence that Enlightenment was developed by my father after he left the same lab at Brecken University where Brandon and I now worked and studied, but Brandon just snorted sarcastically and said, "You did Enlightenment, eh? Well, at least we know then that this explore-your-feelings gig of yours is really how your inner soul wants to waste your life."

My jaw dropped, but Brandon had warned me. He had said he was too busy for this, but I had insisted he come to this. I didn't really like forcing him, but couples counseling was not going to help us get along better if he copped an attitude. Brandon knows very well that my dad's pot product *does indeed* help people find their life's passions just like its name implies, so why was he being this way?

"I rather like to think of exploring feelings as what makes life *not* a waste, but no matter," replied Dr.Pendleton, not the least bit fazed. "You're right, though, young man, and good guess! Enlightenment *did* help me know for sure that psychology is my calling. Amazing stuff, don't you think? Like from another dimension!"

He stood aside and gestured for us to come inside, chuckling like our arrival was the best part of his day. Brandon moved past him but kept a snarky expression on his face. "Sit anywhere, please," said Dr. Pendleton. "No couches here! I long ago rejected Freud's ridiculous couches and his short-sighted and depressing pessimism. It's all Jung or noth-

ing around here, my friends!" Dr. Pendleton's laugh was high
and paired convincingly with his manic appearance.

I smiled at him and followed Brandon across the thresh-
old into his office. There was no smile on Brandon's face. His
torso was tight and his biceps were flexing.

There was a circle of worn Lazy-Boy recliners, so I naturally chose the one that allowed me to look out of the only
window in the otherwise Persian-carpeted and dark-paneled
room. Brandon chose the one across from me with his back
to the window while Dr. Pendleton shut the door and flung
himself down in the recliner between us. His lab coat didn't
quite follow him fully into the recliner, but he didn't bother
to straighten it out any more than he bothered to brush his
hair this morning or shave. Already I liked him. His enthusiasm and earthy disregard for personal grooming reminded me of the favorite men in my life: Dad, for one, who had
a ragged ponytail; his winemaker friend, Bill whom Brandon and I worked for last summer; and also a few of the vet-
eran teachers at our old boarding school, Wandering Pines.
I could tell, though, from Brandon's judgmental expression
and head-shaking that so far he wasn't impressed.

Dr. Pendleton's kooky but genuine smile was illuminated
mainly by the light from the window. The only other light in
the room cutting the darkness was a Tiffany lamp that cast a
red glow on a little table next to the door. I saw gentle smoke
emerging from an infuser next to its base and recognized it as
one of my Dad's latest models. I wondered if it really was just
incense cooking away in there. It smelled like the real stuff to
me.

"So, from your holotext, I gather you are here for consultation on how to survive Brecken mind games and horse crap," said Pendleton.

"You don't like Brecken?" said Brandon, his biceps flexing even harder.

"Of course, I like Brecken, and I happen to know that the program at the bio lab is doing incredibly important work. That doesn't mean the institution doesn't fling a manure-spreader load of horse pucky at you on a daily basis. It's a university, after all. It's to be expected. How are you coping with it?"

"I'm coping with it just fine, thank you," said Brandon. "And I don't agree it's horse pucky. What's *flung* at us are opportunities and challenges. We're here because Ella's just not rising up to them, that's all. If it weren't for me, she would have flunked out long ago."

"Is that true, Ella?" asked Dr. Pendleton, his eyes lingering on Brandon. He turned for my answer, his expression suddenly serious.

"We're a team. He helps me study sometimes. So what? I'm trying as hard as I can."

"What do you mean you're a team? Are you married?"

"No," I continued. "But we live together. It's recent public knowledge, among those who give a crap, that we raised and freed the first quantum-augmented animals into the wild. You know, the new San Rafael Preserve?" Dr. Pendleton nodded. "We applied to the quantum lab program after the preserve went through last summer, and we got in. We're just freshmen, but the Brecken lab needed us and our notoriety as much as we needed Brecken."

"Does Brecken believe that, or is that *your* belief?"

"Ella and I were very lucky to get chosen," piped in Brandon. "The whole thing was luck, really. We both adopted the Brecken lab's cast-off experimental dogs by accident when we were in high school. Then we were just in the right place at the right time at Wandering Pines Academy to be the catalyst to actuate their incredible and unexpected development. But now luck won't cut it anymore. We've got to prove ourselves. The news buzz has faded about the preserve, and Ella doesn't realize that the lab doesn't really need us unless we can actually contribute to the science behind what they created. It's a graduate program, and we're mere undergrads. It's challenging."

"Hence, the horse crap, I see," said the Doctor. "They have all the power."

"Right. They are the masters right now, whether we like it or not. Ella doesn't get that, obviously."

My fingers start tingling sharply, a clear sign that I was missing my psychic fiddle, Lenore, who speaks to me when I'm upset with the guiding spirit of my granddad. This was intense. Aren't therapy sessions supposed to start off slowly? I guess not in Dr. Mad Scientist's office, and with Brandon being his I'm-always-right self as usual, so I decided to salvage my dignity as best I could and just go ahead and say what was on my mind. "You are so full of it, Brandon. There's more to life than *masters and slaves*, and I *get* way more than you give me credit for." My fingers closed into fists, and I had to force my teeth to stop grinding.

Brandon was not backing down. "Then why don't you *get* with the program? There are two tests tomorrow and have you even opened *one* book to prepare for them? No!"

"I told you, Bryson and Vern are not on the right track. Testing us on facts and things that are already known that can be easily blinked on our phoneglasses is a waste of psychic energy. Somehow, you can tolerate those kinds of things, not me."

"You're so stubborn! Psychic energy has nothing to do with it. That's just the way it is. We're not campers at Wandering Pines anymore. This is *college*. You need knowledge, in your *head*, not just on your phoneglasses, to find wisdom," said Brandon.

"That's *your* mantra. Wisdom comes from all kinds of places, including Wandering Pines, which was a pretty good school, psychically and otherwise, and you know it. It may just be a no-name prep school in the boonies to you now, but the hills alone taught us more than this sterile excuse for a college."

I really needed to calm down, but how could Brandon dare discount everything we learned there together? I loved who he was at our old boarding school. He was so open and caring. What happened to the guy who loved animals and nature more than he loved himself? I looked out the window and squeezed the leather arms of my recliner.

Dr. Pendleton twisted a strand of his blond hair and inserted it in his mouth. He took it out and pointed its wet end at Brandon. "Brandon, what do you really want to do right now?"

"You mean with my so-called life?"

"No, I mean literally right now."

"Go study, and think about the mp3 quantum sessions coming up tomorrow for the subjects."

"Then why don't you go and focus on that important work. Ella, can you stay a little longer? I want to hear more of what you have to say about your particular sources of wisdom." Pendleton stood up and Brandon did too, surprised and visibly relieved. Pendleton moved toward the door.

"Brandon, thanks for coming. It's been a pleasure meeting you, and congratulations on the research work you and Ella are doing. All of us are counting on that lab, whether the world or the bureaucracy of the university realizes it or not, and you're sure to be successful. We'll reconnect at a later session, perhaps." He shook his hand.

"Okay, Dr. Pendleton. Fine by me. See you at home, Ella, or at the lab if you *make it* back there."

"I'll *make it* back there, but take my babies for a walk today, please, if I'm late." Brandon's opened the door letting in the harsh light from the hallway.

"Sure, a *walk*," he said over his shoulder. "That's important *if and only if* Bryson asks me to do that." He shut the door firmly behind him, and I took a deep breath of Dr. Pendleton's incense.

"Both of you are off the charts brilliant, aren't you?" Dr. Pendleton said, smiling and settling back into his recliner after Brandon's strong footsteps faded down the hallway.

"I guess. Brandon is anyway."

"Oh, and you are too, I can tell, and I agree that your energy is quite different than his. Your guiding sources are more, shall I say, *holistic*. Do you love him, this bulldog of a boyfriend you have?"

I heard his question and my fingertips tingled as I thought about the history of our relationship, how it was true that I hardly paid attention to him when I first got to Wandering Pines because of his bulldog appearance and mannerisms even though he was the only one there who spoke honestly about himself and his passionate interest in helping animals. Then my whole body shivered as I remembered last year, our senior year at Wandering Pines, and how my feelings changed toward him. I remembered playing Lenore in the school's garden when her magic was in full bloom. How Brandon was playing his banjo, and it was the night I first realized I loved him despite all his quirks. The tunes Lenore played for us in that garden, oh my! She literally gave me psychic permission to make love and guided me into Brandon's arms. Then we flew on horses in a shared orgasm with nature. It was the most romantic experience so far in my whole life.

Then I remembered every detail about afterward helping him achieve his plan to release the abusive neighboring rap star's captive and starving lions, and our shared feelings of sadness and fulfillment when our beloved dogs, Jenny and Max, chose to guide the lion couple away from Renegade into their new life together as a inter-species family in the San Rafael Wilderness. Because of all those amazing things that happened, we got to witness the creation of nothing less than a new order of nature.

Finally, I remembered our excitement at the word leaking out about what happened, the sanctuary being created, and us being invited to come study at Brecken. Things un-raveled between us only when the academics under Professor Bryson started getting serious.

"Do I love him? I suppose you could say that," I said with a sigh.

"But it's faded?"

"Isn't that what happens to all couples? That's what I read, anyway."

"Well, sometimes it does happen, usually when pressures mount, kids arrive, and unforeseen challenges of life get in the way, but it doesn't have to be that way."

"How? How can it not have to be that way? We don't even have any kids yet, and it's *already* happening!" I was up-set, but something in Dr. Pendleton's eyes made me trust him despite his challenging and invasive questions.

"When you nurture the individual connections and pas-sions that originally fueled your coupling, then a partnership can grow and evolve. Have you given anything up recently that was a source of strength to you guys in the past?"

Now my fingertips were really on fire, and I remembered the sound of Brandon strumming his banjo. A lump formed in my throat. It's been a long time since I've heard that. All he does now outside of school is self-readings with his tarot deck.

"I still play a lot, but we haven't made any music *together* since last summer at the winery," I said. "I play the fiddle."

Pendleton looked at my restless hands. "The fiddle, huh? Try something for me, would you please? Show me how you hold your instrument," he said gently. "Just pretend it's here. It doesn't matter that it isn't. Do you mind showing me? It might be good to do that right now with Brandon freshly departed. You play it often when he's gone away from you, right?"

I paused. "Not *it*, Lenore," I finally said, whispering to Pendleton as much as to her, and he's right that I play her a lot when I am lonely and things aren't going well. "Her name's Lenore." I looked out the window at the blue sky above the warehouse across the street. I hated being stuck in this university town of metal and concrete. What happened to all the trees? Pendleton nodded encouragingly.

I raised my arms to hold Lenore's imaginary body in my hands. I felt a little silly, but Pendleton's instincts were right to ask me to do this now. Even though it was just pretend, it felt like I was pulling shivering arms from cold quicksand and thrusting them into the cleansing warmth of the heavens. My left hand curled perfectly over Lenore's smooth neck. I felt with relief the energy of her strings even as I looked Pendleton directly in his eyes. As I played, I closed my eyes, and I saw myself kneeling on the banks of a large slow river. My fingers were ancient Hindu saints caressing the power of lotus flowers before releasing their petals into the current of the Ganges. Petals floated off my fingers with each note like a promise.

"Ah, the music," whispered the doctor, listening.

"Yes," I said.

"I can hear it," he said. "It's bluegrass. The fiddle, I mean Lenore, and something else ..."

"Brandon plays the banjo, or he did," I said.

"Yes! The fiddle is the key, the banjo a backup, like logic to intuition." He listened for a moment to the imaginary music, then sighed. "Okay, you can release her now."

I put my hands back into my lap. Did we really hear the same thing? I felt the spirit of Lenore fly away from me back across buildings and busy city streets to the familiar sanctuary of her tattered case in our apartment. Now, there were not just tingles in my fingers. In the aftermath of her music, fire had erupted in my abdomen. Did Lenore and Dr. Pendleton just hypnotize me or something?

Dr. Pendleton sighed and cracked his own fingers. "I think that's enough for today," he said, looking at me carefully. "But I'm going to give you an assignment."

"An assignment, huh? Will there be a test? Because I really have enough of those in my life right now." I shifted my body in the Lazy Boy, and the fire abated a little bit into something distinctly more pleasurable, maybe a mental release of tension like I get sometimes when I talked with Dad. I trusted this Pendleton. There was more to him than meets the eye. Who knows why, but whatever he's going to give me to do will help, I think. There's some connection between us. Perhaps he was a friend of my Dad's, or maybe he's old enough to have known my Grandfather?

"No worries. No tests from me, and you'll do fine enough on tomorrow's tests, by the way, I am sure of that. Brandon needs to be perfect at them, but you're beyond needing challenges in the same way that he does. Nor does he really need you to need challenges in the same way he does, although he can't see that right now. He sees you as an extension of himself, not unusual in a bulldog. He'll come around.

Be patient with him. He loves you. It's a worthwhile partnership. You'll study enough tonight to pass, but the real work you have to do is *your* work, not yours and Brandon's. When you meet them, all these Brecken challenges and horse pucky will fall back into the balance that is your soulful life. Brecken will suck up only the energy you decide to give to it to receive what you need from the experience to progress." As he spoke, I remembered my grandfather saying almost the exact same thing to me about going to elementary school a long time ago.

I looked at Pendleton's eyes in the darkened room, but his face had morphed, and I saw my beautiful grandfather sitting there instead. But only for a moment. I wiped away a single tear from my left eye and Pendleton was back. Lenore does things like that to my mind sometimes. So does my old golden retriever Jenny, as a matter of fact. Most of the time I have control over what I see and hear, but sometimes I most definitely do not.

"Okay. Sounds good, but is this something I should discuss with Brandon?" Somehow, I felt the need to whisper this, like to talk out loud would ruin a spell of some sort.

"You can or not, as you choose, but personally I wouldn't waste the time and energy. He has a warrior's focus right now. Let him do his thing. It's admirable and possibly necessary what he's doing there at that quantum lab. He'll come around to you again when you regain your strength. The important thing for you right now is to do my assignment."

"Okay, Doc. I'm all in. Spill. What do you want me to do?"

"Get a gig playing Lenore downstairs in Comey's."

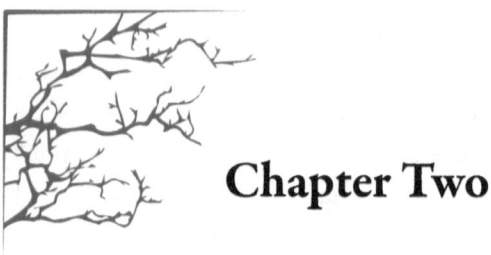

Chapter Two

COFFEE. WHY DO PEOPLE still insist it's not a drug? My mother is a successful artist in Harbor View and drinks complicated lattes literally all day long. I used to think it was just because she liked rolling up her sleeves and tat-chatting with her friends in the Starbucks line, but I now understand the physical addiction. When I first started playing here at Comey's, I took full advantage of the free cups for performers, but then my better Enlightenment sense took over, and now I only want coffee occasionally for the taste. The drug doesn't always work one hundred percent of the time that way for everyone, but when you do Enlightenment, it almost always prevents you from wanting or needing to do drugs ever again. Good thing these days. Classes at the lab never go so well when you don't sleep because you're wired on Comey French Roast from the night before.

Following Pendleton's order was easy in one sense. Comey's has an open-mike every night. Sign up and play. That's it. No try-outs or agents needed. The hard part was right now in front of the microphone. I've been playing every night for three weeks, and you'd think it would get less nerve-wracking the more I bare myself to the eye-boring scrutiny and musical judgment of complete strangers, but sadly it was still terrifying like those dreams where you are stupidly and self-consciously naked while interviewing for an important job or meeting your boyfriend's family for the first time.

Lenore's mind seemed to be focused elsewhere too. I mean once I start playing her, she goes through the motions well enough, and the tunes rock, but I kept expecting to float out of the window and over the ocean for a little flight with her over the bay, and it just never happens like that in this coffee shop. It's a little disappointing, but controlling her is like controlling inspiration – good luck. Sometimes I fly with her and sometimes I don't. She obviously has a mind of her own. For a while I thought the no-flying thing might be because Brandon wasn't playing his banjo with me, but I couldn't test that theory because he refuses to do any-thing but study, care for the test animals, do tarot readings on himself, pet Sybil, and lift barbells in our living room. He tried once to talk me out of Pendleton's assignment for me at Comey's when I asked him to cover my night shifts at the lab, but after I passed all my tests with high B's and paid for our next three month's rent in advance from my trust fund, he backed off.

I looked out over tonight's crowd. As usual it was bigger than the night before. I can't tell if it was my act they liked, or the combination of comedians and other musicians on the program, but the crowds kept getting bigger and bigger, and the manager kept upping the length of my gigs. I don't let it go to my head. If anyone was responsible for it, it was Lenore.

I lifted Lenore to my chin and positioned her in front of the microphone. I noticed the manager turning away people at the door. One of them was a bald administrative-type guy whom I vaguely recognized from Brecken. Somehow, despite his advancing middle age and un-hipster attire, the guy talked his way inside and found a place leaning against the table with the recycled paper napkins and cream and sugar dispensers.

I never know ahead of time what Lenore is going to choose for a set. Tonight she guided my fingers through "Big Sciota," "Cherokee Shuffle," "The Girl I Left Behind," "Laughing Boy," "Take Me Back to Georgia," and a modal tune without a name I heard one time on a YouTube hologram. People were a little dazed at first as they took it in. This usually happens – old time tunes are not the usual coffee shop fare – but by the end everyone was clapping and stomping their feet. I encored with "Year of Jubilo," "Cripple Creek," and "Sally Anne." I finally stopped and people were beaming. The room smelled of Enlightenment rather than of coffee to me now, but, as usual, I didn't see anybody smoking anything. Lenore messes with my olfactory senses that way too sometimes, just like my old golden retriever Jenny used to do. I rubbed my nose with the back of my hand and moved to the side of the stage to make room for the next performer.

"Nice tonight." It was the barista manager also rubbing their nose - unlike mine, they have a bunch of rings in it that itch a lot, I think. They ran their hand through their purple and orange hair and handed me a decaf. Their name is Kanda.

"Thanks," I said. Kanda's always trying to get me to go out with them after their shift, but I told them I was with a hot banjo player and unavailable. Kanda's a sweet person underneath all the hardware, but I'm not sure I could deal with the pronoun thing on a long-term basis. Also, I'm a pretty committed sis-gendered hetero, so I'm sure they would get bored with me fast on a date.

I noticed the balding guy at the condiment table was squeezing his way through the crowd toward me, but before he could reach me, a hot guy in his thirties dressed in jeans snuck up on me as I put Lenore back into her ragged case. I hadn't noticed him before when we were playing. Was he behind me somewhere?

"That's some fine fiddling," he said to me smiling. His teeth were amazing – just the right amount of white without being blinding. The razor shadow on his strong jaw made his blue eyes sparkle even in the darkened cafe. My breathing stopped a moment as I took him in. I know I shouldn't be so affected by things like physical appearance, but I am, so I guess you'll have to shoot me. He's gorgeous, and I'm human.What can I say?

"Well, that's nice of you to say." I smiled at him and returned to my battle with the worn zipper on the violin case. I should get a new case, but this antique canvas one still smelled like my grandfather. He gave me this case and Lenore a long time ago when he died, so I never want to let any part of it go even though the new cases are far better.

"Made me mighty glad I drifted in here to hear y'all. Hey, I'm coming back tomorrow night. You playing again?"

"It's kind of my assignment," I said. I stood up with the case in my hand. Now that he was clearly interested in me, I've sort of lost interest in him.

He laughed. "Well, your teacher knows how to make school fun, then." He reached into his back pocket and handed me a holocard. "Save me a few minutes tomorrow after your set for a cup-a, will you?"

I looked at the card. The background glowed with the Nashville skyline with floating musical notes popping up everywhere. "Lawrence Pinchbeck Agency – Representing Top Talent" it holo-ed. Interest reignited, I looked up at him. He smiled at me and casually stepped back into the crowd. His hair was thick and stylishly long.

As I digested this development, the bald guy in the suit I noticed earlier finally made it through the crowd to the side of the stage. His phoneglasses were hanging from his neck on a red Brecken holder, and I could tell his camera had been on. I hate people who record everything, but what are you going to do? Glasses-shooting is kind of the tech opiate of the masses these days. "Hi," he said. "You're Ella Bradley, right?" I tore my eyes away from a last glimpse of the Nashville guy's amazing physique and looked at this inadequate replacement.

"It's on the play schedule," I said. I stuffed the agent's holocard safely in the pocket of my jeans. Suited bald guy wanted to talk more, unfortunately. "I don't mean to be rude," I went on with him hastily, "but I need to think about something interesting that just happened, and I am in no mood for another lonely college town hanger-on trying to smother a middle-aged crisis with a bar pick-up, if that's what you're after."

"Oh," he said, looking around at the young crowd. "Didn't mean to give you that impression. You get a lot of those? I'm Osho Hannsen from the Dean's office."

"Okay," I said, looking at him more closely. "Something wrong?"

"No, no. Well, *I* don't think so, but I was sent here to give you a message. You don't seem to be checking your campus email lately."

"It's a crime not to check Brecken email obsessively? Most of it is junk, and I've been kinda busy." I picked up Lenore and held her in front of my chest to block his recording.

"Of course. Actually, my mission is to do a little recon *and* deliver a message. I was sent by President Mitchell." Why did he look apologetic?

"Huh? You're kidding. The President has a message for *me*? Why?"

"Well, I just think you'd better please just give his office a call tomorrow morning and set up an appointment." He didn't say anything else.

"That's it? You came all the way from campus to my gig to call me into the principal's office? Come on, what gives? I'm a nothing undergrad!"

"Well, I'm not supposed to say anything, but I guess you could say it has to do with admissions and enrollment. Just make the appointment, okay? My job, such as it is, kind of depends on it." He turned around meekly and left.

"Um, okay," I said. He nodded, not looking back, and I watched him disappear back into the crowd just like the Nashville agent, only this dweeb was a lot easier to track in the crowd because of his shiny bald head. Weird night. I made sure Pinchbeck's card was secure in my pocket, collected my tips, and walked home in the star-less light pollution of the city to do my homework and wait for Brandon to get home from the lab..

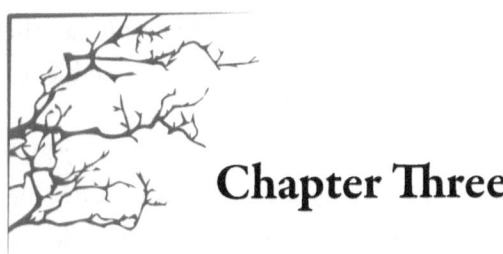

Chapter Three

I WAVED MY GLASSES at the door reader to the biology lab and paused for it to scan my face. The reader had been glitchy lately, but it finally clicked and let me in. The speaker barked at me that I have an appointment with the President at 11:00. "Yes, I got the message!" I barked back. I hoped I would be awake by then.

It had been a late night studying for the tests, but with Brandon's help I got all my work done, plus, when I couldn't sleep afterward, I created a new exercise plan for the subjects that Dr. Vern had given me permission for. I'm paying for all that effort now. Who knows how Brandon keeps his pep and energy with all the work they give us, but that's the way he was in high school too, brilliant and wired. Unlike me, he seemed to get his best thoughts when he's exhausted and under pressure, like two years ago when the brilliant thought of releasing the abused African lions into the California wilderness came to him. At this high-pressure urban school, I'm learning to think and act more efficiently out of similar necessity, but it's a pain. Give me a simple, low-pressure early morning job like picking lettuce in a rural organic garden, and I'm way more centered and happy. Happily, I have another appointment with Dr. Pendleton coming up in a few days. I made a mental note to talk to him about this. His office is like a breath of fresh country air to me despite all the incense. I may need his guidance again if I am in trouble for some reason with President Mitchell.

Brandon has been at the lab a half hour already. He's leaning on the centrifuge having a conversation with Dr. Vern and Dr. Bryson when I pushed open the safety doors. I nodded at them, put on my white coat and went straight to the kennels because I could tell from all the barking and whining that no one had yet bothered to check on them.

My babies! I opened the cages to let them run into the hallway leading to the yard, but they all just enthusiastically mobbed me instead. When these youngsters are in that morning tail-wagging mood, the three female golden retrievers and three male Bernese mountain dogs are no match for my balance. I tumbled over, mostly on purpose, and let them lick my face and arms. I gave them each a hug in turn, with an extra long one for the smallest female, Mavis, my favorite. Don't get me wrong. I worshiped them all, but Mavis had recently developed that intelligent look in her eye that reminded me so much of my old dog, Jenny, who was living the wilderness life of her dreams. It wasn't exactly the same, but sometimes hugging Mavis felt just like hugging Jenny. I want the best for her and all these dogs.

"I'm beginning to think your advice to stick to goldens and mountain dogs was purely self-serving, Ms. Bradley," laughed Dr. Vern approaching our melee.

"Busted!" I managed to say between mouthfuls of dog kisses and tails slapping me across the face. Dr. Vern reached down and petted the backs of each of the test animals.

"Your dad used to play with Jenny and Max like this too when he was here. Sometimes I think his horse-play had as much to do with their eventual psychological success as all the quantum treatments we subjected them to."

"I'm *sure* it did, and you know, frankly, that's what's keeping me going, trying to quantify why that might be so." I resurfaced from the canine scrum and headed for their food bowls. "When we discover that the richness of a home environment is key, maybe we can stop treating these beings as experimental subjects."

"I agree, actually, but what can I say?" he said following me. "Dr. Bryson has the lead on this, and funding is tenuous. If he hadn't cleverly linked it with Alzheimer's research, we might not have any test animals at all. This isn't the sociology department, you know."

" Yeah, I know. Convincing Bryson that the cultural experience of Jenny and Max after Dad sprang them out of here is as important to study as the lab procedures before they were freed is not an easy sell. He's a hard scientist. He likes control over variables. He likes his lab *and* his funding. I get it."

"We're *all* scientists, here, but of what sort, I'm not sure. It's a never-ending quest, you know, like being lost in the woods." He smiled wryly.

"Got time to help me feed these guys, Dr. Vern?" I said. I liked Dr. Vern a lot more than Dr. Bryson. He's not afraid to express his human side to me, whereas Bryson is another matter.

We dumped chunks of bison burger and dry dog food into six stainless steel bowls and mixed them with some fresh goat's milk from the fridge. The play area for the "subjects" was down the hallway with a gate to a grassy outdoor enclosure where the dogs could run a little and get some sunshine. Chew toys were everywhere, and computer screens showed random hologram images of art and nature on every wall.

Dr. Vern and I put out the bowls in six separate places in the play area, and I opened the gate to the outside for when they finished wolfing their bio-enhanced breakfast. As usual, Mavis gulped hers down first, but she was polite enough not to try to sneak bites from anybody else's bowl. The Bernese males were never that considerate. Mavis didn't go outside right away. As usual, she studied me intently, like she was waiting for and expecting something more than what she was getting. Out of all of the subjects, she's the one I think is taking to the quantum meditation tapes like Jenny must have long ago, but I don't know that for sure. I wasn't here when Dad, Bryson and Vern had the monks meditating at them directly. It's just a feeling. Mavis could be hiding her smarts like Jenny did, racking up information in her encyclopedic mind, waiting for her moment to escape. Dr. Vern and Dr. Bryson are still figuring out a way to test the progress of the subjects, but it's not so easy getting inside the minds of dogs, and so far they haven't come up with any reasonable methods of measurement.

"Dr. Vern?" It was Brandon coming to find us. "Dr. Bryson wants to run a session this morning, and follow it up with scans."

"Really?" said Dr. Vern. "I thought we were doing that next week, upping their exercise this week instead?"

Brandon shrugged. "This morning's computer analysis of the amygdala data from the last session indicates anomalies between the subjects, and we want to measure their individual rates of growth more frequently and more precisely to see if there is a generalized pattern or not."

Mavis was paying attention to Brandon and then turned her attention to me. Was she following this? I remembered it took a while to figure out that Jenny could understand conversations, and even when I did, there was no way to prove it. Dogs have evolved to mimic our expressions. If Jenny hadn't figured out how to quantumly transmit scents that turned into meaningful images in my head, I might never have known her true brilliance. So far I have not been sent any messages from Mavis, but I'm listening, and sniffing, for them.

I looked at the shaved parts of Mavis's beautiful golden head and imagined how she would feel if she did understand what was being done to her. The sessions were not easy on the subjects, especially compared to walks outside in the California sunshine. The six dogs have to be separated from each other, receive a shot of sedative, and then sit restrained in darkened rooms with 3D panels flashing at them and mp3 chants playing interminably in their ears. I know *I* would hate it, and she clearly did not look happy right at the moment.

"Okay, I said. I guess that means our own tests are postponed?"

"Oh, well, we'll have to do those next week, Ella," said Dr. Vern.

It would have been nice to know that last night. "I can only work until 10:50 this morning," I said.

"Right, your appointment in the Main Quad," said Brandon. "Should be no problem if we start now. Can you come back after lunch to help with the scans?"

"I hope so," I said meaningfully.

"Should I be worried?" said Dr. Vern kindly.

"No, it's nothing," I said. "It's about admissions, I think. The President probably wants to interview me for a recruiting hologram, or something, I don't know."

"Oh," said Dr. Vern. "The President, huh? Hmm... Well, let me know if you need any help with anything, okay? Now, let's get these guys to the conditioning rooms."

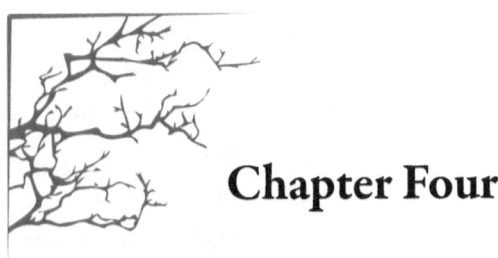

Chapter Four

I DON'T KNOW WHO'S more dangerous on the campus sidewalks, the students wearing phoneglasses riding their transportation devices, or the poorer students on old-fashioned bikes staring at phones they still have to carry in their hands. One thing's for sure, transportation in Brecken culture is officially a secondary activity to holo-texting, so you take your life in your hands every day just to cross campus. There are all kinds of public service holo-vids about this problem, not that anybody pays attention. Today it was especially bad. To get to the admin building from the lab, I had to dodge one guy who was riding an electric skateboard, watching a music holo-video, vaping, and drinking a latte all at the same time. As usual, I refrained from flipping him off after leaping out of his way because I would be flipping people off every day around here if I gave in to that impulse.

Happily, the Main Quad near the President's Office was relatively empty of students at this time of day, and the ones who were actually out of bed were stuffing their faces in the food court. I'd be doing the same thing except I wanted to get this mysterious meeting over with. You'd think that having a trust account, a famous Dad, and two years of boarding school independence under my belt would cure me of my irrational fear of authority figures, but it just wasn't so. Why does the President want to talk to me? I realized my heart was racing, so I decided to sit on a bench in the fall sunshine and take a few deep breaths before approaching his lair.

Despite that courage-building moment, opening the huge oak door to the Admin "vault" still felt like entering a colosseum to face the lions. The air conditioning blasted my face as I closed the monstrous barrier behind me and approached the trim and efficient-looking receptionist with a red and gold name tag sitting at the Brecken-red reception desk. I read her name. The room felt like the lobby of a bank.

"Hi, um, Franken. Ella Bradley to see President Mitchell."

"Oh, hi, Ms. Bradley. They're all waiting for you. Follow me, please." He got up and gestured for me to follow him. They *all*? They was not just a pronoun. I swallowed hard, my courage gone.

He knocked and opened another absurdly beefy door to the President's Office. "She's here," he said and stood aside for me to enter.

The room actually smelled like an oily vault in a bank and also like a pastrami sandwich. There was, indeed, a small crowd of people there. Judging by the empty containers and white butcher paper on the carpeting, lunch had recently been consumed. If I had to guess, the pastrami belonged to the President because he still had bread crumbs on his goatee. Osho Hanssen was there with a clean mouth and a head just as bald as I remembered him from the cafe. He looked uneasy and was the first to rise from a circle of leather chairs where four people were sitting. Besides the President and Osho, there was a graying woman in a St. John's knit outfit like my mother's rich art customers wore when they came to her studio to buy paintings, and a fit younger woman in a Lu- lulemon workout outfit who looked like she had been called in abruptly from a pilates class. The women waited for the President to stand and then followed suit. The President approached me, extending his hand.

"Ms. Bradley, please come in. You know, Mr. Osho, our Dean of Students, I believe, and this is Mrs. Beauregard, our Dean of Admissions, and Ms. Mackenzie from our Board." They also came forward to quickly shake my hand. I managed to smile at them even as their names slipped past my memory.

"Why don't we sit down, please?" President Mitchell went on. I'm sure Ms. Bradley is wondering why we have asked her away from her important work in the lab to see us. Would you like anything to drink, Ms. Bradley? Coffee? Tea? Water, perhaps?" He gestured me toward the circle of sturdy black wooden chairs emblazoned with the Brecken logo.

"No, thanks. I'm fine." *Referring to me in the third person. Can't be good.* They all returned to their seats next to empty coffee cups and drained water bottles. I took the one empty seat left next to Mr. Osho across from the President who stroked his beard and sent the crumbs flying. He sat down and slapped his thighs.

"So, Ms. Bradley, I want to take you through something interesting that is happening to us around here, may I?"

"Sure," I said. No one was smiling back at me anymore, so, greeting time over, I let my face mimic their business-like demeanors.

"Okay. Well, as you know, it is a privilege to go to Brecken. Many deserving scholars dream of going here, but only a few lucky ones, such as yourself, are accepted. Our students are extraordinary scholars, and they go on to amazing careers that change the world. We're very proud of them, and of our ability to serve their needs." Everyone nodded in agreement. "We have, or I should say, *had* an incredible retention rate, thanks to Mrs. Beauregard and Mr. Osho here, but that has changed abruptly this year. Ms. Bradley, do you know what we mean by retention rate?"

"Sure. How many students stay here for all four years?"

"Exactly. Brecken has had a 98% retention rate for many years now. It's so predictable no one even pays it much mind. Once our students arrive here, they don't want to go anywhere else. That's just the way it is when you are a top university like we are. Where else could they *want* to go?" President Mitchell laughed and gestured to his huge window looking out at the quad as if just outside was paradise on earth. I noticed the skateboarder who almost killed me buzzing by again, coming back from lunch probably. My stomach growled. Lingering smells of food, no matter the time and place, always make me hungry. I should have grabbed a sandwich.

"So," he continued, "Imagine our surprise when Mr. Osho here points out that so far this year eighteen percent of our freshman and sophomores have dropped out, and an equal number of juniors and seniors have either dropped out or have radically changed their majors. Do you have any idea, Ms. Bradley, why that might be so?"

"Uh, I don't know, did they get run over on the side-walks? I almost did on the way over here."

"No, there has been no change in our health and wellness statistics for the past five years, even with the uptick in personal mobility devices. Believe me, we have looked into it. No change in dorm conditions, class sign-ups, professors, racial or gender proportions, illness and accident rates, political protests, nothing unusual to explain it. Brecken is the same as it always has been, and this is not happening at Berkeley, Harvard, Yale or even Carleton, well, not to this extent. The rates are up slightly, a point or two nationwide, but we're the only university in double-digit trouble."

"Wow. That's surprising. I'm sorry to hear that," I said.

"Are you? I wonder. Mr. Osho, will you please inform Ms. Bradley here of your research findings?"

"Of course," said Osho next to me. "So, at the request of Mr. Mitchell, and thanks to a grant from Ms. Mackenzie here on behalf of the Board, my office hired Brecken Research Institute to get to the bottom of this. I can't reveal the name of the lead investigator, but they used embedded local agents to track student behaviors. We asked them to look at unusual trends among our students, social activities, food choices, drug and alcohol consumption, political affiliations, etc. We were especially focused on the activities of the students who dropped out or expressed a desire to change majors. It took a bit of digging, and a lot of wading through cell phone tracking data, but I think the results will interest you."

"Enough of the preamble, Osho, get to the point," said Mr. Mitchell.

"Okay, sir. Well, Ella, what everybody has in common is...Comey's."

"What? The coffee shop?"

"Yes, the coffee shop that, as you well know, is quite a ways off campus and suddenly very popular among our students who prior to this year hardly set foot in there at all. Why would they? It's kind of a dump, especially compared to what we provide on campus. And do you know what else we discovered?"

I shook my head.

"They all were there when you were performing. Interesting. Also, students with no fear of C-grade coffee shops who happened to be at Comey's when you *weren't* playing were completely unaffected."

"Brecken people at Comey's? Like you, you mean? You were there when I was there," I said.

"Well, I went specifically to deliver a message to you, but yes, like me."

"Um, so, what's this got to do with me?"

"That's what *we'd* like to know," said Ms. McKenzie, pointing her French-manicured finger. "What exactly are *you* doing to sap these students of their motivation?"

"*What? Doing? Me? Nothing!* What are you accusing me of? Casting a spell on their motivation? *Me?* I don't care one way or another whether people stay or leave Brecken. Why would I ever care about something like that?"

"We don't know," she went on. You want to tell us? Because there is no doubt about the correlation between people listening to your performance at Comey's and having severely damaging thoughts about their academic careers at Brecken. There are no other correlating factors, Ms. Bradley. You are it." Ms. Mackenzie crossed her arms in front of her spandex.

"Well, if that is happening, it is pure coincidence. You guys ever hear of correlation is not causation? You know, *science*? We're the top University for that, right?"

"So this is all new to you, huh?" said President Mitchell looking me in the eye.

"I play old time bluegrass tunes on my grandfather's fiddle and people like to drink coffee at Comey's and tap their feet. So what? What? Do you have something against people liking music?"

"The correlation is clear," said Ms. Mackenzie.

"Well, it's news to me. Your methodology is flawed. You're losing students? Maybe you should lower your tuition. Sounds like you are just looking for someone to blame."

Mr. Osho reached over and touched my shoulder. "No, of course not, Ella, and I don't think anyone is *blaming* you, are we, Ms. Mackenzie? We are just surprised by the results of BRI's very thorough investigation and wanted your thoughts on it, that's all. If this is news to you, then that's fine. We have no reason to believe you are out to sabotage Brecken, by any stretch. You are a very good student. Famous, even. Your father also did memorable work here." I see the President and his board member exchange looks. There was silence for a while, then President Mitchell cleared his throat.

"Okay, Ms. Bradley, I think we are done for now. Thank you for coming by and answering our questions. If anything occurs to you about this mystery that you might want to tell us about, we would love to hear from you. Just contact me or Mr. Osho here. Oh, and would you please keep this confidential? It's important. Our alumni supporters are prone to jumping to conclusions about admissions data and then making life unnecessarily uncomfortable for us. In turn, we wouldn't want anything to interfere with your desire to continue here too, of course, if this gets out." He looked at me meaningfully.

They all stood up and the President opened his office door with a strained smile on his face. Clearly he thought I was lying, but was his threat coming from him or from the other sharks in here? I couldn't tell. I may dislike Brecken, but I'm not *sabotaging* the place for crying out loud! I glared at him and stomped out of there as fast as I could, not trusting my mouth to stay shut. Behind me I heard Mr. Osho speak. "I'm just going to make sure she's okay," and he followed me past the receptionist's desk and out the dungeon door.

"Ms. Bradley, hold on a moment," he said, trotting onto the sunny quad with me.

"I need to get some lunch, Mr. Osho, before I go back to the lab." I was in no mood for any more of this administrative bullshit.

"I know. Just please let me walk you to the food court, okay?"

He looked pained, so I nodded reluctantly but walked even faster.

"You know, I believe that you don't know anything about this, but you should know something important." He was breathing hard.

"Yeah, what is it? That you work for an idiot?" My feet were pounding on the bricks. It was all I could do not to punch him in the face and break into a sprint.

"Well, yes, actually. I'm turning in my resignation this afternoon and moving back to my family farm in Illinois. I never really wanted to be a college administrator."

That stopped me in my tracks. I turned to look at him. He was gasping and even crying a bit, and I realized it was not just because he was out of shape.

"Wait, are you telling me...? You're like...? *Oh my God!*"

"Exactly. I made the decision after hearing you play. I had no idea at the time, but now I know it was because of your music. Thank you so much, Ella, for helping me open my eyes!"

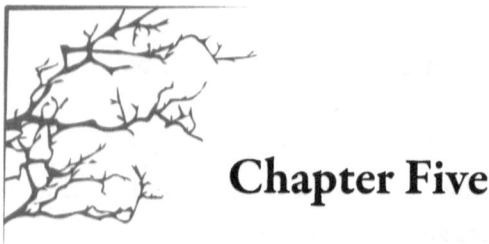

Chapter Five

I GRABBED A TRAY IN the food court but then decided to eat my sandwich outside. I wandered past the geology building to a postage-sized park with some beautiful redwood trees and a bunch of cool indigenous and rather pornographic totem poles from New Zealand. The place was not a wilderness area, by any stretch, but it helped me think more clearly to at least be surrounded by native art in a natural setting. I sat down against a hollowed out log that was carved to drum up spirits when pounded on and attacked my sandwich. Did that really just happen to me, or did I hallucinate it out of extreme hunger?

After wolfing, I dug my phoneglasses out of my backpack and blinked a cll to Dad. He picked up immediately and appeared on my lens screen.

"Ella-Bean! What's up, girl? Two calls in one week. Are you missing your daddy?"

"Hey, Dad. The first one doesn't count, you know, because it was your birthday."

"Right, and you don't go in for holiday obligations. I'm with you on that. Presents mean more when they come unexpectedly, not when they are reinforcing commercial holiday guilt. So, I should be thrilled. You are calling me for no reason whatsoever other than to make my day?"

"Well, yes and no. Sorry to disappoint you."

"Anytime you call is a happy day for me, my dear, no matter what the reason. What's going on?"

"BRI. Brecken Research Institute. What do you know about them?"

"Think tank. Well funded. Had their hands in all kinds of cold war things, many of them tech. Some psychic research, LSD. They tried to weaponize clairvoyance. Stuff like that. They were interested in funding the Enlightenment Project, but I escaped their claws when I went off on my own. They were the ones pressuring Bryson and the lab team for quick results when I rescued Jenny and brought her home for you. What's going on? Is the lab tapping them for funding again?"

"No, well, I don't know. Maybe. Money is tight, but Dr. Bryson keeps his cards pretty close to his chest. How Jenny and Max ever escaped his control-freak clutches is beyond me. Honestly, how'd you ever get them out of there?"

"Oh, it was all Dr. Vern. He had heard of and respected my experiments with endocannabinoid receptors in relation to quantum physics and meditational communication and was dying to get a hold of a sample of Enlightenment. When the funding dried up, Bryson was hell-bent on burning the place to the ground to cover his seeming failure. The end seemed inevitable. BRI was livid at the lack of results. Vern played along with Bryson for a while because he didn't have any other choice. Then I gave him a sample in exchange for him slipping Jenny into my van and taking Max to a pet store when Bryson wasn't looking. It didn't take Enlightenment long to reinforce the correctness of his decision, and he got the last laugh when you and Brandon helped Jenny and Max gather their animal allies to live successfully in the wilderness."

"So Bryson never smoked any?"

"Not that I know of. I don't think Vern dared to share it with him or even tell him about it. Bryson is brilliant, but it's all about Bryson for him. He must have been sorely deprived of love as a child or something. Keep him at a distance like I told you before but learn as much as you can from him. He's brilliant, smarter than all of us, but not someone you want to go hiking in the woods alone with, if you know what I mean."

"I do. Yuck! Brandon worships him, though."

"That's okay. Bryson's kind of like a little God who demands worship. I refused to stroke his ego, so eventually I had to go. Enlightenment might have been better researched, though, because of him had I stayed."

"Well, that is my second question, Dad." I thumped the log behind me for help in how to phrase this next thought without making Dad worry too much. "What do you know about Enlightenment causing major disruptions in people's lives?"

"Are you talking about anyone in particular?"

"No."

"We're getting good reports, but mostly from addiction centers who have seen a huge drop-off in meth and opioid addictions since Enlightenment hit the market."

"That's good. But what about people who are in the mainstream? People who are on fulfilling career tracks with families and obligations and stuff? What about people like, say school administrators who vape it and then realize they really want to do something else, like farming for instance? What if it is too late for them to change careers?"

"Well, Yeah. Those are harder cases. The longer a person sails with something cosmically incorrect, the more difficult it becomes to right the ship. It can cause disruption for them and for others. That doesn't mean it still isn't a worthwhile course correction, however."

"Cosmically incorrect, huh? I just wish there was a more scientific way to express that. It's all so vague."

"The relationship between energy and matter is complicated, my dear. Einstein proved beyond a doubt that there is a relationship between the two, and we take it for granted that there are all kinds of different forms of matter from cannonballs to ice cream, but do we all have the same innate ability to recognize different forms of energy? Of course not. Some people do, some don't. Those that do are labeled psychics. Cats see ultraviolet light. We can't. Does that mean ultraviolet light doesn't exist? No. Can humans learn to sense and read ultraviolet light eventually in the same way? Possibly. Psychic powers can be developed. But learning to sense energy is one thing. Figuring out the relationship between energy fields, motivation, and human thought, is much more mysterious and difficult, especially when it comes to making wise career choices and finding fulfillment."

"Hence the need for vague terms like cosmically incorrect."

"Yes, but we're getting closer to a more precise understanding in relation to genetics and upbringing every day."

"Dad, could Enlightenment be causing an unusual number of people to drop out of Brecken?"

"Maybe. For students searching for colleges, Brecken has a strong romance attached to it and all the appearances of a sure path to fulfillment, but Brecken is just a small slice of the multiverse pie, my dear, with its own particular taste. It's not for everyone."

Ironically, an admissions tour chose this time to stop right in front of my log, so I asked Dad to hold on while I moved. The student tour guide and overly earnest parents talked in loud voices while pointedly ignoring the generous totem genitalia on full erect display in front of them, but for the middle-school-aged siblings in tow, the carvings were obviously the highlight of their otherwise tedious tour. I smiled at their giggles and headed back toward the lab.

"Well, thanks, Dad. I have to get back to work now. We're playing the tapes to the pups all the time now. It's so intense. If *I'm* feeling the pressure, I can't imagine how Mavis and the other dogs feel."

"How do they feel when the chanting tapes are on?"

"Engrossed, of course, but not exactly happy. I'm sure it's helping them grow, but it just feels like it is too much too fast to me, that's all."

"I hear you. Jenny might have developed as much brain power resting at home with us after leaving Brecken as she did at the lab. We just don't know. Here's what I think. Speak your mind, girl. You've got as much to contribute as everyone else does in that lab, maybe more."

"Thanks, Dad, but right now I feel that playing Lenore might be a better path."

"Do you want to quit?"

"No, I love those dogs, and Brandon needs me too, although he thinks I need him more than he needs me."

"Sounds complicated."

"It is."

"Well, give it time. Go with your heart. I know you love those dogs. You'll find your way. You always do."

"I love *you*, Dad."

"I love you too, Ells. I'm headed to Europe for a while. Hang in there. I'll call when I get back."

"My father, the international business tycoon."

"Hardly. Just an old hippie trying to help the world a little bit before I move on to greener pastures."

"You're the best, Pops."

"Not compared to you, my dear. Say hi to Brandon for me. Love you! Ciao!"

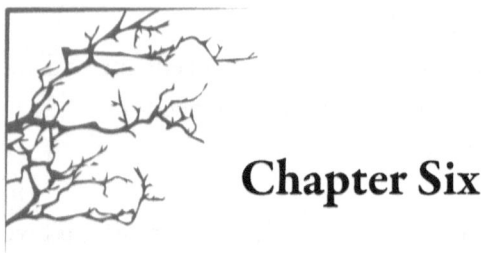

Chapter Six

BACK AT THE LAB, MAVIS and the other pups were all doggie-Xanaxed and strapped in their individual sensory cubicles. Brandon and Dr. Vern had headphones on and were working the input controls that looked like a high-tech soundboard in a recording studio, and Dr. Bryon perched in front of the brain monitors like a mad gamer intent on world domination. If I didn't force myself to tolerate his passionate personality as I do, the drool leaking from the side of his mouth would seriously scare me. Dr. Vern nodded at me and pointed to the third headset. I slipped it on over my windblown blonde hair.

"We're trying to double theta waves in the inferior frontal gyrus," said Dr. Vern in my ear. "But it's not going so well. As usual, the tapes are diffusive in their effects."

"Yes, diffusive, but by the time we analyze the patterns for optimality, the window of plasticity will be long passed, so if we can find the core area of sensitization during the inoculation, we will save a lot of time," said Bryson. "Up the volume in the visual center again, Vern. Ten degrees this time. Brandon, you on this?"

"Level is at 30 right now and holding steady for all subjects. Wait, no. Mavis is at 25."

"Okay, go ahead, Vern. Let's see if it is a visual feed, or if it's all aural."

"Upping visuals now," says Dr. Vern. I saw the ambient glow in the cubicles increase as the wraparound screens responded to the stimulus. Ever since Bryson figured out that visuals keyed to sound colors upped the response wave in the subjects' communicative centers, he has been on a tear to augment the meditation tapes. Personally, I would augment the subjects' experience by bringing back the monks from Tibet instead, but there wasn't the budget for that, and all the communication sensors indicated that there were no measurable differences between a sound feed run by the mp3's and live meditation and chanting sessions. Personally, I think some differences can't be measured scientifically, but what do I know? This is a science lab. Bryson and Vern are more adept at controlling computers and brain probes than at controlling Buddhist monks. Give scientists a chance to geek out over variables, computers, and data, and they'll take it every time, even when past successes are scientifically unquantifiable. I looked at Mavis's lower response levels again. Is she fighting this? If so, why?

"So you've been at this for an hour already?" I asked.

"Yes," says Vern, "And their vitals are holding steady. No sign of agitation, except for Mavis, of course."

"Always the outlier," says Brandon.

"Outliers are where the real knowledge comes from," I said.

"Sometimes," said Bryson. "I know what you're thinking, Ella. We'll give them a break in a minute. Let's go with a ten percent increase in aural now and make one more set of measurements."

"Okay," said Vern. "Aural at 75 dB. Visuals holding steady at 1200 lux."

I flipped the background feed to what the subjects were hearing. Bryson didn't want us to do that since the effects of the monk's chanting have not been quantified for humans, but I figured a little bit couldn't hurt me, and I wanted to know what Mavis and the others were experiencing.

What I heard made me jump in my chair. The monks were doing their throat singing thing, and at that high volume setting, it felt like a Mack truck engine rumbling in my head. The powerful sound reminded me of an unpleasant version of the background noise I heard when Lenore took me and Brandon in her musical arms and let us fly with her across the wilderness last year at Wandering Pines. It vibrated in my head like the energy of the cosmic brain that runs the universe cranked up way higher than it should be. It grabbed my head and lifted me from my chair.

I looked at Brandon intently, focused on the monitor in front of him, and in my mind we were flying together again like when we first realized our love for each other. The sound was lifting both of us. I reached for him and we held each other tightly and banged into the walls and windows of the lab trying to get out. I wanted the experience of flying to freedom again, but I couldn't have it. *No, not here! Not now! Not while we're trapped by these laboratory walls!* I fought the power of the noise and willed my fingers to back-click the mouse still gripped in my hand. The sound cut off and a weight of grief, love, and frustration lifted from my chest as I landed back down into my body in front of the monitor. *What had just happened?* Discreetly, I wiped a tear from my eye with the sleeve of my lab coat and steadied my breath and looked around. Bryson and Vern were still focused, but Brandon was frowning and looking right at me. I managed a reassuring smile, and his face relaxed a bit, but he kept looking at me.

"You got enough?" said Vern.

"Just about," answered Bryson. "Mapping the salience network differentiations now. Okay. Got it. Cut 'em off now. Ella, you and Brandon can release the subjects."

"Got it," said Brandon. Apparently satisfied that I was okay, he turned back to his monitor and cut the feed to the dogs. We hung up our headphones and headed to the cubicles. I was a little unsteady on my feet, but Brandon's attention was back to the business at hand. As usual, he skipped Mavis's cubicle, knowing that's where I always headed first after sessions.

Now that the big push is over, we could focus on the dogs' comfort and recovery, thank goodness. Because I listened, I now had a clue about what we were putting them through in these sessions and why they must hate it. I need to talk to Brandon about my little trip later. Brandon was serious about the experiments, but the instinct to take kind care of animals also runs deep in him. He's the greatest when he follows that instinct. I hope he'll listen to me. "I think it's warm enough for a swim today," he said. "Let's get them in the water."

"Roger that, partner," I said. "They can bob for tennis balls. They'll like that way more than surfing the universe in a box."

When I entered Mavis's cubicle, she was already back to consensus reality. Bryson was really pushing the Xanax limits these days squeezing in sessions longer than the drug's half life. Mavis pawed at the electrodes pasted on her head and strained against the strap holding her chest to the table. I had the feeling that if she had had a mouse she would have clicked it like I did to end the session a long time ago.

"Easy, girl. It's okay, I'll have you out of there in a jiffy. Hold on, okay?" I pulled a Milk Bone treat out of the pocket of my lab coat and placed it by her nose to sniff. It slowed her down just enough that I could untape the wires from her head and release the safety buckle. She sprang to her feet, and I lifted her down before she could jump. She's a little unsteady, like I was a moment ago, so I hugged her on the floor for a bit and gave her her treat again. She took it in her mouth. "Easy, easy, Mavis. You're a good girl. Want to go outside? Ready for a swim?" Somehow I felt she also felt the desperate feeling of being trapped that just happened to me. After Jenny left this place, her passion was to be free in the wilderness, and I could feel the same need developing in Mavis. The sessions were improving her brain, but also frustrating her at the same time. I could understand why.

Bryson insisted on leashes around here, but I always claimed that the pups were too fast for me and used that as an excuse to let them run around with abandon. Mavis was the first to reach the door to the outside containment area. If Bryson tore his gaze away from the new data stream to check out the chaos of dog toenails skittering on the linoleum, I don't care. He can glare all he wants. Mavis won't hurt any of his precious instruments just dancing around wagging her tail.

I helped Brandon release the other five subjects, two more golden females and three Bernese males. We could barely wade through them to get to the door handle. It's a bad design that the door opened inward because we always had to pull it hard to move all the groggy but anticipatory dog flesh out of the way. Once they got their noses into the fresh air, though, there was no stopping their recovering energy. It was a tornado of spinning dogs out there. The barking was thunderous and joyful. I urged them on, laughing. About once a week we get reports from the provost about complaints from the sleep lab next door. Too bad, suckers. These guys earned their fun.

Brandon snaked the hose to the wading pool, and I opened the storage bin for the tennis balls. Of course, the goldens go nuts over the balls, and even some of the Bernese males acknowledge the entertainment potential of fluorescent green balls. The whole pack mouths them like a team of canine Cyclops chomping on tasty sailors. Brandon sprayed water into the air making a cooling rain, and I threw the slimy orbs for the dogs one after another like a pitching machine gone wild. If these animals are the new hope for an intellectually dominant planetary species, at least we can be glad they maintain a healthy reverence for play.

Mavis was the first to calm down. She came to sit next to me to monitor the other dogs still obsessively chasing balls. Sometimes I have to ice my arm after these recesses, and I can't even play Lenore when I get home, but it's the least I can do for these poked and prodded pups. Brandon shut off the hose and came to sit next to me. We watched the dogs gamboling in the wading pool.

"So, how'd the meeting go?"

I'm glad he asked about this instead of what happened to me just now in the lab. Did he feel me flying with him again? Is that why he was staring at me? I know I need to find out, but I was afraid to ask.

"They're blaming my fiddle playing for a mysterious rise in campus dropouts," I said.

"*What?*"

" Yeah, you heard right. Lenore. Breaking Brecken's precious 98% satisfaction rate."

"You're kidding me."

"Nope. Apparently people go to Comey's, drink coffee, eat a croissant, listen to my set, and then decide to do something better with their lives. They "researched" this. Pick a correlative causation. *They* did. It's got to be my music, right? Not anything else. No. Couldn't possibly be the Costa Rican coffee or the French pastries, no sir. Or even something outside of Comey's like sunshine or a workout at the gym. Or the fact that Brecken might just suck. Or even Enlightenment ..."

"Oh, of course. Well, it probably *is* Enlightenment."

"*I* know that, but these are crusty old central-quad administrators terrified of their financial spreadsheets and mega-rich pilates-obsessed board members."

"Sounds horrible. So, what's next? Should we hire a bodyguard?"

"I'm thinking about hooking up one of dad's infusors to their ventilation system over there."

"Ha! Good idea. Only, it belies the variable of intention. They've got to choose it, want it, right, for Enlightenment to change their lives?"

"I don't know anymore. Like what we're doing here? Do we really understand intentionality? Where's Mavis's intention in all this? Or any of the pups' for that matter? Or Bryson's? What's *his* intention?"

"I agree. There are a lot of mysteries and variables. You can't blame Bryson for trying to narrow them down, though, can you?"

"I guess not. But, can you *ever* take the mystery out of mystery?"

"Well, that's the goal, isn't it? To find out. Control mystery. Use it to make things better."

"Yeah, *control*. As I said, intentions are important."

Brandon raised his eyebrows. "So what are you saying, that we are somehow insulting the universe by trying to figure it out?"

I reached down and petted Mavis who seemed to be following our every word. I can't be sure she is, though. Like my old dog, Jenny, Mavis hides things pretty well. I thought Jenny was just a mildly-advanced dog, and then she ended up teaming up with Max and controlling lions to form a sophisticated survivalist community in the wilderness. Talk about a mystery!

"I don't know, Brandon. Who can ever know? We don't really know what we're messing with here."

"Ella, do you remember that joke that Bryson told us?"

"Bryson told us a joke? Oh, you mean the God thing?"

"Yeah, when we first got here and he was showing us around. The joke about the religious dude on the Titanic."

"I didn't remember it as the Titanic ..."

"Well, a sinking ship, the waters are rising and the dude thumps his bible and says he won't panic because he has faith that God will save him."

"Right, and then he doesn't put on a life jacket, ignores the helicopter, refuses to get on the raft, and then drowns like an idiot."

"Yes. He gets to heaven and complains to God that God didn't save him despite how faithful he was, and God, exasperated, asks him what more he could have done beyond sending him a life jacket, a helicopter, and a raft. Remember Bryson telling us that one?"

"Yes, I do now. It was in the chapel. He was loud and a little irreverent in that silent zone, I might add."

"Okay, so what? Everyone talks there. But my point is opportunities are worthless if you don't act on them."

"Yes, we've been through this before. "He who hesitates is lost" beats out "haste makes waste," or so you believe."

"I *do* believe that. Don't you?"

"Like I said, not always, but what's your point?" I laughed at Mavis using her back feet to kick water on all the other dogs.

He lowered his voice. "My point is that I snuck Sybil in here this morning, and I want you to help me with her after everyone is gone." I turned to look at Brandon directly to see if he was serious. I should have known he was up to something considering his ponderous and silent mood lately. It's been weeks since we last went out to share a beer.

"You brought your python in here?!" I looked back at the lab.

"Shh," he said. "Not so loud."

"How the hell did you get her in here without anybody noticing?" I whispered.

"I Ubered this morning before you were conscious of the waking world. You didn't even notice her missing, did you? or your suitcase?" He's smiling, and it's so cute to see his smile again. I moved closer to him on the grass so we could whisper more easily.

"You know, Brandon, I stopped being a morning person since we left the winery last summer. My mind was empty this morning I guess, like Sybil's cage. You *Ubered* him over here? Why?"

"Extra credit. I want to try the tapes on a reptile." His eyes didn't waver from mine for a moment.

Suddenly a feeling of lightness hit my chest. My recently annoyingly overly-conventional, kiss-ass boyfriend finally has a radical and rebellious idea to jazz up our four-year sentence at this staid and stuck-up institution! Quantumly alter our pet python right under the noses of two of the world's most renowned neurophysiological research scientists? Who wouldn't jump at the chance to stir the pot like that? Yes! Throw professional scientific decorum to the wind! I planted a big kiss on Brandon's luscious mouth.

Chapter Seven

KISSING BRANDON WAS a relief, like our relationship was finally back on track, and my mind was now in high gear. One good thing in our favor, pythons don't require a sedative to keep them still. If Brandon's old dog Max were around, he could control her, but Max was off with Jenny in the wilderness controlling lions and deer right now and raising their intelligent-as-human pups.

Unlike the past few weeks when Brandon's constant goal to impress Bryson clashed with my growing disillusionment with school, there was suddenly, for the moment anyway, no feeling of separation between us. I felt his joy at knowing I was all in with him on this wild plan. This felt the same as when we freed the lions last year. We clicked into action.

"When we get inside, tell Bryson and Ken we need to backup data and check the calibrations on the cubicles tonight," I said.

"Yes, and you look in the supply room for a heating pad."

"Right. Also, why don't we ask them if they'll allow us to do an extra audio relaxation session for Mavis tonight? We could propose that her outlying data set could be due to simple anxiety."

"Great idea. We're not controlling their stress levels, so it won't skew the results to give her a little extra meditative love. If they go for it, that will get us prolonged access to the controls. It will be easy to plug her in while we zap Sybil."

"If they go for it."

"They will. They want our input, remember?"

"Okay. I'll work on Ken. He's easier for me. You work on Bryson."

We left Mavis and the other dogs to their romping time outside and headed back into the lab. Bryson and Ken were still concentrating behind the controls uploading and analyzing the new data. It was overwhelmingly complicated what they were trying to accomplish. Six dog brains, each mapped out into hundreds of distinct areas cross checked for activity spikes in relation to each other and in relation to the neurological gene expressions of the individual subjects. Every discovered anomaly had to be mapped in relation to every immersion session to check for patterns. It was difficult and tedious work, but the school's super-computers could handle it, provided the data was inputted correctly and the variables controlled as well as possible. If the creation of quantum powers in canine brains could ever be scientifically explained, this decked-out lab had the best chance of doing so.

What Dr. Bryson and Dr. Ken might *do* with that knowledge once they obtained it was another question. I suspected that Bryson had more up his sleeve than just seeing his name shimmering on the cover of a breakthrough scientific study. Looking at them behind their computers intently clicking away made me wonder if all this analysis was simply an expensive way of missing the point. Dogs listened to chanting monks and developed unreal intelligence and persuasive powers. What could be more simple? You could fly the monks here again and chant to the dogs outside by the phallic totem poles, get the same results, and save a ton of money. Who cares *how* it works? It just works. It doesn't make sense to me. I'm really not cut out for this science business. People like Bryson trying so hard to prove things all the time seemed pointless, not to mention expensive and impractical.

We approached the scientists and stood by the monitors. Brandon tilted his head toward the hallway and said, "So you're going to check on the food and stuff? I'll be right here when you finish." Dr. Vern looked up at us, nodded, and made room for Brandon to sit down with them, but Dr. Bryson stayed laser-focused on the computer screen. I wouldn't doubt it if someone told me Bryson was on the autism spectrum because his single-minded powers of concentration were scarily impressive. A bomb could go off right now, and he wouldn't notice. He wiped drool off his chin again with the sleeve of his lab coat.

"Motor skills normal on the subjects post treatment?" Bryson asked without looking up.

"Yes," said Brandon. "They're doing fine."

"Okay, log on and run numbers on the inferior frontal gyri data. We need to decide if we have consistency and what to focus on tomorrow."

"Yep. Got it. Thanks."

Dr. Vern looked at me again and smiled before returning his attention to the data. I moved off toward the hallway and the offices and storerooms at the back of the lab. I passed the centrifuge and the hooded electron microscope. It smelled awful back there. For all the expensive equipment that existed in labs like this around the world, no one has yet to invent a way to effectively control the putrid scent of caged rats.

The reek intensified as I passed Bryson's big office, Ken's smaller one, and the dozens of cages lining the hallway. Most of these leftover rats were being kept alive just to get a set of long-term data for ongoing experiments, none of which had any real worth to the advancement of science as far as I could tell except as data mines for acquiring more grants. Poor animals. So much politics and unnecessary cruelty goes on here, but if I ever released the rodent prisoners just to make myself feel better, I would get prosecuted to the full extent of the law, and it would be a waste of effort anyway because the poor demented things wouldn't even know how to forage for themselves.

I noticed Bryson's door was open and his computer was still on. Busy guy. Forgot to shut his door. Too bad. The stench will be as awful in his office as it is in the hallway by the time he gets back here tonight.

I opened the solid metal door to the equipment storeroom at the end of the hallway and flicked on the fluorescent lights. This huge room was not where we stored the dog food, but everyone was busy, so I had some time to poke around. Sometimes heating pads are used under the rat cages to keep baby rats warm, so I was pretty sure I could find one even though I hadn't been in there for weeks.

I looked around. Something was different. Raising my eyes, I saw that the area in the back looked like a tornado had hit it. Strange, this storeroom was immaculately ordered the last time I was here. Now it's a huge mess. Someone was clearly in a rush, and that someone could only be Bryson. Ken is way too fastidious to be the cause of this disaster. Petri dishes lay broken on the floor, and small lab machines of various types teetered haphazardly on the shelves with their cords hanging down. Towers of shipping boxes of every size and condition were growing like stalagmites from the covered floor.

I pushed myself past a pile of boxes and quietly moved lab equipment around on the shelves looking for a heating pad. Nothing. I moved farther into the room avoiding the glass on the floor. Still no luck, but at the very back I spotted a clear vinyl curtain stretched from wall to wall. *Weird.* A full-on hazmat suit was hanging on a hook just outside the curtain looking like some kind of sci-fi effigy. *Definitely weird.* Next to the suit was a big empty box with molded styrofoam still on the inside. Obviously it had just been opened. CRISPR Unit #93950 it said on the label.

"What are you doing in here, Ella?" It was Bryson appearing behind me.

"Oh, Dr. Bryson, you scared me! The door was open, so I thought I'd get a heating pad." I learned a long time ago from sneaking out of my parents' house that when caught doing something you shouldn't, you can buy time to make up a story by immediately confessing a partial truth.

"They're right in front of you." He reached behind me and pulled one out by the cord. It had rat hair on it but was otherwise in good shape. He handed it to me and looked me in the eye. "What do you need it for?"

"Oh, Brandon didn't ask you? We're thinking an extrawarm cubicle for Mavis to rest inside tonight while listening to pure relaxation tapes might help her for tomorrow's session. What do you think?"

" Yeah, he just mentioned it to me. It's a good idea. That's why I came back here. You need extra blankets, right?" He shoved aside more junk on the shelf and dug out a red pile blanket with a Cardinal printed on it.

"Oh, thanks," I said. "Hey, what's with the curtain? I didn't know there was a lab back here." Another survival tactic I learned was to put parents on the defensive.

"Just a little bread and butter side project of mine. Nothing special." He handed me the blanket.

"Not the best ventilation ..." Also, keep them talking.

" Yeah, well it looks worse than it is. I'm experimenting with some bio-preservative agents for my friends at Tyson. Salmonella, you know. Can't be too careful, but it doesn't spread through the air, so we're safe. Just being extra cautious, that's all."

"Is Brandon helping you with this?"

"No, but I'm about to ask him, and maybe you. It's all I can do to keep up."

" Yeah, I noticed," I said, kicking at some broken glass under my foot.

" Yeah, I know it's a mess. Well, you got what you need now?"

"Oh, yes, thanks!" I headed back out the door with the heating pad cord trailing behind me. Bryson followed me, flicked off the light, and locked the door behind him. I headed back to the control center.

"You're checking on the dog food?" he said.

"Right! Thanks. I forgot." I turned back to the smaller store room where we normally kept the food supplies.

"See you back out front, Ella."

"I'll be there in a moment." His eyes stayed on me until I disappeared into the food closet.

Chapter Eight

THERE'S PLENTY OF FOOD in that small storeroom. I already knew that, of course, but I dragged a few bags and boxes around to make noise for Bryson's benefit and snapped off an inventory order form from the clipboard by the door. Holding the blanket, the heating pad, and the order form, I headed back out into the hallway. The coast was clear. I waited a few moments more to be sure, then dropped everything except the requisition form against the wall by Bryson's office and slipped inside for a quick snoop. CRISPR machines are for making fast and dirty genetic alterations. They cost a fortune and are usually purchased with great fanfare. Bryson was up to something, and I wanted to know what.

I picked a black pen from a Brecken coffee cup on his desk and partially filled in the order form just to have an excuse for being there in case he comes back and startled me again. His computer screen glowed brightly on his messy desk. *Convenient.* After a quick glance at the door, I grabbed the mouse and clicked open his tabs.

You know how snowflakes are all basically the same but different? That's what the hundreds of pages that popped up on his tabs looked like, each one a snowstorm of genetic micro-structures with accompanying data. There were column after column of genetic patterns all with numerical tags, ar-

cane descriptions, and codified locations on the double he-
lix. Whatever he was looking for was not obvious or computer searchable. *Hmm...He must really want something to plow
through all this data by hand.*

I heard a chair squeak loudly in the distance. Someone
was standing up in the lab. Quickly I clicked out of the tabs,
dropped the mouse, grabbed my order form, and dashed
back out the door. I scooped up the blanket and heating pad
just as Brandon (whew) appeared at the end of the hallway.

"Hey, we really need you," he said. Clearly he is saying
that for Bryson's benefit because he was smiling at what I had
in my hand.

"Yep, coming. I found enough extra bags of food, the
premium stuff from the previous order." I winked at him.

"Can you bring the dogs back in and feed them, please?
If I can stay on the computer, we should have the data done
in a half hour or so."

"Sounds like a plan," I said. I handed him the blanket
and heating pad. "Put these by the cubicle, okay?" I whispered to him.

"Sure thing, babe." *Babe!* It was good to feel like a team
again.

If it weren't for their primal hunger for food, getting
these smart dogs back into the lab from their little play area
would be impossible. Not that it was all that vastly stimulating for them out there, but anything outdoors was worlds
better than their cramped and stinking indoor kennels. I've
done my best to argue for lots of toys and time in the schedule to take them for walks, but there were economic limits
to how much stimulation a university could ever really offer

young lab pups, especially when Bryson was squeezing CRISPR machines out of the budget for his own personal use.

I filled the plastic Brecken-red dog bowls with TruDog raw dog kibbles and noticed that one of the bowls was chewed up again. It's a bad habit one of the Bernese dogs, Sam, got into when Bryson and Ken previously insisted we feed them the cooked big name puppy chow with the checkerboards on the package to save money. They relented when I pointed out the ridiculous amount of inert filler in their formula and that Jenny and Max, their only successes so far, thrived on real dog food in the wilderness–pig and deer flesh. When healthy subjects are absolutely needed for re-search purposes, you would think that scientists would know that quality food was worth the extra money. Dad always says that when it comes to nutrition you either pay for good food now, or for medical bills later. "Do you want to eat your wealth or give it to doctors?" he always asked me when dol-ing out my morning supplements.

I've come to agree with Dad, actually. That's why I still swallow a handful of spirulina tablets with my oatmeal in the morning. It's pure food made from sunshine and healthy minerals, a bit like fresh salad in a pill. Skimping on our most basic connection with nature's complex web of nutri-tion is a short-sighted way to save money, in my opinion. Mom doesn't give nutrition a second thought, unless it's to wonder how many calories there are in her lattes and glasses of chardonnay. Brandon agrees with me and Dad in princi-ple, but getting him to focus on anything but protein bombs and raw eggs in the morning is difficult. He's such an old-fashioned Rocky Boy. To each his own, I guess.

I threw the chewed up bowl away and pulled another one off the stack for Sam. Poor guy. I'd be too neurotic to be cramped up in this lab. I measured out everyone's food, recorded the amounts in the kitchen log, then added another scoop to each bowl for good measure. The dogs have beds in separate quarters with a run connecting them. When we leave their room doors open, sometimes they drag one or two beds together, or cuddle together in the hallway, but most of the time we find them in their own separate spaces by morning.

I opened their individual gates and placed a bowl in front of each bed. Then I called them in from outside. I've learned to open the door to the outside all the way before yelling "dinner." They can be quite explosive in their mad dash to the food bowls. Tonight they got stuck in the run all trying to be the first to the food. "Hey, easy!" I yelled at them. Sam was the only one who looked at me guiltily and moved back to let the others squeeze ahead of him. He's a sweetheart. I'd take him and Mavis home with me tomorrow if I could.

You know those reptile holovids where a group of crocodiles devour a hapless zebra in about thirty seconds? Well, that's what it's like to see these dogs go at their food. It's good cheap entertainment, but after a few moments I closed them in and grabbed the pooper scooper. This was my least favorite chore. Not that I minded poop. It's what I have to do with it that bothers me, throw it away. If I had my way I would take the daily accumulation over to the school's cactus garden for fertilizer, but Brecken is, unfortunately, not our old boarding school. At Wandering Pines they let me do a junior project using human urine to fertilize lettuce and corn in the school's organic vegetable garden. It worked great. Best lettuce I ever ate. Here at Brecken I have to wrap the dog waste in petroleum-based plastic and throw it in the dumpster where it will eventually leach out of a landfill somewhere and pollute the groundwater. It's depressing.

But at least I can be outside while doing this chore. Well, in a dog yard outside, but at least there are a few trees, some people riding bikes, and some yellow daisy-like flowers blooming on that lonely bush on the other side of the fence. I chose to be here at this Brecken lab, but there are limits. Freedom of choice as a human is nice, but why did I choose to be so busy? I still can't do nature hikes here, or even have a social life other than forcing myself to go to Comey's for my therapy gigs. I know every tree and cactus still left standing in the jungle of concrete sterility that is Brecken Vista. They seem sometimes like my only friends.

I emptied the wading pool and dragged it back into the outside shed. I glanced over at the path to the administration building. Did Lenore and I really convince that bald-headed admissions guy, Osho, to quit his job? What if his farm fails or he gets hurt? I'm not sure I want that responsibility. It's one thing to mess with the minds of animals, but humans?

Back inside I dropped the massive evening's collection of reeking nutrient-rich poop in the garbage, rinsed off the scooper, and went to look for Brandon. I found him alone at his computer by the control panel. "Hey," I said. "Everyone leave?"

"Ken did. Heading to Mug-a's to meet his wife for a decaf mocha. He won't be back. Bryson's still here, though, in his office."

I don't say anything because I knew how voices carried around here. If Bryson was back there searching those pages on his computer, we might have to wait a while. Oh well. Nothing else to do but act out our cover-up plan for Mavis. Sybil's meditation session will just have to wait until Bryson's eyeballs get burned out enough to force him to go home.

"Ready to pay a little extra attention to Mavis?" I said. "I'm actually thinking maybe Sam could use the same treatment. He's been chewing his bowl to smithereens again and could use some relaxation."

"Yes. Good idea. Do we have two blankets?"

"Well, no, but they can share, don't you think?"

"Yeah, probably. They get along pretty well. Let's give 'er a try."

"After we get them settled, I think I'll give the others some bones," I said. "We don't need them to get jealous."

"Sure, but will they even know?"

"You can never tell what these guys know and don't know." I gave Brandon a little rub on the shoulder.

"Yeah, you're certainly right about that. Mysterious creatures. I swear there must be a gene in them for pretending to be normal dogs, or else they were born with Mercury in retrograde. Their brain scans are so promising, but it's hard to verify any behavioral progress."

"Like Jenny and Max."

"Exactly. Failures on the outside. Geniuses on the inside, maybe."

"I wonder how they're doing."

"Max and Jenny? Me too. Living the California good life in the heart of what's left of the best of mother nature."

"I worry about them."

"You do? Worry about *us*, Ella. They have birds and African lions protecting them."

"I know, and they are where they want to be, which is wonderful. Maybe I just miss them."

"Yep. Me too." His hand reached for mine on his shoulder. "It would be nice to have them here for this little Sybil experiment, actually," he went on. "Max and Sybil have a special bond, and he would tell her what to do. But Max and Jenny are doing their part in the wilderness to save life on earth, and we need to keep doing our part here. At least it beats succumbing to total climate-change depression."

I squeezed his shoulder sharply and put my finger to my lips to remind him that Bryson was still around, and he nodded. He hit the send button and logged off his computer.

"Let's get a relaxation tape queued and settle them in," Brandon said, pushing back his chair. I held him for a moment longer, swiveling him to face me. The world may be ending, but his lips tasted like a memory of fresh garden sweetness mixed with the savory energy of horses in full flying gallup. No stinky rat smell on them at all.

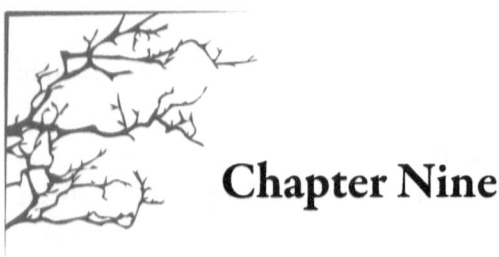

Chapter Nine

IT ISN'T TOO HARD TO get Mavis and Sam back out of their cages. They were done eating and happy at the prospect of a little extra time to run around. They followed me into the lab while Brandon sneaked some bones to the other dogs to keep them occupied. I herded Mavis and Sam toward the closest inoculation cubicle, but as soon as I opened its door, both of them sat down on the linoleum and refused to budge.

"It's not a session, guys," I said to them. They didn't look convinced. "Just the relaxing part. No electrodes or bright lights. Promise." They both lied down and covered their ears with their paws. I kept expecting a scent to hit my nose and an image of horse poop to appear before my eyes, but that's the way my old dog, Jenny, used to communicate when she was stubborn or had an opinion. Jenny figured out that paintings could deliver messages after hanging around Mom in her art studio. These guys, perceptive as they were some-times, still seemed stuck using body language and whimpers to express their feelings. If and when they ever learn to use physically manipulative quantum-communications tech-niques to communicate with humans as Jenny and Max did, it will probably manifest itself in some way other than the transmission of smells that turned into images of fine art.

How much they'll be able to control us, as Jenny controlled my eyesight and Max controlled the will-power of other animals, remained to be seen. So many mysteries.

"Okay, fine. Stay!" I told them and went back to the control panel where I had dumped the heating pad and blanket next to Bryson. The heating pad was for Sybil, but I picked up the fuzzy red blanket. Brandon came back from the kennels. "They're being stubborn," I said. "They think we're giving them an extra inoculation session." Bryson looked up and grunted and then followed us back toward the cubicles. He hung back with Brandon when we got near Mavis and Sam. I stepped around them and took the blanket into the cubicle.

"See, warm cuddly blanket. Come on, let's go lie on it." The dogs looked at me skeptically. "I'm not even going to shut the door, you guys. You're free to leave anytime you want. Brandon, start the spa music, please. We're going to have ourselves a little siesta!" Brandon glanced at Bryson, gave me the thumbs up and went back to the controls. I folded the blanket in two and lay down on it on the floor. "Come on you guys, join me!"

Bryson, uncomfortable and bored, turned to leave, and seeing him depart, Mavis and Sam got up and followed their noses into the cubicle to join me. Maybe they sensed that I really did understand their reluctance. They've had a lot of intense sessions lately. I reached out and petted them both on their bony heads. Brandon's music came on softly. It's old new-age stuff full of pan flute riffs, Tibetan throat singing, and relaxing subliminal vocalizations. The dogs liked it, and in my exhausted state it didn't take long for it to work on me too. I was half asleep before Mavis and Sam finally did their snake dance twirls and cuddled up against me. They must have decided my offer of cuddling beat standing on the cold linoleum in the hallway. Their bodies were warm and hairy against me, but their breath still smells like dog food. *Covers up the smell of the ratty lab, at least.*

Even with all the excitement Brandon and I had planned for Sybil tonight, I was ready to conk out. I'm worn out, and naps always work best for me when I take them in unexpected places. At home, if I try to take a nap in my regular bed, forget it. I have to be on the floor of the living room or out on the grass under a tree somewhere. One time I took a nap curled up on the kitchen counter. It was a great snooze, and I didn't even fall off. Sleeping in this usually bustling sensory cubicle with Mavis and Sam is an equally weird and perfect place for me to let go.

I drifted off with the music, and I felt my body lighten again like it was a party balloon slowly filling with helium dog breath. As I floated upward in my sleep, I realized that the music was gradually coming under my control. Lenore appeared. I grabbed her and floated near the fluorescent lights staring down and at the sleeping pups and playing music to them. Lenore's bow kept up with the music, and the sounds coming out of Lenore were not just violin sounds but the sounds of many instruments. Deep hypnotic voices blended and mixed with these sounds of Lenore's instruments in bizarre but sensible-seeming ways. The music even hooked into my eye-blinking mechanism like electrodes hooking into a controller for a computer. Every note became a blink that I felt compelled to keep up. Something clicked in my head too, and I realized the music was actually being generated by my eyelids as much as by the sawing of Lenore's bow.

The clicks continue and a mild anxiety sets in. My back banged against the metal covering of the hanging lights. My eyes were going wild. I couldn't keep up the blinking! But I must, because between blinks I now can see brief images of things I really want to see. Is that Jenny appearing there? Oh, hi Jenny! I see you. Blink! I want to shut my eyes to see her all the time, but I have to keep blinking or the music will stop. I can't let the music stop. It's not my place! Oh, goodbye, Jenny. Open, blink! I see you again. Open, blink! Goodbye! I love you. Open, blink! I see you. Goodbye! Open, blink! Oh, I want to be with you. I want to know your life in the wilderness! Open, blink! Jenny, be safe in your cavern home with Max and all your loyal subjects! Open, blink! Goodbye, Jenny! Thank you! Open, blink! I love you! Open, blink! Music! Open, blink! Art! Open, blink! Nature! Open, blink! Understanding? Open, blink! Goodbye! Open, blink! I love you, Jenny! Open, blink, open, blink, open, blink! Oh, Music!" Open...., bliiiiiink....Falling!

A gentle hand was shaking my shoulder. "Ella, wake up. You fell asleep with the dogs. Bryson has left for the night."

"Brandon. Oh, my God, I fell asleep playing Lenore! I fell from the ceiling!" I looked up at him standing strongly above me.

"Ella, Lenore's not here. You were twitching and dreaming. We're in the lab."

"I know. In my *dream*. Lenore, and Jenny. I was with *Jenny*!"

"Okay. Sit up, dog-woman. We can talk about that later. It's time to work on Sybil while these guys are asleep."

Brandon helped me rise from the warm nest of dog bodies on the blanket. Mavis looked at me reprovingly like "why would you ever want to leave?" and then resigned herself to cuddling with Sam.

"This has been good for them," I said.

"You mean good for *you*," said Brandon.

"That too." I rubbed my eyes. "These lights are harsh here."

"They're as dim as they can get and still be on. I've got the heating pad set up in the cubicle next door. Are you ready?"

"Yes, but I have to pee first."

"Why am I not surprised? I'll get the sequences ready."

In the bathroom I shook off the uncomfortable feeling of the dream and my longing for Jenny. Two dreams in one day. Am I losing my mind? I've played Lenore long enough to know that when she decides to show me something I better pay attention, even if I'm just playing her in a dream. Yes, I really needed to think about this blinking thing later. The toilet flushed automatically when I stood up. I waved my hands under the sink faucet and splashed water on my face. No need to touch anything in here. As usual, that fact pissed me off. Our bodies are basically warm bags of dancing germs that thrive on variety, yet modern architects are deluded into imposing on us energy-sucking bathroom fixtures to provide automatic sterility in the name of health and sanitation. What a misguided waste of money!

I found Brandon in the second cubicle, and Sybil was already out of the rolling suitcase Brandon borrowed from me without permission to bring her over here. She was looped over his shoulder, tongue darting in and out tasting the air. Must smell pretty antiseptic in here for a snake. I blinked and my own tongue tasted like metal all of a sudden. Did I just connect with her? *I did. Maybe I'm still not completely back from my dream with Lenore.*

"I found another blanket and put the heating pad on medium underneath it," said Brandon. I looked at the platform where the sedated dogs were usually strapped in.

"Are you going to try to strap her in?

"I don't think we can without hurting her or freaking her out. Hopefully the heat will lull her sufficiently."

"Is she hungry?"

"What? You want to feed her one of Bryson's rats?"

"Ha! Yes, I really *do*, but never mind. I forgot you fed her last night."

"You're easy to entertain. If bouncing over here in this piece of crap luggage hasn't rattled her too much, she should settle down on this blanket."

In deference to our togetherness, I decided not to defend my thrift-store taste in luggage. Brandon dipped his shoulder gently and guided Sybil's head onto the platform. As soon as she felt the fuzzy heat on her head, she bent her neck sideways and pulled the rest of her body off of Brandon with a thud.

"Whoa, that was quick," I said.

"Yeah, she can move fast when she wants to, like all reptiles."

"Scary."

"Yes, especially now that she has gotten so big, but look at her settle in now!"

It was true. Sybil coiled herself in a huge spiral with her head resting on her abdomen. We couldn't have strapped her into a better position to catch the visuals than the one she just chose accidentally by herself. Or was it an accident? *Did she connect with my mind and figure out what's going on?*

"Shall we get some popcorn for her? I think she's ready for the show!" I said.

"Popped rat heads? Free refills if she orders the largest size with a large soda?"

"Exactly." I laugh. "What do you want me to do?"

"Come with me and watch her on the cam while I monitor the levels. Let me know if she changes positions, okay? Let's go!"

We shut her into the cubicle, checked on the sleeping dogs, and headed back to the control panel. I logged in next to Brandon and pulled up the surveillance suite. I clicked on Cubicle B and there she was on camera from two angles. "She's holding her position," I said.

"Good," said Brandon. I looked over and saw the chanting and visual sequence he had up on his monitor. It's the same one the dogs went through today. No reason for it not to be. There really is basically just one tape that has proven effective, the one recorded from the breakthrough treatments on Jenny and Max four years ago. Because the meditation and quantum sounds from the monks worked on Jenny and Max, even though Jenny and Max cleverly hid the results from them to win their freedom from the lab, the thrust of the lab's research since has been to figure out why. Bryson and Ken were focusing on measuring and analyzing the tape's effects on the dog brains of the new subjects rather than on dissecting and analyzing the sounds on the tape itself.

Personally, I had my doubts about this approach, scientific or not. The monks originally chanted directly at the pups to try to elevate their awareness and communications skills. The recordings were made mostly just for record keeping. Still it was true that after the monks were sent back to Nepal, Bryson and Ken stubbornly kept replaying the tapes for Jenny and Max over and over, so who knows what really worked? Even though, as Bryson says, there is no detectable scientific difference between the sound of the recorded sessions and the original sound and visual stimulation the dogs received, I have my doubts. Human intentionality is a real thing, I feel, even if it can't exactly be measured scientifically. The *will* of the monks might be somehow missing on the tapes, no matter how exacting they were originally recorded, especially now because the subjects are Mavis, Sam, and the four others, not Jenny and Max whom the monks knew personally.

That's my argument, anyway. I get it, though, that it is too expensive to keep a bunch of chanting monks around for years on end. And, I admit, I could be very wrong about my argument. When I first inherited Lenore, for instance, I found a picture of my grandfather buried deep in a hidden pocket of her worn-out case. The yellowed and faded black and white portrait had obviously been taken long before I was born, yet every time I look at Granddad's beautiful young face in the photo, I know deep in my heart that he had that picture taken expressly so that he could squirrel it away with Lenore just to send his love to me. Who knows what powers the monks were really playing with when they came to chant in the Brecken lab? What did they *really* intend? Did they even know themselves? Were they motivated by prescience? By a sense of hope? Or perhaps only by their perception that the consensus world we live in was about to radically change forever? When you think about it, intentionality and the deeper realities that selfless dedicated meditators move in are probably way more complex than we far-less-enlightened mortals may ever really know.

I looked at Sybil resting on the heating pad when the sequence kicked in. Brandon brought the visuals up slowly so as not to startle her. She lifted her head, but didn't change her coil position. "Holding steady," I said.

"Good. Bringing up the audio now."

"Can she even hear it?"

"No. Not like the pups can. She'll register the vibrations, though, that's about all. Her sense of smell, now *that's* different. Undoubtedly she can smell every living thing that has ever breathed in that cubicle."

"Wow. Still steady. How can we tell if this changes her?"

"No idea, but I doubt if she has the social intelligence to hide changes like Jenny did. Snakes can sneak around and camouflage themselves pretty well, but in the open they aren't very good at hiding their emotions or empathizing with other animals. They're power creatures. If this changes her, I suspect we'll see the signs right away."

"Like when I played Lenore for her the other night?"

"Yeah. Correct. She kept looking from you to me and back again like a reptilian bobble head."

"Yes, for a whole hour, then she stopped when I stopped playing." Suddenly, I felt my tongue tasting metallic again.

"I think I tasted what she was smelling in there a moment ago."

"Really? Hmm....What's she doing now?"

"Still steady, except she's bobbing and weaving her head a little bit."

"Okay. I'm going to full levels now. Keep watching."

The head bobbing continued but Sybil stayed put on the blanket. "She's still good," I said, but my tongue was tasting mushrooms now and dirt from a musty forest floor. "I think I'm definitely connecting with her sense of taste."

"Keep watching. We're halfway there."

"What if she decides she doesn't want to go back into the luggage afterwards?"

"I guess the lab will have a new resident, then, until we can figure out a good dose of sedative and a safe way to administer it."

"Maybe we should have done that already?" Brandon nodded but didn't say anything. I looked at the clock icon on my screen. It was getting late, and I was predictably hungry again despite the weird jungle tastes coming in and out of my mouth. It's not easy being a night eater. Well, actually, I'm an anytime eater and in large quantities. That's just me. What can I say? I'm getting a pizza after this no matter what it might taste like after this and whether Brandon agrees to wheel Sybil into the all-night food court or not.

Ten minutes later the tape wound down and the chanting faded. Just as the visuals cut out, Sybil unwound herself
and slithered to the edge of the table. "Brandon. She's on the
move!"

"Okay, I'll go grab her and put her in the luggage. We
can check her out at home. Cut the music to the dogs, will
you? We'll need to wake them up and put them into their
kennels before we go."

"Oh really? We need to do that? No duh? Thanks for letting me know the obvious, Mansplainer." I think I'm getting
hangry.

"Right, sorry to sound like I am giving orders. It's getting
late. I need to get some rest."

"Food first, then rest, Bwana."

"You're right. I'm starving, too. Order ahead, will you?"
I moved over to his computer and instigated the shutdown
for the relaxation tapes, then moved back to mine to look
at the monitors. Mavis and Sam were still sacked out. We
could just let them stay there tonight. No. Bryson would
have a fit. I watched Brandon enter Sybil's cubicle pulling my
suitcase behind him. My luggage is going to smell like snake
now. Why couldn't he have used his own suitcase? Sybil was
stretched up at the side of the table looking like she was going to fall off at any minute. I saw Brandon approach her and
rub the side of her head the way he does to invite her onto his shoulders. She responded immediately and slithered
up his arm swinging her heavy body onto his torso. I shut
down the computers and got up to wake Mavis and Sam. I
paused at my backpack hanging in the hallway and pulled
out my phoneglasses. Just as I was blinking the toppings onto

my pizza order at the food court, I heard a frightened shout from Brandon.

"Sybil, stop! Stop! No! No! Aaargh!"

I ran down the hall and almost tripped over Mavis and Sam dashing out of their cubicle. I did a little hop on one leg to avoid crashing into them and ducked into Sybil's cubicle. There she was, wrapped around Brandon in a full-on death squeeze. He had dropped to his knees and was beating and pulling at the coil closest to his neck. His biceps were bulging with desperation, but they were no match for Sybil's taut strength. She was waving her head above his with a far-off look in her eyes and pulsing her muscles like she was having some kind of bowel movement–the killing instinct.

"Brandon! What should I do?" No answer. He can't even breathe. I had to kill this snake before she killed Brandon. I pounded on Sybil with my fists and looked around desperately, but there's nothing in the cubicle more lethal than the heating pad cord. "Hang on. I'm going to the kitchen to get a knife!"

I tore out of there into the hallway. Should I hit the fire alarm? No, not yet. There's a box knife in the kitchen. *Maybe if I stab her, she'll let go!*

I ripped open the kitchen drawer and rummaged frantically for the box knife that I know is in there. It's not there. I go to the next drawer that has the plastic bags and zip ties. It's there. *Bryson, he never puts things back where they belong!* I fumbled the thing in my hands until I jammed the safety slide into the full open position. "I got it. I'm coming, Brandon!" I shouted. I heard a muffled response and a thud. I sprinted back down the hall.

I flew into the cubicle ready to bury the knife deeply into Sybil's flesh only to find her unwound and relaxed on the floor with Mavis and Max licking her gently. Brandon was slumped against the legs of the platform rubbing his neck and taking deep breaths.

"Oh my God! What happened? Should I kill her?"

"No!" Brandon gasped, raising his hand to stop me. "She's under control. Leave her be!" He stood up and leaned on the platform rubbing his neck, breathing deeply. "The dogs did it. Amazing," he said. I looked at Mavis and Max. Mavis turned to look at me triumphantly, her brown eyes glowing. She licked Sybil.

"I'm okay. A little shaken, that's all. She was so quick!" He reached down to pet Max.

I took in the ramifications. Animal control, just like Max. "Wow. A breakthrough! Just not how we expected," I said to Brandon when he stood up like nothing's happened. He's more than okay. He laughed and rubbed his neck.

"Or they were holding out on us, but now we know we have a couple of new masters on our hands," he said, eyeing Mavis and Sam with grateful admiration. "Good thing we had them close by!"

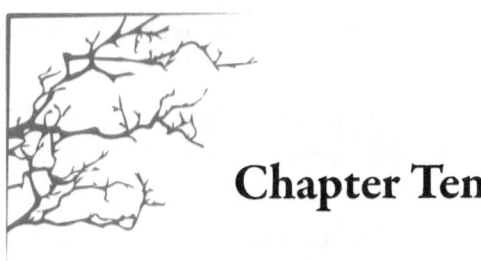

Chapter Ten

"YOUR DAD WARNED ME that you two would shake things up around here," said Dr. Bryson staring in the window of the cubicle at Mavis and Sam curled up with Sybil on the blanket. "And, I should have listened to him. The only scientific evidence you have is flimsy at best given that you two operated with a rogue plan and didn't even bother to record the surveillance footage."

"You don't believe us?" said Brandon.

"Sure I believe you. You would have just taken the snake home had it not happened instead of dragging me out of bed to see this trainwreck. The point isn't *me* believing it, but the world." He ran his hand through his balding head, frowning.

"Sybil had me in a death grip and was not letting go. The dogs hear my cry. They walk in and she relaxes, completely contradicting everything we know about pythons once they get a grip on prey," said Brandon.

Bryson growls. "Don't you think I know that? But you're just an undergrad looking to make a *big* impact not caring about protocol or professionalism. No one is going to believe you, or me for that matter. Your *girlfriend* is your witness to all this? It's laughable."

"So what do we do, try to get Sybil to choke me again while you record it on your phoneglasses? Because I don't care. I'll do it again." Brandon's biceps were flexing again. *We should have kept this to ourselves.*

"How do you know the dogs would save you again? It's not ethical to put yourself deliberately in danger like that. All of us would get kicked out of here if we tried your foolishness again even if they saved you repeatedly, and we clearly can't go public with what already has happened due to lack of evidence. No, we need real evidence of the tape's quantum manipulation, *if* that's what really happened. In the meantime, we've got to keep quiet about this and test them in some other way."

"Okay, but how?" I said.

"I don't know yet. I'll have to think about it. Don't mention this to Dr. Vern, either. We don't need him getting on *his* high horse any higher than he already is. If we get further evidence, fine, but not until then. In the meantime we need a safe place for our little pet here."

"I'll just take her back home," said Brandon.

"Well, that's brave of you, but I don't think so. Unless you want another chiropractic adjustment from serpentes pythonditae here."

"We can take Mavis and Sam home too," I said, looking at Brandon.

"No way. I already told you, too dangerous. Also that would blow all our environmental controls."

"But what if a lab environment is the thing that's holding them back? What if they *need* a human environment to progress?" I pressed, hearing my Dad's voice in my head.

"Hmm. I know what you're thinking, that the successful subjects might not have developed their skills until after they left the lab, but that's why we brought you guys here and spent so much money on a homey environment in the lab. It's the best we can do and still control the parameters. We'll never know exactly what we're doing if we don't stick to our controls!"

"So much *money?* Come on! A few dog toys? A wading pool? Jenny and Max had *so* much more. Jenny learned art history, for crying out loud! Who are you kidding?" Homey? What's *your* home like? Have you ever even owned a dog!

"Calm down, Miss. Do you think I don't *know* a lab's not not the same as a true home environment?"

I take a deep breath. *The important thing is the animals.* "Okay, sorry, Dr. Bryson. This is probably a debate for when we're not all dead tired. So you have a plan for right now?"

"Sybil, it's a female, right?"

"Know a lot of men named Sybil?" I said. Brandon gave me a warning look. I took a slow deep breath.

"Ella, please," said Bryson, running his hand over his head again. "I do have an idea. I've been working with Dr. Olaf in animal pathology on invasive species control. He has a male python over there in a rainforest room with enough space for a guest. I'll have him send his graduate students over here in the morning to scoop up your new donation to his department. He'll thank me for tracking this snake down. He's actually been looking for one that can't be traced to a black market."

I looked at Brandon and he shrugged. "What about the dogs?" I said.

"They look comfortable enough. Let them stay in there with the snake for right now. Bring them some food and water before you go, and get here early tomorrow before Dr. Ken. I'm staying here. Don't worry. I'm too wound up to sleep, and I've always got lab work to do. We'll talk about what happened tomorrow over a gallon of coffee. At the very least we need new scans for these two dogs. What are their names? It doesn't matter. I suspect we'll see major growth in their frontal cortices in comparison to the other subjects."

"Their *names* are Mavis and Sam. You've been working with them for *months*. Invasive species, huh? Does this Dr. Olaf maybe have a thing against snakes?" I can't help it. Once I get angry it takes me a long time to reboot my trust in those who set me off. I got another look from Brandon. *Why'd I let him talk me into waking Bryson up about this?*

"On the contrary, snakes are important predators. Intelligently introduced, they can hold down populations of rats and other destructive pests. Sybil will be well taken care of. Might even get to have a family, Ella. It's the best we can do right now unless you've got a better idea, which you don't. Glad you didn't get killed, Brandon. Now, go home, you two. You've done enough damage for one night. I'll get the subjects water and food. If we're lucky this *might* turn out to have been a helpful evening, even if it, unfortunately, has to remain a secret." Bryson put his hands on his hips. "Be glad you have an understanding supervisor or you'd both be out on your undergraduate butts applying to the music department or something equally useless."

"Music is the highest form of art, Dr. Bryson. Maybe you should listen to it sometime," I said.

Brandon took my arm. "Ella, will you please calm down? He didn't mean anything by it. He's giving us a break, you know. I'm sure he loves music," said Brandon. "Thanks for understanding, Dr. Bryson, and for keeping us around. Sorry we messed up. We're going to figure this out with your help. Thanks. It's going to work out and be good. It's in the cards. See you early tomorrow. Come on, Ella, let's go get that pizza. I need you to help me celebrate the joy of breathing."

Only because I was exhausted and wasn't the one who almost died, I let Brandon stear me out of the lab and away from Bryson and my babies. I hoped he would remember to feed them.

Chapter Eleven

I WAS IN THE FOOD COURT uni-sex bathroom washing my hands like Lady Macbeth. Back at Wandering Pines I would never wash my hands before eating, even after working in the organic garden, because I wanted the earth's biome inside me connecting me to all that is healthy, but around Brecken it's very different. No matter how much I scrub or shower, I can never get the stench of laboratory chemicals and caged rats off of me. Or maybe it's permanently embedded in my sinuses, I don't know.

Another late-night eater joined me at the sinks, so I had to cut my ablutions short, but not before I also splashed some water on my face. Too late I remember this bathroom only has jet-powered hand dryers, so I rubbed the water out of my eyes with my knuckles and crammed my hands into the unnatural energy-wasting hurricane. All these urban bathroom fixtures are supposed to protect you from germs, but the mist from hands fly everywhere and everyone has to pull on the same door handle to get out of here, so again I ask what's the point? I hated this place.

Back at the table, the pizza has arrived perched on a stainless steel throne with an inviting spatula ready to serve the first slice. "What are you waiting for? Not hungry?" I said sitting down.

"No, you first. I'm still wondering if my throat is wide enough to swallow."

"Does it hurt? Maybe we should go to the clinic? Tell them Bryson tried to choke you."

"Nah, I'm fine. I just can't believe I let you talk me into anchovies again." He picked up the spatula, folded a piece horizontally, and crammed the end of it into his mouth. I followed suit. The cheesy fishy deliciousness was amazing and immediately fixed my rotten mood.

"Look, Brandon. We've got to rescue Mavis and Sam," I said, swallowing, "but first we've got to talk about Bryson. Should we trust him? He doesn't seem to have much respect for Ken." I belched and started on a second piece. I marveled that the most serious things in the world could never supersede eating for me. That's one addiction Enlightenment didn't cure me of. In fact, I needed to ask Dad if using it gave me a permanent case of the munchies. Not that I'm complaining, mind you. This pizza was *so* good.

"They just have different styles and, frankly, interests. Ken is an academic, kind but plodding. Probably ready to retire, but genuinely interested in the new research. Bryson tries harder, I think, because he's more brilliant. Fire in the belly, you know? Thinking outside the box." There's grease all over Brandon's upper lip. He needs a shave. I think about what he's like in bed. Grrr. Now I know I am feeling better.

"Well, so what's he so fired up about? I mean, in his little Wizard of Oz lab behind the curtain?"

Brandon laughed. "Nothing to see here, folks! Just ignore the man behind the visqueen curtain!"

"Right. Exactly. And he's skipping sleep to pull levers back there, on a CRISPR machine no less. What's up?"

"Oh, you noticed that, huh?" Brandon scooped up another piece and crammed it in his mouth. "Gwanageddanobelprive ..."

"What? Swallow, please, then talk." I handed him a napkin.

"Sorry, Nobel Prize. He's going to get one, I think."

"Are you kidding? What an egomaniac!"

"No, he's not *aiming* for that. It's not even on his mind. *I* just think he's going to get one. Or probably should. For putting nature back in balance."

"Well, if humans wipe themselves out, and the Mavises and Sams of the world take over like we hope they can, I doubt if they will care about prizes and continuing with that fine Norwegian tradition."

"Likely true. Still, the world needs more than just an intelligent master species capable of adapting. It needs rebalancing and some major repairs at all levels."

"Bryson is repairing things?"

"Well, I don't know everything yet, but I'm gaining his trust."

"So, spill, what is he working on? How are you gaining his trust?"

"Look. You've got to keep this under your hat. He could never get funding for what he is working on."

"So he *is* leaching from the budget. I knew it!"

"It's not like everyone else around here doesn't do the same thing. Science moves way faster than grant awards can ever keep up. You do what you have to do." Brandon shrugged.

"And he thinks it's justified because he is saving the world."

"Well, yeah. He's never outright said that, but he may very well be secretly doing that very thing. Rebalancing. Don't you think that's a Nobel Prize thing to do? Putting things back into balance?"

I take a moment to think about this. "He's sneaky, like we were when we released Lyca and Siam from Renegade's zoo into the wilderness?"

"Yes, and Lyca and Siam are doing pretty great out there with Jenny and Max. Anyone who cares about what is happening to our damaged earth is going to have to act in whatever ways are still open to us, ethical or otherwise." I nodded and grabbed another slice.

"Well, as unindicted co-conspirator for the release of Renegade's famous lions into the California wilderness, I guess I have to hear you out. What's Bryson up to?"

"Well, I'm not positive, but since I have been staying in the lab extra hours–sorry about that, I know it hasn't been good for our, ah-hem, love life–I think I've put it together. He's bioengineering pathogens to control invasive species."

"Pathogens, huh? Is he working with that snake guy, Dr. Olaf, on that?"

"Yes, well, not directly. I don't think anyone at Brecken really knows about his CRISPR lab in the storeroom. I've never seen Olaf in there, but, whatever he is doing, it is clear that Bryson is overwhelmed and needs help. Maybe he's waiting until he really has something legit before dragging in anyone else, but I think he'll let me help him out if I keep working for him the way I have been."

"You mean obsessively?" He raised his eyebrows, not disagreeing. "Well, Ken must know what's up?" I continued.

"No, I don't think so. Ken has only four places he goes: the cubicle control room, his office, Starbucks, and home, wherever that is, a faculty apartment in the old section, I think. Oh, and nice guy lessons at the chapel on Sundays. That's five."

"I've seen him go to the restroom a few times."

"And the restroom. He's definitely not in on Bryson's extra-curricular activities."

"Want to order another one?" I picked off a few cheese dribbles stuck to the spatula.

"No, but since we finished our pizza dinner like good boys and girls, I think we deserve an ice cream sandwich for the walk home, don't you?"

"Let's go get Mavis and Sam first. They're miserable there."

"I understand your impulse, but I think we'd better just let them babysit Sybil tonight like we decided. We can talk about them tomorrow after we get some sleep."

Chapter Twelve

AS WE TURNED THE KEY to our apartment my finger-tips tingled, and not just from the delicious and numbing-ly cold Klondike bar I devoured on the walk home. I see Lenore's case leaning against the couch. Oh no, did I miss my gig at Comey's?

"Brandon! My gig! Is it Friday?"

"No, Thursday, I think. Yes, Thursday. Well, very early Friday morning, actually."

"Whew, I thought I missed it."

"You really need some sleep, babe. You play tomorrow night, or tonight, however you want to say it. In about eigh-teen hours." He put his hand around my shoulder.

"Yeah, I'm just going to play a tune or two to beam down, okay?"

"Okay, I'm taking a shower. I reek."

"Let me in there first, okay? I have to pee."

"Of course." He smiled at me, but he looked as wiped out as I felt. I can't blame him. Any day a brain-zapped python squeezes you around the neck would probably exhaust me too.

I peed and washed my face for real this time, a decent scrub. It felt great. I'll shower in the morning. I really needed to play Lenore.

When I came out, Brandon was waiting there undressed for the shower. His body was carved and beautiful like Michelangelo's statue of David. I'm glad I didn't lose him. As we passed each other in the doorway, I slapped him affectionately on his muscular butt like the Brecken football coach does to his favorite players. Touching Brandon's body makes my fingers tingle even more for Lenore.

I unzipped Lenore from her case and went into our extra bedroom. A luxury, I know, for a couple of undergrads, but my Dad has an old friend in the housing office, so we got a sweet apartment. Sybil's empty cage was in here, and the room was pretty soundproof, so it's okay to play fiddle tunes at odd hours even though there were probably a hundred people asleep nearby. It's not like playing in the mountains at Wandering Pines, but what are you going to do?

I rosined up the bow and put Lenore to my chin. As usual she was in perfect tune. I don't tell anybody this, but I haven't ever had to tune her or even replace her strings since inheriting her from Granddad. I'm not even sure the pegs still work in her peg box. Probably they would if they ever had to.

Sometimes playing Lenore is intense like having sex, but tonight when I worked her bow she was in a different mood than I was, a focusing outward mood, a different kind of passionate longing. Was she feeling cooped up too maybe? The green hills of the Irish countryside seemed to be on her mind. Perhaps a memory of hers? A previous owner a long time ago? Guided by Lenore, my fingers find "Drowsy Maggie,""Nellie Mahoney,""Gerr the Rigor," and a bunch of other Celtic classics. I played until I could no longer hold up my head. She released me reluctantly. I put her back in her case, peed again, and crawled into bed with Brandon who was snoring. His snoring style was endearing, the noise subtle like a kitten's purr. I've never told him that he does this, and I suddenly wonder why. Do I know that he is afraid to have a gentle side, a receiving side? Or am *I* the one afraid to acknowledge that side of him exists. Is my fear of letting him express it openly why he doesn't very often? I sighed. *Relationships are so complicated.*

Head on my pillow, I listened to the unconscious deep feline purring of my boyfriend and wondered if Jenny and Max heard the same thing cuddling at night with Lyca and the lions. I looked at Brandon's beautiful neck and flashed on Sybil's terrifying death grip. How could he possibly sleep so soundly after that experience? Could *I* even get to sleep?

The Brecken Vista nighttime semi-darkness made the white room look sickly yellow, like the skin of some dying person in a nursing home. Shaking the image, I focused instead on Lenore's tunes still playing in my head. I snuggled up to Brandon's muscular body as the wind picked up and fluttered the curtains with a welcome breeze from the ocean shore too many buildings away from here. I fell asleep feeling about as safe as I could manage in my concrete prison.

Chapter Thirteen

BRANDON'S PHONEGLASSES go off just as dawn was turning the room a slightly warmer shade of urine yellow. "Oh, let me stay on the sand!" moaned Brandon. He waved his hands to stop the drum-beat alarm he insisted upon waking up to.

"Huh?" I said, my head reverberating.

"We were swimming on a big white beach in Hawaii to celebrate," he shouted.

"Go back to sleep, Brandon. Please. Hawaii? Celebrate what? Our honeymoon?"

"No, this was on the Big Island, not Waikiki, dreamer." He sat up and pulled the covers right off me. This was a regular occurrence.

"People get married on the Big Island too," I said. I was about to point out to my overloud boyfriend that *he* was the one dreaming just now, then I remembered. Sybil and the lab! "We've got to go meet Bryson!" I shouted and sat up.

"Yes, but I need to tell you about this dream first. It felt *so* real." *Why does he have to talk so loud in the morning?*

"Dreams usually do," I said, lying down again and gently pulling back my share of blanket warmth. Far be it from me to be the one to boing out of bed even if there *is* an emergency.

"No, this one was different, Ella. It felt like our garden dream back at Wandering Pines."

Lenore. She was reaching out to him too? Now I am interested. "Okay, tell me what you saw. Did you hear me playing last night through the wall?"

"Yes, for a minute before I fell asleep. Irish, right?"

"Right." I waited. Brandon's more of a doer than a talker, so when he gets in a chatting mood, I've learned to give him plenty of time. Brandon put his hands behind his head, and in the momentary silence I was amazed that this tough but beautiful man had shared a bed with me for the last half year. He had just the right amount of hair on his muscular chest, and those *abs. Calm down!*

"Sybil was around my neck. Of course I would dream about that after what happened. But she wasn't hurting me in my dream. She was uncoiling and pulling me upward, like she could fly and wanted me to join her. And she was waving her head back and forth chanting something. It sounded Polynesian, like that old Disney movie you insisted we watch at the winery last summer, you know, the one named after the Hawaiian volcano?"

"Moana."

"Yes, a chant from that, but more real, not cartoon-like. Like shamans were calling to her from outside of her while singing inside her throat at the same time."

"Okay... ?" I looked at his throat and the talisman of a coiled snake he wore on a silver chain around his neck. No one knows more about tarot than Brandon does, although lately he doesn't talk much about it with me like he did in high school.

"That's about it, except we blinked our way over there and released her deep in the rainforest. No, we let two Sybils go. There were two of her somehow. And it felt like a huge accomplishment, like bringing what she was singing into reality. We were celebrating alone on a huge white beach."

"Were we naked?" I put my hand on his belly.

"I don't remember, but I woke up before we could go swimming in the warm surf." He cuddled back down next to me and kissed me.

"A swim in Hawaii sounds pretty good to me right about now," I purred. Brandon's smell makes me think about the refreshing reservoir we used to swim in at Wandering Pines and the long hikes on the school's wilderness ranch. I missed it almost as much as hikes by the ocean in Harbor Vista. "Let's go there right now. About the last thing I needed on my day's agenda was a crowded lab and a coffee shop with no trees or fresh air."

"I hear you, but be here now, babe. Pretend that you *want* to go to Brecken, and focus on the good. Come on, let's go. The work is important. Enough dreaming. Bryson and the dogs need us." He pulled his body away from mine and started getting dressed enthusiastically. Was this display of sincere dedication to the work we have to do calculated to sweep me up in his wake? The possibility annoyed me. What's wrong with a little morning messing around? Still, I can see that at least part of his body was trying to convince him to stay right there in our bedroom and relax. Better than nothing, I guess.

"Should we stop and get an aloha shirt for Sybil?" I managed to quip, watching him pull on his shorts and black jeans.

"At the local surf shop for talented reptiles? Sure, babe! Come on, I'll make the coffee."

Chapter Fourteen

WE SWIPED OUR WAY INTO the lab around 7:30, and the caged pups all started barking at once. *Poor things.* I let them out of their cells and herded them toward the door outside. No matter how much abuse humans, especially scientific humans, dump on them, these guys still loved to greet us and each new day with energy and enthusiasm. Bryson emerged from the storage room wearing his lab coat and nodded at us curtly over the scrum. In contrast, Ken usually verbalized a greeting, but he was nowhere to be seen yet. No surprise. He never showed up before 9:00 no matter what's going on.

"I'll get the food bowls ready," said Brandon.

"Check on Mavis and Sam," I said. I grabbed the pooper scooper and a bucket and herded the pups into the outside pen. Behind me, I saw Brandon following Bryson into the cubicle where we left Sybil.

It took about five minutes for the pups to do their business. I followed them around on the grass like I was some deranged character hunting for Easter eggs, then went back inside to dump my stinky haul into the garbage can. I rinsed my hands without soap and walked toward the cubicle.

"Oh, you ready? I haven't set out the food yet," said Brandon from the control computers. He and Bryson were looking at one of his many pages of obscure data. Again, Bryson nodded a gruff greeting at me.

"That's all right. I'm going to let them just play out there until we get around to them. How are our snake sitters doing?"

"Alive, well," said Brandon. "I fed them. Sybil is sleeping on the heating pad."

"I'll go let them out with the others."

"That would be good. We need to move the snake subject before anyone else arrives. Olaf is opening his lab for us at 8:00," said Bryson.

I left them and entered the cubicle where Mavis and Sam said good morning by practically licking me to death. Mavis knew better than to jump up on me, but Sam hadn't quite gotten the message yet. He planted his front paws squarely on my chest. Ouch! *Boys, developmentally a bit behind and always aiming for the chest.* I pushed him off me and rubbed him playfully around the ears. My face was soaked with dog kisses.

Sybil may be asleep, but her tongue was moving in and out and her eyes were half open. The rolling suitcase was right next to her on the floor. Hopefully she won't be in a mood to strangle again when we try to stuff her back in there.

"Thanks for saving Brandon last night you guys," I said to the dogs when they settled down, and I've used a Kleenex on my face. "Come on. Want to go outside?" Mavis looked at me like, "Are you kidding? Yes, I have to pee!"

I let them outside with the other pups, washed my face, and rejoined Brandon and Bryson at the computer. Bryson looked exhausted. He had swollen red eyes just like the tortured young interns around here who shuffled back and forth from their exhausting residencies.

"So what's the plan?" I said.

"Let's go," said Bryson, ignoring my question. "We'll scan everyone when we get back. See where Mavis and Sam stand out."

"Shall I print this?" asked Brandon.

"Yes, one copy for Olaf. Just this page," said Bryson. He pulled out his phoneglasses and blinked through his texts. "All right. He's there waiting for us."

"Maybe we want Mavis and Sam to go with us, just in case...?" I asked. Brandon shook his head.

"Won't hurt. Go get them. Wait, are they outside? You let them *out?*" said Bryson.

"Bodily needs, Dr. Bryson. Even these dogs have them too, you know. I'll go get them."

"Forget it," said Brandon. "Don't need them."

"Really? Are you kidding? It's no problem. I'm getting them! They could use a change of scenery whether they save your life again or not," I said.

"Stop fighting," said Bryson. "I said it wouldn't hurt. At this point, those two are in a control category of their own. Come on, Brandon. Let's put your pet into that transporter."

All I have to do is flash a leash outside and the dogs all lined up hoping to be the ones chosen for a walk and a rare chance to get out of there for a while. Here we were trying to breed super intelligent dogs, and Bryson kept them in a super low-stimulation lab environment because of not wanting to violate established Brecken protocols for animal subjects and thereby lose his funding. It made about as much sense as the protocol of testing promising cancer drugs only on desperate people about to die anyway when the subjects you really need to test new drugs on are the legally more risky patients who are only marginally sick and have a genuine chance to be healed. Medicine and science, is this the best humanity can come up with? I snapped the leashes on Mavis and Sam and left the other very disappointed dogs outside in the yard.

By the time I got back to the cubicle, Brandon was zipping up my bulging suitcase. "She'll be harder to handle after we bounce her over there, but at least I got her in the suitcase while she was still waking up," he said.

"Well, I guess Sybil and I have that in common, morning doldrums," I said. Mavis and Sam sniffed the zipper of the suitcase enthusiastically. They say snakes don't have any identifiable scent, but that doesn't appear to be true for Sybil, apparently.

"Let's get going!" said Bryson.

The suitcase was noisy bouncing over the millions of bricks in the central quad and across the labyrinth of cement walking paths that led to Olaf's lab building. Mavis and Sam lurched after every squirrel they saw, making my shoulder sockets pop, but I managed to hang on to them. The sun was already generating significant heat. It will definitely be bright and hot outside today, but we won't even notice with all the air conditioning and fluorescent lighting. I thought of the dogs stuck back in the lab. I really needed to walk with them in the mountains or something very soon.

Bryson swiped us into Olaf's zoology complex, and we rolled Sybil past a long hallway of stuffed and live animals in glass displays until we got to the main zoology lab. Just like our lab, of course, it smelled of rat. The smell was mingled a bit with monkey poop, but definitely still primarily rat, the universal stench of biology labs everywhere.

"Bryson!" yelled Olaf. "Over here!" Olaf, true to his name, was one of those Scandinavian types with light hair and a perpetually youthful appearance. He could be thirty or he could be sixty, hard to tell, but it was clear he ate salads with lots of avocados, exercised regularly on a NordicTrack, and took long saunas at the gym. Make the mistake of challenging Olaf to a cross country ski race, and he'll hand you your hamstrings on a stretcher. Does he miss ice and snow living here in Silicon Valley?

"Dr. Olaf. This is Brandon and Ella. You know, the special undergrads working with me on the quantum project."

"Oh, I know them. Pleased to meet both of you," said Dr Olaf shaking our hands. "Impressive what you did with the first dogs, Jenny and Max, correct?"

"Yes. Thank you," I said, surprised he knew their names. "But, they kind of did it themselves."

"Well, yes and no is what I heard about *that*. Glad to have you with us here at Brecken. What have you brought me?"

"Don't play games, Olaf. You know what's here. Let's get this python situated before all your cronies show up and ask too many questions," said Bryson.

"Relax, Bryson. We're more than set for your specimen. We have a little Garden of Eden for her, in fact, only the snakes are the ones we hope will bite the apple! Follow me, please."

"I have something else for you too," said Bryson. "Brandon?" Brandon hands Olaf the print out. Olaf gave it an eager glance, then shook his head.

"Still plugging the micro route to save us all, eh, Bryson? I'll give it to you, you never stop trying."

"It's easier to alter the genome of a virus than of a monkey, Olaf. This is progress."

"True, but monkeys are easier to track down if something goes wrong. I see that you have leashes on these canine experiments. Ever try to leash a bacterium?"

"Try making that argument to the Hawaiians who now have a mongoose problem to solve as well as a rat problem," countered Bryson.

Hawaii? Weird. I raised my eyebrows at Brandon.

"Yes, that was an unfortunate miscalculation. They were on the right track, though. Just not enough observational information and control. Microorganisms, on the other hand, can evolve even faster into something far more disastrous."

"Well, it's *already* a disaster out there no matter what is released, and you know it," said Bryson. "Just make sure you take a close look at that readout. I think it might just be what we are looking for. Sufficiently pathological, but with an expiration date."

"Telomerical inhibition? You found a way?!" Olaf takes another peek at the printout.

"Have CRISPR will travel. Old mice to experiment on helped too. We have a lot of them over there right now."

"Hmm ..." said Olaf.

I glanced at Brandon to see if was following all this. He frowned, scratched his head, and shrugged at me, but I could tell his brilliant mind was thinking hard about it. Olaf opened a double door, and we entered a hallway behind the animal displays. Mavis and Sam sniffed and hesitated, but followed me inside. Brandon rolled Sybil ahead of us behind Olaf and Bryson. We passed fifty pound bags of pellet food resting in metal garbage cans, hoses coiled on walls, and shelves filled with medicines, boxes of gloves, and hand tools for cleaning cages. I recognized the same type of pooper scooper I use hanging on a tool rack.

"Here we are," said Olaf. He opened the metal door to the python cage. "Sheldon, my fine fellow. You have a visitor!" he said. There was a ramp leading from the open door upward onto the floor of the display. "He's hiding, probably in his cave. Sheldon, come meet your new friend...what's her name?"

"Sybil," said Brandon. "She's been with me for over five years."

"Well, she'll be treated well here. Thank you. She'll feel at home among the humidity and native rainforest plants. You can let her out now. Just roll her up in there. Open it and just leave the suitcase. We'll retrieve it later when she's out."

Brandon rolled the suitcase up the ramp and unzipped the front flap. Sybil oozed out onto the straw floor like a prize fighter entering the ring. "Be a good girl," said Brandon. He watched her slither to the front display glass, her tongue working in and out to catch the scents. Brandon walked back down the ramp. He seemed a little sad. Sybil had been with him a long time. "Can we observe her from the front now?" he said.

"Of course. Let's go," said Olaf. He locked the door to the cage and nodded back the way we came.

We exited the access hallway and circled to the front of the display. Sybil had half her body up on the glass, and Sheldon was emerging from his plastic cave shelter. He's a little bigger than she was. In other words, huge. We watched him raise himself up to Sybil's height and slither up next to her against the glass. Their undersides are a light vanilla yellow. The two snake tongues flitted in and out wildly, and their eyes were wide, observing each other.

"They seem to almost be the same size, so that's good," said Olaf.

"So they'll probably just fight to a mutual death?" said Bryson.

"If they were going to fight, they would probably already be doing so. Reptiles move surprisingly fast, you know, when they are motivated by fear or aggression."

"Don't I know that!" said Brandon rubbing the back of his neck. Is he relieved or sad to be done with Sybil?

"Look what they are doing now!" said Bryson. The two were dancing, swaying back and forth against the glass.

"That's cobra behavior," said Olaf. "I've never seen that before in pythons. Amazing!"

"Look, it's coordinated!" I said. The snakes were moving as if choreographed in a complicated undulating rhythm.

"Mating ritual?" Bryson asked.

"Possibly, or a greeting ritual, but I've never read about or seen anything like this," said Olaf pulling out his phone-glasses to start a recording.

A pulsing tug in my fingers told me to tear my eyes away from the hypnotizing snake dance to look down at Mavis and Sam. Mavis was staring straight at Sam, and Sam was moving his head ever so slightly in rhythm with the snakes while staring intently at Sheldon and Sybil. I touched Brandon on the shoulder and pointed at Sam.

"Oh," said Brandon. "Wow."

"Yeah, *wow*," I said.

"What?" said Dr. Olaf.

"Let's just say that these two dogs have a special connection to the mystery of your dancing couple in there."

Chapter Fifteen

"SO, YOU DON'T THINK the snakes will ever attack humans again?" asked Olaf. We are all sitting in his private office. Bryson looked like lack of sleep was finally catching up to him. Mavis and Sam were by the closed door to the hallway lapping water from a semi-clean bowl Olaf found for them.

"No," said Brandon. "Because Mavis and Sam are masters now."

"But what does that mean, masters?" snapped Bryson. Apparently he's more awake than I gave him credit for.

"It means that since they telegraphically stopped Sybil from strangling me, chances are good she will never try strangling a human being again, at least not me."

"So it's a teaching thing?" said Bryson, yawning again without covering his mouth.

"Yes. Well, more than that. Max, my old Bernese Mountain Dog from the first group of subjects years ago was a master. I discovered his quantum powers because of Sybil's strange behavior. At first I noticed that she wouldn't eat unless Max was around. Then I noticed she wouldn't eat unless Max *barked*, so the next time, just to test him, I commanded Max not to bark, and lo and behold no eating, even though Sybil was long due for a feeding and laser-focused on the prey. Eventually I had to take the poor mouse out of her cage to prevent it from dying of stress. Eventually, Max and Sybil were so in tune with each other at feeding time that all I had to do was give Max permission to give Sybil permission to eat and bingo, it happened, eventually even without barking. After Max left with Jenny, Sybil never ate another mouse."

"So what do you feed her?"

"Rats. She only eats rats now. Look, I don't know exactly how it works, okay? I just know that because of exposure to the meditational chants in the lab, Max, and now Sam, probably in partnership with Mavis, are quantumly tapping into the logic and executive functioning centers of Sybil's reptilian brain. They are elevating the snake's cognitive and decision making abilities to a higher level through what we can only assume is some sort of quantum telepathic language they learned from the tapes. There's a reason Sybil and Suzy danced synchronized like that. A simple message of "don't kill each other" might have only left them ignoring each other. Instead the words from the master elevated their intelligence around that idea and turned it into a greater and more creative evolutionary suggestion involving choreography, art, *marriage* even, if you will. In other words, by stimulating a higher level of intelligence, something akin to human intelligence, a creative spiritual awareness of self and others was engendered that crossed the normal cognitive barriers of their breed."

"So, a super race of thinking pythons," said Bryson, rubbing his eyes. "With emotional awareness and intelligence, provided they hang around Mavis and Sam long enough?"

"Yes. It's just a theory, but we have evidence. The zoo lions that our first subjects, Max and Jenny, now live with in the wilderness are under their control but are passing learning milestones every day, most likely," I said.

"So, this is your hope for the future," said Olaf.

"Well, that's what we've been working on. Obviously humans are doing a piss-poor job of being intelligent and knowing our true place in the world," said Bryson. He picked up a Hamlet skull mug from Olaf's desk and pointed at it meaningfully. It would have been a funny reference if he didn't look a little dead himself right now.

"Yeah, dogs, snakes and lions probably wouldn't create climate change, greed, and global warfare," said Olaf.

"Exactly," said Bryson.

Olaf took a moment to look at me and Brandon in the eye. He breathed once deeply and let it out slowly. "So, we'll need to bring these two up to date on our pact, won't we, Bryson, since we have all been witnesses to what just happened in Sheldon's cage."

"Okay, but we need to sit on this, observe, and think for a while," said Bryson. "This development may change things, or it may not. To be sure, we need to see the snakes operating in the field. Olaf, about your staff, why don't we keep the cognitive developments in the new arrivals a secret for right now and let the two pythons get used to each other. Brandon, Olaf and I need to get new scans and readouts on these two subjects, the Golden and the Bernese, what are their names?" He glanced at me. "Oh, right, Mavis and Sam. Collate them, will you please, and report to me your thoughts? Come on, let's get back to the lab." He started to stand up.

My fingertips tingle and before I had a chance to stop myself, I blurted out, "Um, excuse me! If I'm to be a part of this mysterious pact, maybe you might be interested in what's on *my* mind right now, besides just purely wondering what all this is all about?"

Bryson sat back down reluctantly and closed his eyes, but Olaf looked at me attentively. I took a breath and adjusted my tone.

"With all due respect, look at us right now. We've been through a lot. Dr. Bryson, you can't even keep your eyes open. Clearly we are all too wiped out to do anything more than just go home to bed for a while. Don't you think we've done enough for one day and night? These pups are feeling it too. They need a walk outside more than they need to be hooked up to an MRI machine right now. Whatever you guys have up your sleeve for saving the world, non-stop action has a law of diminishing returns, you know? Let's go home and *think*. I know I personally need a little time to do that. Then together tomorrow we can kick some ass." The tingling moved up my left arm into my shoulder. *The hell with thinking. I need to get home and play Lenore!*

Bryson just stared at me with his mouth hanging open, but I returned his stare unwavering. He blinked, probably too tired to marshal a convincing argument against me. Brandon smiled.

"You need a day off, huh? We'll see you in the lab bright and early tomorrow then," said Bryson, frowning and rubbing his forehead. "Rest? Screw that. I'm going home for a scotch."

"Keep me up to date, people, and *no one else*!" said Olaf. Bryson nodded, and Olaf gently rescued his tilting skull mug from Bryson's tenuous grip.

Chapter Sixteen

YAWNING AT FIRST, BRANDON and I took all the pups on a walk around campus. Their favorite place was the forest surrounding the mausoleum where the Breckens were buried. The ornate structure resides in a remote corner of the huge property where few people ventured. The dogs' joy to be out of the lab and into the late afternoon sun was energizing. Even Brandon, the lab rat, was smiling to be outside with them finally. The leashes tug relentlessly.

"I don't care. I'm too tired to fight them anymore. I'm letting them go," I said. "Mavis, keep them nearby and under control." Sam looked at me like I had violated Canine Union Equal Employment Opportunity rules. "Yes, and you too, Sam. I'm depending on you too." He growled joyfully and nipped Mavis behind the ears.

"Ha, busted! You always were a little overly partial to the female element," said Brandon.

"What can I say? They're more dependable," I said. "Bryson could use a dose of figuring that out too."

"Well, I'm sure he's thinking about your feminism right now as he sips his Laphroaig."

We let Mavis and Sam off their leashes first, then the others as quickly as we could to save our shoulders from further dislocation. Like a pack of wolves, they circled the mausoleum and then lifted their legs in unison on the Brecken family statue.

"So disrespectful! Shame on you!" I shouted at them laughing.

"If women are so obviously better, why is it that Mrs. Brecken is looking up demurely at Mr. Brecken like he is the masterful hero?"

"Don't get me started," I said. "Power and virtue have not always marched hand in hand."

"Hmm," said Brandon. We left the sculpture to take off after the galavanting dogs.

The dogs were clearly following Mavis and Sam's lead exploring a small eucalyptus grove and winding their way quickly through narrow and labyrinthine paths in the cactus garden. They must have powers of quantum vision and bodily control now too since we heard no squeals of pain from cactus encounters. We followed them, the unnecessary and humiliating leashes draped over our arms. Mavis and Sam kept them pretty close to us, but still the extra mileage the wound-up pack covered going to the same places we went was impressive.

"I don't think anyone has ever gotten away with telling Bryson what to do before," said Brandon as we paused to watch the canine gang take turns sniffing some interesting excretion at the base of a eucalyptus tree.

"Sorry, I got a Lenore hit and couldn't help myself. I also couldn't help myself because frankly he looked like a junkie in need of a fix. Ridiculous. Is he married, or what's his deal?"

"Married to the lab. There's a daughter somewhere, but no spouse. He keeps his life pretty private. Anyway, thanks for making him slow down. Another session today would have driven *me* crazy, not to mention Mavis and Sam. Lenore, eh?"

"It's been intensifying lately, ever since I started playing at Comey's. We'll see about Bryson. Don't thank me unless he actually did go home to sleep. So, what's this pact thing he's got going with Olaf?"

"Oh, the pact? He's... Wait! Don't you have a gig right now?"

I check my phoneglasses. "Shit, you're right! I'm late."

Brandon gestured to take the leashes from my hand. "Just go. I'll take them back to the lab and settle them in. See you at home after."

"Let me at least help you get them corralled first. Mavis! Sam! Come here! Time to go!" Immediately, I saw the pack heading back to me passing a lonely and mildly terrified jogger.

"To answer your question, the pact is about saving the world."

"That would be nice," I said. "It could use it." *Bryson wanted to save the world? Really? He could barely take care of himself.*

Like an army patrol reporting for duty, the canines lined up behind Mavis and Sam and sat down obediently to wait for their leashes.

Well, if nothing else comes of this, we could at least open a dog obedience school!" Brandon said. One after the other, we snapped the leashes back onto their red Brecken collars. Brandon looped the leashes onto his tattooed forearm.

"See you later, Brandon. Thanks," I said.

I ran like mad to our apartment and changed into a cleaner shirt. The jeans I have on will have to do even if they smelled a bit ratty from the lab. Who ever has the time to do laundry and wait for jeans to dry? Not me. Half the time I just scrub them down in the shower and use our Goodwill furniture as drying racks. Brandon would like to do the same thing, except he usually doesn't have the time for even that little nod to quasi-acceptable hygiene. I loved him anyway. Cleanliness was overrated. After all, half the world's allergies were caused by people being too sanitary. I grabbed Lenore and headed to the coffee shop.

The crowd was so big I had to hold Lenore's case in front of me and push through the group surrounding the front door of Comey's. *What's going on?*

"Man, am I glad to see you," yelled Kanda from the counter. I squeezed through the crowd packing every table and ducked behind them's counter. "Jason is extending his set. They're being polite to him, but they really just want you."

"You're kidding me." I looked at Jason on the puny little stage and caught his eye. I raised my eyebrows and opened my hand to indicate five minutes. He nodded and launched into a John Prine cover.

"What are you drinking?" They must have seven coffee concoctions going all at once.

"Oh, just water, Kanda. Thanks. I've got to sleep tonight."

They pulls down a mug. "You're getting at least a hot chocolate. Owner's going to retire early because of you if this keeps up."

I laughed and removed Lenore from her tattered case. "If you insist, but I told you I'm only doing this to placate my therapist. These people are here for *your* artistry, not mine."

"As much as I can't stand bluegrass and would like to agree with your assessment, it's just not true, but don't worry, your secret's safe with me, toots. Enjoy your set." They lands a cocoa on the counter next to me and goes back to they's intricate dance with the espresso machine.

With Lenore in one hand and the cocoa in another, I looked out over the crowd as Jason sang. Clearly, we're way over the occupation limit of this broken down fire trap. College kids were perched on couch arms, sitting cross-legged on tables, and doubling up on the wooden chairs. Glad this isn't Europe or the whole place would probably be filled with cigarette smoke. I can't say that for sure, though, because I have never been to Europe. My Dad went to Ireland a long time ago with Granddad, and they both said the pub music there cleaned their brains but soiled their lungs. Here my nose picks up a hint of Enlightenment, maybe wafting down from Dr. Pendleton's office, but mainly the air smelled of the fetid breath of way too many people. Jason's song ended and the applause was raucous.

"Thank you. Thank you," said Jason into the mic. "And next up is Ella Bradley playing Edgar Allen Poe's very own fiddle, Lenore!" I smiled and put down my mug. Kanda was right, the cocoa was just what my courage needed. Still, the tiny Comey stage felt like a leaky life raft in an ocean of Brecken Vista sharks tonight. People were clapping, but I couldn't see their faces because of all the hands waving about.

It's a weird vibe. *So many strangers in this city. So many people in the world.*

I took the mic from Jason and sat on the stool. "Thanks, Jason. And thank you all for coming. Really, Poe's Lenore is a raven, and the fiddle was my grandfather's, but kudos for picking up on the reference anyway. It's not easy to be highbrow enough to be accepted in this sanctuary of so-called educational enlightenment, eh?" Chuckles from the audience, and my fingers tingle. "By the way, I didn't name her Lenore, actually, so I come by any highbrow status her name conveys purely by accident. He did. My grandfather, named her that is, not Poe. Actually she named *herself*, I think, considering that she has a pretty strong mind of her own." Laughter, and the tingles spread to my belly. "Let's see what she wants to play tonight, shall we?" The audience cheered, and now my whole body was on fire.

Again, Lenore is in a Celtic mood with a lot up her sleeve. From the first note I almost passed out from what was happening to my nervous system. Oh, I knew where I was and what I was doing, sort of. I knew I was on the Comey's stage, and I didn't fall down, but my mind had left logic behind and was traveling fast with the music to unknown places. It's been a while since Lenore has taken me with her like this. I was a little dizzy on the stool, and I felt my nipples harden and smolder. *Is my shirt thick enough?* I pushed that thought away. The lights were dim enough. *Go with it. Lenore owns you right now.* Flames shot from my fingers and burned my clothes. *Well, I guess that settles that. Okay, now that you're naked, just keep playing.*

Usually Lenore's journeys happened in nature. This time there was a distinctly urban feel to Lenore's insistent and passionate love. Tonight her tunes were clearly keeping us right here in Comey's, not escaping out the windows and heading for the woods like whatever logical sliver of my brain that was left expected them to do. *She must really have something here that she wants me to see right now.*

My fingers moved on their own, fast, slow, modulated, emphatic, the tone sometimes matched the tune, sometimes contrasted with it. I went with it, no longer having any say over the music I was creating. I knew people were looking at my naked body, but I didn't care. *I must do this for them.*

The music was a variation of "Sullivan's March" that Lenore had never played before. It was melodic and hypnotizing. I could feel Lenore reaching out for the audience like she's doing some kind of mantric yoga stretch, but she's also pulling me along with her on the sound waves she's creating. I was the player, but I was also the soundwaves themselves. Lenore and I were the agent *and* the message. We tickled the audience and then heated the ears of everyone, entering their minds and then their sacred warm places. *So hot in here!* We breathed, connected, and traveled through lava channels deep into a planet of brains and bodies like alien tentacles searching, pulsating, wondering.

Lenore played tune after tune, one, it seems, for each person in the audience. Then her music changed in a disturbing way, and a sweaty chill ran through my body. Somehow Bryson had powered into the music holding first his Brecken coffee mug and then the skull mug. His spirit was mingling in my audience's brains, coloring my connection with them into a cooler shade of red. Lenore's tunes become discordant, harsh. *This is my concert, Bryson! You don't even play!* But his breath of overly-caffeinated espresso fogged the audience completely and repelled me back to the stage. Lenore and I retreated from the cancer he had turned our passion into because we smelled death, and death's cold chill was repulsive, intolerable. Huddled on the stage, part of me still felt him out there whispering to *my* audience. Still warm and loving, Lenore has shifted somewhat, doubting her own music a bit now, doubting her intimacy. *Too many people, she seemed to be whispering to me.*

Above me I saw a blue light spreading down over Comey's. I urged Lenore on, begging her to try playing inside the new light to reconnect with the audience. *Olaf! Olaf is the blue light! Olaf will get them back!* Cool blue, sensible Olaf was out there exhaling decaf, warring with Bryson. Lenore and I moved toward his intellectual energy with hope and connection. *Relief!* But also boring sensibleness, just brain cells sparking without the comfort of a body. Lenore pulled back. We tried, but his blue light was just too cold, the red light too hot. Who were we playing for? Maybe no one. We were drifting again, hovering in the coffee shop, disconnected. Lenore mercifully ended the song.

My mind snapped back onto the stage. I looked down, relieved that I still had my clothes on, but Kanda was staring at me with a smirk, as the audience applauded wildly. *Did they see me naked?* I stood up from the stool and laughed nervously into the microphone, telling some joke my stage mind made up about blue and red politics. They laughed, and I climbed back on the stool and tried to ride Lenore's tunes again. She tried hard to take me flying with her, but my body was suddenly heavy, my clothes like metal armor. Our music penetrated the waves of blue and red light flowing everywhere now around and between the swaying people in the crowd, but it kept circling back to the stage, back to me cemented stupidly on the stool.

Lenore choses a modal tune, dark and foreboding, but it was like she was playing it herself, disappointed in something. Abandoned on the stage and disliking the colors, I flexed the muscles in my biceps like Brandon does sometimes and tried to power-bow my way back to Lenore. *Forget the colors!* But the colors are upset now. Huge mouths bathed in red blew fire back at me and mouths awash in blue spat icebergs. The fire and ice didn't cancel each other out. They just pummeled me on the stage. They blasted through my armor and hurt equally in their cold and hot way all over my body. *Lenore let me out of this!*

Then I was singing. Somehow I was singing. I *never* sing at my gigs. Lenore was making me, trying to answer me, help me, somehow. She was making me sing questions, many painful questions that were somehow lyrics, perfectly rhymed lyrics, lyrics that perfectly fit her music, but still were mysteriously unclear in their meaning and intent. I was some kind of bluegrass rapper right now, my mouth was as out of control as my hands were on the strings of Lenore. The questions I was singing, what are they about? That itself became one of the questions I was singing. I didn't know. I can barely hear the questions I was asking myself. I knew they couldn't be answered, none of the questions could ever be answered, no matter how clearly I tried to sing them.

The colors in Comey's shrink to tiny capillaries, two networks connecting bodies of everyone in the audience to me. I was their heart. What flowed through the red network from me to them and back again was dust. What flowed through the blue network is at least moist, but icy cold. Where was my comfort? My salvation? My body was drying from red capillary pain and freezing from blue capillary ice, and yet I was still the heartbeat of Comey's, their leader, keeping them alive and beating in time to Lenore's music. Each question I rapped, each pounding of my heart, pulled moisture and heat from my chest simultaneously until my voice was just a tortured squeak in the microphone like Lenore's e-string tightened to its limit, ready to snap. *Lenore, are you betraying me? What is this? Why am I not flying through the totality of nature?*

The dryness in the red capillaries spread into the blue network making the blues desperate. In a last ditch effort, the blue flooded Lenore's music with every piece of ice they had, draining the souls of the audience and leaving only empty shadows behind. Their icebergs turned to snakes intent on swallowing anything in their way. Dozens of Sybil-like snakes swam like desperate sperms down the capillaries toward the brains of the red people in the audience. "Look out!" I sang.

The red brains, desperate too, with not much moisture left to lose, shrank and dried completely into the smallest particles imaginable and blew like a tornado of viruses to meet the snakes' attack. They clashed in the capillaries and the quantum dust storm drove the snakes back into my heart, deep into Lenore's river of sound.

The Sybils flipped and flopped with each beat of the music, their skins now covered disastrously with red, their deaths inevitable. I couldn't stop it or avoid them. It was happening right on stage to the music in my heart. The combatants flailed against each other and against my ribs, dying, their pain multiplying like a nuclear bomb. Lenore's beat wavered and faded, then exploded in a massive final chord. The pain blasted open my chest and sliced open my arms. The questions in my mouth turned to mumbles, my voice to a whisper. *I am falling!* I dropped Lenore and clutched my chest desperately. *Stop! Stop, for God's sake! This is insanity!*

I WOKE UP LYING ON something very hard. I was lost, but someone familiar was right above me shouting. "Ella! Ella! Are you all right? Oh my God, your hand! Jason call 911! Ella, wake up! Oh no, it's the shoulder too. She's bleeding! Don't panic, people! Get me a towel somebody!"

I heard screaming and chairs falling over, people in a hurry. *Huh?* A vaguely familiar person was trying to get my attention.

"Ella, wake up! Stay with me! It's Kanda. You've been shot, I think, but everything's going to be okay. Help is on the way. I'm right here." *What? Shot? Where am I?*

"Lenore?" I said. I tried to sit up, but an excruciating heat in my shoulder slammed me back to the floor. *What the hell?* I felt wetness. *Weird. Wasn't I really dry just now?* The fire spread to my right hand. I lifted it from my chest and looked at it. Blood. Blood was pouring from my palm. *Why isn't it boiling?*

The person was shouting at me again. *Was it a man or a woman?* "That's right, elevate that hand if you can. Somebody grab me a dish towel! Oh shit, they've all panicked. Jason, dish towel! Stay with me, Ella. Cover your hand with your other hand, with this!"

The person squeezed the bar towel into my left hand, and I did as I was told. A different person pressed another towel hard onto my right shoulder. I looked at him. *Jason. That's Jason. Oh, that's Kanda? Comey's? I'm in Comey's. Right, I was playing in Comey's! But where is Lenore?!* I looked around me on the stage, but the intense pain in my shoulder made my eyes quiver. There was blood and spilled cocoa all around me, but no Lenore. "Kanda, Lenore!" I said. They looked at me and frowned. "It's going to be okay," they said.

Then sirens with red and blue flashing vehicles arrived disgorging people in crisp uniforms. Other people were shouting with guns drawn, and I woke up enough to know I felt distinctly not okay. I felt raped, beaten, and in pain. Hands in starched shirts lifted me onto a starchy stretcher, then into an ambulance. Lights were flashing blue and red. There were so many questions coming at me that I couldn't answer. "Am I going to die?" I asked, "And where the hell is Lenore?"

# Chapter Seventeen

I WAS IN THE BRECKEN Vista Hospital. Brandon, has been trying to get the nurse to let me use my phoneglasses. She's finally relented.

"Okay, but just to call her Dad, *briefly*. She needs rest, and I can't keep turning away these investigators if they hear her blabbing in here on the phone," said the nurse. He was big enough to work as a bouncer, so Brandon wisely just smiled from his chair next to me and thanked him. It's a miracle they even let Brandon be in the room. I imagined he lied to them and said he was my husband. I didn't care what he told them. I'm just glad he's here.

I struggled to pull the phoneglasses onto my head with my left hand. Brandon reached over to help.

"Want me to blink him for you?"

"No, I got it," I said. My whole right torso was swathed in bandages from my shoulder down to my hand. There was an IV stuck in my other arm feeding me a cocktail of who knows what. It's making the pain disappear, though, so I'm not complaining. I blinked on Dad and waited for him to pick up.

"Dad, it's Ella." His image was clear. He was driving his truck.

"Ella. Hold on, let me put this on auto-drive. What the hell happened? Are you okay?"

"Yes, I'm fine. They're taking good care of me. You don't have a news feed up there? I was shot."

"So you *were* shot. They said on my feed that no one heard anything. They are saying they haven't found a bullet or a suspect yet."

"Dad, the bullet entered my right hand while I was playing and then my shoulder. Here, look." I blinked the camera lens toward my bandages.

"Oh my God. Did it hit your lungs? Your heart?"

"No, it went through my thumb webbing and then my trapezius. Missed my collar bone, and my heart, obviously. Flesh wounds only. They just sewed up the holes and said I was lucky."

"Yeah, I guess. Lucky enough to get shot. In Brecken Vista of all places! That's luck?"

"Dad, I'm alive. Stop complaining."

"Sorry. Look I'm coming down. I decided to drive since the flights are ridiculous. Fierce turbulence basically shut down the schedule again. Your Mom is in Kenya with her Gauguin group."

"I know. Don't tell her until after her safari. Hopefully she's in a place with lots of nature and art and no news feed."

"I'll be there later tonight or tomorrow, depending on storms and how busy the charging stations are."

"It's okay, Dad. Don't push it. I'm fine. Brandon's here. Just have to deal with all the cops and reporters. There was a stupid reporter drone out the window a moment ago that was preventing us from opening the curtains."

"Those damn things are so obnoxious."

"Brandon complained for me about it. The buzzing should be gone soon, I hope. I really need some air and sunshine."

The nurse marched back into the room and gave me a dirty look.

"Dad, I better go. They want me to rest."

"I'm so sorry this happened to you. Let them take care of you. Hello to Brandon. I'll be there soon!"

"Love you, Dad."

"Love you, Ells."

The nurse squeezed yet another syringe full of something into my IV. "Nap time, girl," he said. I rolled my eyes at him.

"Brandon, before I pass out again for who knows how long, please go find Lenore. Obviously, I'm going to be okay here. Those cops don't care about her. Someone shot me and grabbed her. Phoneglasses were everywhere in Comey's last night. Someone is sure to have a recording."

"All right," he said looking meaningfully at the nurse. "I'm on it, babe." He smiled at me. "I'll find Lenore for you. Don't worry."

# Chapter Eighteen

THE DETECTIVE HAD BLONDE hair and a face like Scarlett Johansson. She didn't mince any words, though, or play on her good looks. They discharged me, and she pounced like a superhero before I could even leave the hospital lobby.

"Look, Ms. Bradley. Are you sure there is no one with a motive to attack you?"

"I told you, the Brecken admin blames me for people dropping out or changing majors."

"You think that's a motivation for first degree attempted murder?"

"No, of course not. Not in any sane world you or I can imagine." I glanced across the lobby at Brandon and my concerned Dad waiting patiently for me.

"Have any of them threatened you previously in any way?"

"No."

"Have you ever been followed on campus?"

"Not that I'm aware of."

"Harassed, flirted with inappropriately, been unusually uncomfortable somewhere?"

"I'm an attractive person. So are you. Do you really think I can answer no to that question?" The meds were wearing off. I could feel the pain seeping back into my hand and shoulder. They promised that rehab would be memorably painful too.

"Well, more than the usual man-gazing?"

"No."

"Well, there are no suspects, and the incident occurred during an unusual breakdown in the feed so there are no recordings. In fact, everyone's device was erased in that whole quadrant during that time frame."

"You don't find that suspicious in and of itself?"

"Of course I do. But frankly these blackouts are more common now due to the storms. Also, more internet traffic flows through rickety old houses owned by aging techies around here than the server warehouses of New York. Could just be coincidence or old infrastructure. Now, maybe if you were a Russian spy... ?"

"I told you. I'm a student."

"A special admit, I know. A public relations coup for the Brecken Admission Department. Famous lab rat with a knack for attracting miracles."

"I wouldn't go that far. I just have an influential parent."

"Right. Enlightenment. Hmm. So, done anything else lately to piss someone off? I mean more than playing music to already disaffected students ready for personal transformation?"

"I let a pack of dogs run loose on campus, and they all peed on Mr. and Mrs. Brecken."

"Every dog in Brecken Vista has pissed on that statue, and in my front yard, I might add." She paused to look at me pensively.

"Is that all?" I asked. *I need to get outside.*

"Well, there's one more little niggling detail. No bullet."

"You want to inspect my wounds, detective?"

She shifted her body in the chair, still eyeing me.

"No, the wounds are real. I've seen the report, and it happens sometimes that we can't find a bullet. It's probably nothing. It could have embedded in the crack of a wall panel, or been kicked off the stage somewhere, maybe down a floor drain. How much was your missing violin insured for?"

"What, do you think I staged this somehow to collect insurance? Nothing. The fiddle is German, maybe a few thousand dollars. No insurance, but I would really like it back, by the way. It belonged to my grandfather, his dad." I gestured with my good hand toward Dad and Brandon.

"Okay, Ms. Bradley. I doubt whether you would have purposefully done this to yourself in any case. We'll do our best to find your violin for you. Thank you for your time. We were lucky, you know. You're going to be fine, and just scrapes and bruises for the others in the exodus. Panic usually kills. Not this time, though. Comey's will need a bigger door installed, but, lucky for them with the planning commission that there is no video record of the number of people in attendance. Clearly too many according to the barista, but no records. That's how it rolls sometimes in a blackout. The owner is cooperating, and he better because the over-capacity fine he deserves would probably put him out of business."

"Well, crowded or not, all those people were there to hear my music, and I'm out of business without my fiddle, detective."

"Maybe you can get Brecken to buy you a new one. Their dorm guards make more than I do." She ran her hand through her long hair and stood up, smiling. Her eyes were deep blue and gorgeous.

I shook her hand awkwardly with my left hand and watched her strut confidently out the door. *I'll bet she catches a lot of Brecken johns when she poses as a hooker, but maybe not, in this age of Hola-Tinder.*

I walked back to Dad and Brandon who had moved toward the cafeteria. "Come on," I said. Hospital food sucks, and I'm starving. Let's go get a sandwich at Muga-Joe's."

Chapter Nineteen

AS PREDICTED, THE PHYSICAL therapy sucked, especially because I refused to take addictive pain meds. Ever since Dad's Enlightenment pot hit my system in high school and I discovered playing Lenore, reality was just fine however it rolled, thank you very much. Up until this last Lenore "trip" that is.

It's my afternoon session. The sweat from my hands made it hard to grip the dumbbell. "Two more times, Ella. I know it hurts. You can do it," said the therapist. She let Brandon sit in on the therapy so he could learn the routine and help me on-going. He gave me the thumbs up. I grunted and crossed the dumbbell across my chest again. It burned my shoulder like a blow torch.

I finished the session and stayed on my back on the yoga mat. I'm supposed to squeeze a tennis ball all the time for my hand. It sat idle on my stomach. I never thought something so simple could inflict such pain. I sighed. "Any hits on our ad?"

"Nothing yet," said Brandon. I sat up and he handed me water. "But the Daily mentioned Lenore in their article, so that's good, at least."

"Thanks for looking. She's gone. I just know it." A wave of sadness hit my stomach again.

"Maybe, but we're not giving up yet."

"How are the dogs doing?"

"Fine. We took Mavis and Sam over to see Sybil and Suzy this morning. Same old thing, coordinated dancing, but nothing further. Olaf is getting antsy. He's looking forward to you coming back."

"Why?"

"I don't know. Except I told him more about Lenore and the details about Jenny and Max."

"I'm no miracle worker, Brandon. In fact, I might be a riot maker if recent events are any indication."

"Don't be so hard on yourself. It was just some nut who couldn't handle the vibes. Probably a meth head, or another person going psychotic over climate change."

"I'm not so sure. Kanda never heard any shots, and no bullet. Maybe I'm the one that's psychotic."

"No, but maybe you need to go see that psychologist, Pendleton, again. He's the one who got you into this, right?"

"You know, that's not a bad idea, but tomorrow I'm coming back to work. I miss Mavis."

"And Sam?" He gave me a look.

"Yes, and Sam too, of course."

Chapter Twenty

WALKING BACK ONTO CAMPUS I felt self-conscious, like walking onto a stage again, except instead of carrying Lenore I am carrying bandages wrapped on my hands and shoulder. It's all in my head, though. No one paid me any mind as I headed to Bryson's lab. Sure, my picture was in the Brecken Daily a few days running, but since my shooting wasn't deemed terror-related or racist, the community has already moved on to whatever new news has popped up next in their feeds. Today's, undoubtedly, was the freak hurricane headed for San Diego.

Bryson, his hair a mess, was sitting next to Brandon behind the computers and didn't even move his eyes away from the screen when I arrived. He just said, "About time you got here. Take Mavis and Sam over to Olaf's. He's got plans for you and Brandon. Can't say I'm on board, but he insists, and he says I owe him one, so see ya."

Brandon looked at Bryson incredulously, but Bryson got up and headed for his private storeroom without another word. He disappeared down the back hallway a little shakily like he'd pulled an all-nighter again.

The dogs were in the outside enclosure. We got two leashes, but it's just for show. Mavis and Sam let the other dogs greet us for a minute and then nodded them out of the way and followed us to the back gate like they already knew what's up. They were calm and focused, like they were high school seniors going for an admissions tour of the facility instead of dogs for a dog walk. They kept up the serious attitude all the way to the Zoology building too, ignoring other dogs on leashes who were clearly jealous of their freedom. They knew exactly where we were headed and didn't even stop to sniff at the usual dog messaging spots. *They're like four-legged humans now. Do they feel self-conscious without clothes? Probably too evolved for that, unlike humans.*

Brandon swiped us into Olaf's lab, and we found him in his office sipping coffee from his skull mug with a shaky hand. He jumped up like someone fired a starting gun when he saw us. "Ella!" he said. "I am very glad you're not dead!"

"Me too, Dr. Olaf. Believe me." Dr. Olaf reached out to touch my bandaged hand briefly, then looked urgently at Brandon.

"Did you bring that suitcase with you, Brandon? No matter. Probably too small for both of them. We'll use a carrier and the feed cart." He's talking very fast.

Brandon looked befuddled. "What's going on?" he asks. "Are the snakes going somewhere?"

"We all are, and soon." As if that's all the explanation needed, Olaf put on his phoneglasses and blinked a number. Someone picked up. I could just see a slice of a holograph dude popping into view through the side of his glasses. "Yes, they're here...no, I'll text him...in back, by the alley...uh huh...yep...hurry!"

"Come on. No time to lose." We followed him out into the lab. He's obviously blinking a text while walking, so we didn't interrupt him. It's hard to keep up with the spring in his step, so different from Bryson's this morning. We passed some graduate students holding a hooded bird in the office next to his. He gave them a thumbs up, sent the text, and flipped his phoneglasses back onto his forehead. "Brandon, dump out the junk from this carrier and put it on the cart right through here. Come on!" He opened the access door to the zoo displays and held it wide for Brandon. Olaf drummed his hands on the door knob impatiently as Brandon did what he asked. The dogs sprinted inside ahead of us to get out of the way.

"Where are we going with them, Dr. Olaf?" I asked, stepping in after Brandon.

"Shh... Hawaii," he whispered. "Time for phase one. You ready to

fix an island?"

Chapter Twenty-One

WE COULDN'T SLOW DR. Olaf down enough to get much of an explanation about what he meant about fixing Hawaii. I could have asked Brandon to tackle him and insist he tell us more, and I would have if he had said we were going to fix someplace like Siberia, but since apparently we were going to Hawaii, who wanted to argue with him? Olaf barked one order after another at us until Sybil and Suzi were both safe and snug in the carrier.

"Okay, they're ready, but what about us? What about packing?" said Brandon.

"You don't need anything," he said. "My partner is very thorough."

"You mean Bryson?" I asked.

"No, not him. My *partner* partner. Can you handle the dogs with your good hand, Ella? Okay, then. Come on, let's go!" He blinked back onto his phoneglasses, and led us to the loading dock at the back of the lab. *Handle the dogs? They are about as focused as Olaf is right now.* I threw their leashes into the garbage. They watched me do that and looked at me like "What took you so long?"

Backed up to the loading dock there was a white van with "SRI" printed discreetly in Brecken red on the driver's side door. The driver wore dark sunglasses and stayed put in the seat with the engine running. "Roll them right in, Brandon, and leave the carrier on the wagon. Use those straps and clips," said Olaf. Through the metal grating of the carrier I saw Sybil and Suzy looking out together flicking their tongues.

"Okay, Ella, get in the middle with the dogs. Let's go!" I buckled into a side-facing seat next to the carrier. *Feels like an ambulance.* Olaf and Brandon shut the back door and climbed into the front bench seat with the driver.

"We don't have much time," said Olaf. "Hurry, but don't get pulled over." The driver nodded and peeled away from the loading dock.

The roller coaster ride to the airport was noisy but short. Olaf didn't say much, but he's texting like mad the whole time. There's no window where I was sitting, but in the front the morning sun illuminated Brandon's beautiful hair. Brandon turned around to focus his gorgeous blue eyes on me. He raised his eyebrows and shrugged.

The van careened into the airport and headed for the private jet corral. The attendant waved us through the gate, and the driver sped toward the long row of unmarked Gulfstream silver and whites. At the very end of the row, he turned abruptly and hit the brakes. The straps tightened on the carrier, and Mavis and Sam slammed into my knees.

"Okay, people. All aboard!" said Olaf.

Before Olaf was even out himself, the back door flew open, and in the sudden brightness a man with white frizzy hair was standing there smiling at me. Immediately a waft of Enlightenment hit my nostrils.

"Dr. Pendleton! What are you doing here?!"

"Letting my personal life mess with my professional one for a good cause. Nice to see you again, Ella. You've been missing your appointments. Come on. We can catch up on the plane." He offered me his hand, and I jumped out with the dogs. Looking around, I felt like I was in an aviation museum. Even Howard Hughes would be impressed by the wealth of expensive flyers towering all around us. The jet that we were obviously taking, a G650, whatever that means, was waiting with open doors. A few blades of grass grow bravely in the cracks of the tarmac in this otherwise sterile sanctuary of technology and monetary power. As if knowing what they would soon be facing, Mavis and Sam finally let themselves sniff around and relieve themselves, thus doubling the chance of that little patch of grass surviving until the next onslaught of airport glyphosate. I looked away from them and back at Pendleton. The air stunk of jet fuel.

Pendleton jumped into the van, unstrapped the carrier, and rolled it into the arms of Brandon and Olaf who grunted and lifted it and the cart onto the tarmac and rolled it toward the cargo door. Two uniformed pilots were there and helped them muscle the carrier off the cart and onto a conveyor belt that carried it into the hold of the white and red-trimmed private bird. Olaf and Brandon lifted and sent the cart after, and it was grabbed by unseen hands that secured everything inside. A slim but muscular young man climbed out of the hold and onto the conveyor belt, closed and locked the door to the fuselage, and then wheeled the conveyor belt away.

"Come on, people. Time's a-wastin," said Olaf sprinting up the passenger ramp into the jet. The pilots waited for us on the tarmac and then followed us on board, not phased at all to have two dogs trotting ahead of them. Dr. Pendleton was the last to climb the stairs, a hot breeze playing with his white hair. There were so many questions I wanted to ask, I didn't know where to begin, but clearly my need to know was not a top priority right now. Still, I was dying to know what my therapist was doing here? *What exactly does Olaf think we're going to do in Hawaii anyway?*

Unlike on a commercial flight, it took only a brief moment for the pilots to secure the hatch, buckle themselves into the cockpit, and fire up the engines. One of them turned around to speak to us, but then decided to use the speaker and said, "Buckle up for take-off, please," and the jet was taxiing before I even had a chance to move into the cabin and look around. All the seats were leather recliners with their own stocked mini bars and viewing screens. I chose one across from Pendleton, and Brandon and Olaf buckled in on the other side of the aisle. With Mavis and Sam at my feet, it felt like I was in some rich person's personal theater, or man-cave, rather than on a jet. I looked up and noticed there were mirrors tastefully positioned to allow everyone to see everyone else. Good for in-flight business meetings, I guess.

"First time on a Lear Jet?" said Pendleton.

I stuck my nose in the air as I petted Mavis's head like she was some spoiled celebrity poodle. "Maybe this particular one. I don't seem to recognize its decor. I was going to take my monthly jet-weekend to Sardinia last week, but my regular pilots got caught in a climate storm in the Caribbean, so I had to settle for Rome. How about you, Dr. Pendleton? Where do *you* usually go for fun in your G-650?"

Pendleton laughed. "I guess I deserve that, but I really *am* a therapist most of the time, if that's what you're wondering."

"When you're not doing research for Brecken Research Institute?" I was just guessing here, but obviously he's got connections significantly above his facade as a low-grade therapist. Everyone knows BRI is a secretive research think tank on campus with strong historical connections to industry and government. They have next to nothing to do with students on campus, but it's a popular party game on campus to speculate what they're up to these days, and where they spend all their rumored money.

"Smart girl. Yes, but now it's mostly projects on whatever strikes my fancy. Today I am simply doing a favor for my handsome Danish partner, there. Not like the good old days when putting LSD in the water fountains of the Kremlin was a serious proposition. It's been a few months since I last booked this baby for anything, I have to admit, and the maintenance department *has* remodeled the inside, I notice." He looked around a bit, and then point made, reached into his minibar and popped open a can of imported bloody mary mix. "Ah, tomato juice always tastes best on an airplane, you know. We figured out why a few years ago, too," he said, smiling. He took a big swig and saluted me with the can.

I was too busy taking it all in to think of anything clever to say back to him, so I opened my own mini-bar and chose a ginger ale. The jet taxied efficiently, and before I could even scope out where my cup holder was, it turned onto a straightaway and accelerated. No waiting in line for this bird, apparently. The jet was quick and powerful on the runway and whisper-quiet once the landing gears retracted. It banked west and nosed out over the hills toward the Pacific.

"Onward to paradise!" said Olaf. "Or what was once paradise, at least." He got up and put his hand on Pendleton's shoulder. "Thanks for doing this on short notice. I know it was probably expensive." Pendleton put his free hand over Olaf's and gives it an affectionate squeeze.

"Not at all, and no way to do it conventionally," said Pendleton. "Not with this cargo. Half the BRI governance board is on the Big Island right now playing golf at Schwab's, so I'm just a little late to the party. I did book a conventional van, though, to keep this discreet, and our rooms are at the Hapuna Prince."

"Ah, lovely resort. It laid waste to a perfectly good nude beach when it was built last century, but that's the way it goes, I guess," said Olaf. "Thanks, again for your help. Let's try to not take any of those golfers with us for the release, though."

"I'm way ahead of you. They don't need to know *anything* until the quarterly report."

"Good."

"Anybody got time now to let the lowly undergrads and their dogs in on what's going on?" I said. "This secret society talk is really starting to bug me. I half expect a Kardashian to walk out of the powder room back there." Brandon shot me a warning look, but I don't care if he's wowed by this jet. He's not the one who took a mysterious bullet for no discernible reason. *I want some answers.*

No one seemed to mind my question or my attitude. "Glad you asked, but I'm afraid there aren't any easy answers," said Pendleton. *Did he read my mind just now?* "If there are any, I suspect they reside in *your* heads, actually, not in ours, despite our abundant resources and intense curiosity."

"How do you mean?" said Brandon.

"Well, where were you when Ella got injured, Brandon?" asked Pendleton.

"I stayed late in the lab with Bryson," said Brandon, glancing at me worried.

"But I thought you took the dogs back and then went home," I said.

"Yeah, um, that's what I *wanted* to do, but Bryson came back, so we did some more work with the CRISPR."

"He came back! But he was exhausted, needing a drink!"

"I know but he took a NoDoz or something. He wasn't that bad, really. The guy's a doctor; he is immune to sleep, and he feels he is really on to something."

"I don't know why he is so obsessed with that CRISPR and the lower forms of life," said Olaf, rolling his eyes. "The ecological disaster is not bacteriological. It's the higher life forms that are out of balance and going extinct."

"I don't know," said Brandon. "But there are more incidental genes of microorganisms in animals' bodies than there are their own inherited genes. Maybe he thinks adaptive manipulations to gut biomes would be more efficient than pure animal genetics."

"Sounds plausible," said Olaf. "Such a germ guy! I guess we'll just have to wait to see."

"Yes, and in the meantime we'll plant the seed of a top predator in Hawaii and watch it work its magic," said Pendleton. "Providing the programming these subjects provide is reliable."

"Their names are Mavis and Sam, by the way. And likely they are developing the ability Jenny and Max have to understand English, so you might want to stop calling them *subjects*." Mavis got up to lick my hand at that, appearing to prove my point. Pendleton's jaw dropped.

"Was that intentional? Was she just reacting to hearing her name? Or are you saying this one actually *understands* our conversations?"

"It's hard to know for certain. It took me a while to figure out that Jenny had human language figured it out, but I could never prove it, nor did I try, or *want* her to go through the torture she would have to go through as a science experiment in order for humanity to find out. She could send smells to me that turned into pictures of fine art. Neat trick, eh? Who knows what she has learned to do now after a few months in the wilderness? Let's hope a lot because she and her cooperative family have a better chance of surviving and preserving conscious intelligence after the climate catastrophe than we do. As for these guys, we do know that one or both of these *subjects* had a breakthrough and can totally control the pythons, and even *teach* them, which already means they are more advanced in their capabilities than humans will ever be. Trained any snakes lately, Dr. Pendleton?"

"No, Ella. I have not, and I get your point, but what's this about images of fine art."

"You don't have to go through this all again, Ella, if you don't want to," said Brandon.

"Why? Because you still don't totally believe me? I believed *you* about Max controlling Sybil last year. Have you forgotten it was Jenny who convinced us we wouldn't get eaten when we let the lions out?"

"Didn't convince *me*. We were safe because Max had that whole Lyca/Siam situation at Renegade's ranch under control," said Brandon.

"Oh, so that's the way you see that, huh? It was all *Max* and his being a *master*? Well, that's bullshit. If anyone was in control of Lyca and Siam it was Jenny. She is so much smarter than *Max*. Max couldn't even communicate with us. Jenny's the one who solved the whole situation, figured out how to free the lions *and* herself at the same time."

"Ella, I love you, but you're wrong. If Max wasn't the master over those hungry lions, Jenny would have been their first meal when we swung the gates open."

"Do you see why humanity is doomed, Dr. Pendleton? It's because of *men* who can't see beyond their 'fight their way out of the colosseum' mentality. *Control*, what an illusion. Real control comes from insight, compassion, and *love*, not just power."

"How do you know love isn't power?" asked Pendleton.

"Oh, okay, you've got it all figured out, Mr. Ultra-Connected Washed-Up Science Guy who likes drugs. I took you for something better." I got up and stormed into the bathroom, but I couldn't slam the sliding door behind me like I wanted to because Mavis and Sam rushed to squeeze in there with me. With those two inside, there was barely enough room. I bent down and hugged both of them with my one good arm. I know I needed to cool it with my anger. *But what the hell happened to Lenore?*

Chapter Twenty-Two

AS USUAL, I HAD CLARIFYING thoughts on the toilet. It's always been that way with me. There's something about the process of peeing that forces me to reconnect with my body when I am upset and have too much in my head. This time was no different. Happily, the sink water on my face and hands was also grounding, if "grounding" is even a possible thing on an airplane at thirty-five thousand feet. Suddenly, I was ready to forgive Pendleton because whatever else he might be at Brecken Research Institute, I felt in my gut that he was a genuinely caring person, but I do have some questions he needs to answer.

The only sound was the faint roar of the engines as I crossed the plush carpeting to my seat again. I took a sip of my ginger ale, and petted Mavis and Sam at my feet. "Okay, sorry everyone for my little breakdown, but can someone please tell us the plan? And, it would also help, Dr. Pendleton, to know if your little therapy assignment for me had anything to do with my being shot and losing Lenore."

"Good questions. I'm not sure why I gave you the assignment to play at Comey's, Ella. It just came to me, like things sometimes do when I am in tune. You know what I'm talking about, I'm sure. Humans may no longer have the connection to nature that dogs and other animals still have, but Enlightenment and meditation can bring us closer, give us glimmers and hints at truth. I'm sorry my assignment led to your injury."

"Well, I liked playing there at first, and then it was a complete bummer."

"Yes, I can imagine you are devastated about losing your family's fiddle. Lenore, right? We are looking hard for her, you know, my whole team and the sheriff's office. We interviewed everyone who was there. Nothing. We even put our in-house psychics onto the problem. We're looking for her online and in all possible pawn shops, fencing operations, and music stores world-wide, but as far as we can tell, she just vanished, kind of like the bullet that hit you."

"Why do you care about Lenore so much?"

"Same reason you do. You're not really surprised she was a hit at Comey's, are you? I didn't think so. You may not know why exactly, and we don't know either. But there is no denying she profoundly affected everyone in the audience. Like she's a portal to something. My associates at KRI disagree with me, but I'm not ready to dismiss my hunch that what happened to cause the Jenny and Max breakthrough was due to some sort of quantum energy transfer through Lenore. Your granddad was a pioneer in that sort of stuff, you know. Meditational channeling. Cosmic waves. Dark matter and energy. The collective unconscious. Stranger things have happened."

"So you wanted her nearby to observe her in action, huh? Catch first hand the messages of higher consciousness riding on her vibe? Convenient, that you gave me the assignment to play gigs in the coffee shop right below your office. I should have known it wasn't just for me. What, were you up in your office listening through the heating ducts, or did you have hidden cams recording everything without permission?"

"BRI doesn't need permission for surveillance, but no, not cams, otherwise we'd know what happened to Lenore. Just a few devices that can't be picked up by phone cam detectors - psychometers, magnetic resonance meters in the light fixtures, a few of our human psychics in the audience every night ...''

"Were the psychics the ones in the cheesy Brecken baseball caps who were always asking me for dates, by any chance?"

"No, please, give me some credit. We needed someone you trusted who could actually check in on how you were feeling."

"Oh, my God, Kanda!"

"Oh, you're good. You're *very* good. Yes, Kanda. They's been with us for years. Very bright and spot-on in the field. I might actually have to hire you for they's intuitive team when you graduate."

"Hmm. Let me think about that. Work for Kanda? No thanks. So spill, what did you and your undercover barista learn besides how to make a wicked French roast latte? What do you know about how Lenore got her powers? Does she control them, or is she a conduit of some sort? Do you know the limits of what she can do?"

"No, and even though you have experienced her powers more than anyone else, I'm not sure you know the answers to these questions either. Do you? I didn't think so. Language isn't too helpful when it comes to things like this, but maybe you can tell *me* a little bit about what really happened that night from your perspective, and we can figure out this corner of the cosmos together?"

I glanced at Brandon. He looked like he thought both of us were just dealt new-age loser cards from the bottom of his tarot deck, like our flaky conversation was a waste of the cabin's oxygen. I dropped my jaw at him. *Really? That's his attitude right now? His tarot cards are not flaky? No wonder I've been hesitant to tell him what really happened to me at Comey's, the crazy lights, the dryness in my veins, the pain and sheer terror of my wounds. He thinks I'm nuts! Well, screw you, Brandon. Tarot's not a science either. It's just an excuse for justifying power. Were you lying to me that you flew with me on Lenore's music back at Wandering Pines?* He could see that I was pissed at him, but he just shook his head and put on his phoneglasses.

The furious part of me, which was nearly all of me these days since losing Lenore, wanted to get up and rip the phoneglasses from Brandon's gorgeous head, but I decided it would feel better to just spill everything I'm thinking to Pendleton, share some intimacy with someone else instead of trying to get through to Brandon. It's exhausting to hold things in. I don't trust Pendleton, Bryson, Vern back at the lab, or even Pendleton's apparent loverboy Dr. Olaf over there, but at least Pendleton sort-of knows how to speak my language. Judging by his gadgets, he seemed to have studied these things for years, and he might be able to help me understand Lenore better, even if she's never found and I won't ever be able to play her sweet strings again. Tears gathered in my eyes as I thought about facing the future without her.

"It sucks being in Brecken Vista, Dr. Pendleton, and I don't think Lenore liked it very much either. There's a reason we played mostly old time bluegrass music. It's pure country, nature's rhythms, the smell of pine trees, refreshing spring water, you know? Also Irish tunes straight from the rolling green hills of the old country. What's Brecken music about? Car exhaust, streets that never get dark, sterile laboratories, purposeless academic ambition, cement hallways lit only by buzzing fluorescent light fixtures. It's *horrible*."

Pendleton nodded and looked over at Olaf as if I had just articulated a discussion they were intimately familiar with. He turned back to me. "So this is a perfect time for a little beach time in Hawaii, eh? Actually, there is no need for us to rush back right after the release. We can take a few days to relax on BRI's tab, maybe go swimming with the dolphins or turtles."

"If they aren't all dead from swallowing too much plastic. I don't know what's worse, living in a sterile urban environment, or being in nature and witnessing first hand her destruction."

"Yes, it's definitely depressing, although the turtles in Hawaii have been brought back from the brink, at least around Kiholo Bay. But, yes, climate destruction, species decimation, that's why we're trying to do something about it, upping the intelligence of animals who have a sporting chance of surviving and maybe even evolving into something better than humans."

"Did vaping Enlightenment bring you to that conclusion?"

"It motivated me to look beyond the limits of ecological
science, yes."

"So what's the plan for Sybil? She and Sheldon might be
able to do something about the rat problem in Hawaii, but
the pigs are also causing havoc. Last time I looked, sows are
too big to be swallowed whole by anything."

"Well, yes, true, but we don't know how quantumly aug-
mented intelligence might adapt and develop in animals still
close to nature's truths. Balance can be achieved in many different ways."

"Like snakes cooking pork chops?"

"Something like that, but likely more subtle, more reflec-
tive of the forces that have empowered Lenore. Powers that
can guide beings somehow toward balance and true fulfillment, like the culling and digestion of pigs before they get
too huge,"

"Frankly, I don't know why you don't just go the route
Jenny did and release some feline predators to tame the
Hawaiian pig problem."

"How do you know we won't? This is just phase one of
a global makeover. Panthers, actually, are what I personally
think would be the right choice."

"I can see that."

"But only if enough of Bryson's and Ken's next batch of
masters break through like these two have apparently done."

Masters, that word again. I looked down at Mavis and
Max and wondered if they were following all this. My head
said no they weren't. Max's head was resting on Mavis's front

paw. Just two regular dogs on a plain old Learjet. My heart, though, is sure they know more than they are letting on. *Maybe I should ask* them *what happened to Lenore...*

"Masters, huh? You buy Brandon's take on all this then?"

"The subjects do seem to take full charge once they evolve and go free don't they? We're not getting any calls for help from Jenny and Max are we? Because of their team with the lions, the San Rafael Wilderness is already showing satellite evidence of improved riparian habitat. By any objective standard, that release you orchestrated has been a booming success, an encouraging bright spot in a world of bad news."

"They're surviving. Like trees survive in a forest. Doesn't mean any of them are "masters" any more than any surviving being is a master over their own way of living.

"They are if they are dependent on controlling others for their survival. Without the lions, Jenny and Max would probably starve out there."

I looked over at Brandon who had his eyes closed listening to music. Is his faith in this "masters" philosophy coming from an evolved consciousness or is it just a tarot-filled excuse for the worship of power? *How much control does he think he really has over his life? Over me? How much control do I have over* myself?

As if to answer my question, a patch of turbulence lurched the jet. The fuselage shuttered and Mavis and Sam flew upwards and onto their feet. The drinks were goners, and it was all I could do to hold onto the dogs and stay strapped into my bouncing seat for the rest of the five hour flight. I was a mess when we landed, but Brandon, Pendleton, and Olaf seemed strangely rested, as if the out-of-control chaos of the turbulence was just par for the course for them now in the game of modern world fixing.

Chapter Twenty-Three

I FIGURED THE SCIENTISTS would be in a panic about the pythons in the hold, but I was wrong. Their strange sense of calm persisted all the way through exiting the plane into an amazing blast of tropical heat, opening the cargo hold, and unloading the crate into a waiting van, this one with hibiscus flowers painted on the door panels instead of the Brecken logo. Sybil and Sheldon were just fine, of course. A little violent rock and roll can't hurt those human-length tubes of grisled muscle. The dogs, though, were bruised and very happy to be off the jet.

The pilots tipped their hats at us and Olaf drove the van out the back entrance of the airport and into the flow of traffic on the main two-lane highway that circles the island. Pendleton sat in the front and Brandon sat in the back with me but avoided my eyes. I could hear the snakes slithering behind me in their crate. I looked out at the never-ending expanse of black lava fields going by. *Where's the jungle? The beaches?*

Brandon's silent treatment persisted all the way north to Hapuna. I could see patches of green and coconut trees far to the west where the lava met the ocean, but it wasn't until we pulled up to the Hapuna Prince did we see an actual beach.

It was white as a diamond shimmering in the late afternoon sun.

"Now don't get too anxious, kids," said Olaf. "There's time for swimming after we get our cargo settled and find our rooms." He pulled the van up behind the resort near the kitchen and maintenance area. A huge dark-skinned guy in an Hawaiian shirt waved the van to an open garage door. We pulled completely inside before Olaf cut the engine. A blast of air conditioning hit us as we stepped out.

"Too cold, Kanoa," said Olaf to the mountainous man.

"Aloha, Doctor," said the man in a surprisingly falsetto voice.

" Yeah, aloha and all that," said Olaf. "We need it to be around eighty in here, okay? How long will it take?"

"Today? Just a moment or two with the door open."

"Good," said Olaf. "Risk it, but let's secure it right after."

"You got it, Doctor," said the man.

After the crate was unloaded and Olaf was busy putzing with it, Pendelton took us into the lobby and checked us in. We all had separate rooms which under other circumstances I might have objected to, but since Brandon was being Mr. Know-It-All-Silent-Treatment Guy, I was happy to have my very own space for once. Not that I really needed a room. After Brecken Vista, I could easily just hang out in the lobby, swim in the pool, and watch the sun glitter on the ocean all day. Brandon was looking out at the ocean too, but maybe it was just so he didn't have to look at me. It sure didn't take much to end that little resurgence of affection and mutual purpose we felt when we were charging up Sybil back at the lab. One little overly new-agey conversation with Pendleton was all it took, apparently.

"I'm in the Plumeria Suite," said Pendelton. "You guys go for a swim, change, and meet me there. There's some tapes Bryson wants you guys to listen to tomorrow before the release. Do you have everything you need for the dogs, Ella?"

"I don't know, do I?" I said.

"Well, check it out. Olaf said he arranged all the food to go to your room. Put the service dog vests on them when you get there. Otherwise no dogs are allowed here. They should be with the food. They're fake, but no one will know the difference around here." He handed me a key card with a pineapple printed on it. "You're in 212."

I snatched the card and headed straight for the elevator with the dogs. Finally, a place I could be by myself. I didn't even look back to see what room Brandon was assigned. He could go off and drown in the swimming pool for all I cared. How dare he ignore me?

I waved the card in front of the reader and the door popped open. Such retro technology. They really expected us to hang onto a card key? I tossed the card on the queen bed next to a pile of clothes that actually looked my size and a box full of dog food that immediately drew the interest of Mavis and Max.

"You guys must be hungry. Let's see what we've got here." I opened the bag of raw dry Kibbles and dumped a generous portion into two red bowls, obviously procured from the labs at Brecken. I filled another bowl with water and headed for the lanai.

The view of the ocean was even more spectacular up here, but I was feeling too down to really enjoy it. *What's going on with me? I'm so angry now, all the time. I should be happy I'm not dead but all I can think about is how out of control everything in my life has become since getting shot at Comey's. And Pendleton? Who is this guy? Can I trust him? Is Brandon right to be wary of him? He lies and covers things up, that's for sure. How do I know he isn't lying to me? Did he or one of his agents shoot me to steal Lenore? And where is Lenore? God, I need to play her!* My psyche felt like the days before Wandering Pines when I would lock myself in my room and play Lenore for hours to avoid my family, or, as I came to know later, to avoid thinking about my problems, my depression. Do I want to do the same thing now? You bet I did!

I thought Brandon was someone who would understand me, but he feels more like my mother to me now, always with a better idea about life and how to live it, judgemental about things I have feelings about but can't defend yet well enough. But maybe that's unfair. Who knows what he's thinking? When we connect we are on the same page, and my heart still flutters when he kisses me. When we don't connect, well it sucks. I don't want his lips anywhere near mine right now, that's for sure. Great attitude to have in Hawaii. I wonder if this ever happens to other couples and newlyweds when they get here?

There's a lot of magic in our lives. The miracle of Jenny and Max, Enlightenment, the effect Lenore has on people's knowledge and priorities, the Tibetan meditation tapes. It's good and bad, mostly good, I guess, but what's wrong with trying to figure out feeling-wise what that magic really is?

I liked knowing answers as much as the next person, but I don't like *not* knowing answers and then acting like I do, like Brandon's doing right now, not to mention these other science geeks with their deep pockets and fancy jets. One thing I know for sure, action alone might *feel* good, but not if you haven't thought things through enough. The mystery has to *feel* like it makes sense to really make sense.

In the pile of clothes there was a one-piece Brecken swimming suit that Olaf probably swiped from the athletic department. It's made for a skinny person on her way to the Olympics, but I ditched my bandages and managed to squeeze into it, and it had the virtue of at least covering up my angry shoulder scar. I rubbed my hand where the bullet passed through. It was healed but still pretty sore. Maybe a salt water swim would make me feel better, but then I looked down at Mavis and Sam and I realized we weren't here for fun in the sun. Are we really going to go through with this? Let a breeding pair of pythons loose in the Hawaiian rainforest? Who the hell do we think we are?

What if the snake thing backfired and screwed everything up even more than things are screwed up right now? And worse, what if Mavis and Sam are stuck in the middle of it, lonely and afraid? Jenny and Max, they *wanted* to go live in the wild, well, Jenny at least. I'm not so sure these guys were entirely on board.

I looked down at them finishing up their Kibbles. What do they really want out of life? So they get to be really smart and connected with nature more than we are, does that have to mean they don't want to still be pets? Do they really want the pressure of being the planet's next dominant species, the healers of all that humankind has screwed up? Mavis looked up at me. What options did she really have? It's not really about living in the rainforest vs. being a pet. If she and Sam don't go with Sybil and Sheldon, they'll spend the rest of their lives in the lab getting zapped and dissected by Bryson. And for what? To be pawns in the pursuit of logic and rationality. To deliver power into the hands of those wanting to control nature. Hasn't mankind done enough of that already?

There was a beach towel in the closet, but I was still torn about going out into the sun. It would relax me, but it felt safer locked in here with the dogs and my thoughts, confusing as they might be. That was the good thing about having Lenore to play in situations like this. You could be confused as hell but playing her somehow made everything feel like it would work out anyway. Like how she helped me accept that my old English and fiddle teacher, Mr. Bearman, who was as rational and action-obsessed as any of them, could be forgiven for loving me even though I was old enough to be his granddaughter. Or that Brandon was the right person for me because his generous passion for helping the lions escape Renegade's cruel vanity zoo was just so right and helped me see that letting Jenny fulfill her dream was the hidden pathway to my own liberation. That was pretty action-oriented, wasn't it? Not to mention probably felony theft material if we had gotten caught in the act. Sometimes this screwy world just *needs* a little edgy action.

Like the two presidents solution. The country was on the brink of civil war, the republican president refused to step down, and the democrats convinced the generals to point their tanks at the White House. It took action and compromise on the part of a few senators to avert death and mayhem. No time to wallow in feelings there. Feelings are what got the country into the mess in the first place. But how do you know that action taken in the heat of conflict is ever going to work out? You don't. The presidents are still always at odds with each other over every little decision and the world's climate continues to go down the toilet.

I looked out at the beach again. So what do I have that I can count on in this world right now? What's *my* plan?

The sad truth was that I didn't have one. Being mad at Brandon is my plan, I guess. Doubting my professors who are way more educated than I am. *God, I'm such a selfish shit!*

I picked up the clunky phone at the side of the bed and asked for Brandon's room, praying that he'd pick up. I needed to get in the ocean.

Chapter Twenty-Four

"PENDLETON'S BEEN IN touch with Bryson and wants us up in his suite after this," Brandon said over the noise of the swirling water.

"We don't have to go," I said. We were standing up to our necks in glorious warmth, the little ocean swells coming by with just enough height to make us tread the bathwater every once in a while. After I called him, I went to his room. Here's how the conversation went there that got us back on track:

"Look, I know you're mad at me for trying to explore with Pendleton this whole missing Lenore thing, but I'm a little mad at you for bull-headedly wanting to do this little eco-rearranging snake release plan without fully being sure, psychically, that it's the right thing."

"That's not it at all, Ella."

"Well, what is it, then?"

"You've just been spending a lot of time with Pendleton, that's all."

"You're jealous?!"

"Protective is more like it. Or, mad that I can't protect you."

"Protect me? How? You spend every waking minute in the lab with Bryson!"

"He's a master."

"God, Brandon, get over the master thing, *will you*? What, and Pendleton is an evil master or something?"

"Maybe, I don't know. We'll see what happens."

"What, you think he's like Bearman or something? In love with me?"

"No, maybe, I don't know. He's got a lot of power and holds his cards close. I just don't trust him, that's all. Not all masters are benevolent."

"Well I guess I'd be foolish not to agree with you about that. Brandon, I'm sorry. I'm just trying to figure all this out, you know? Getting shot, Lenore getting stolen, being in Hawaii all of a sudden with BRI people doing secret things to the environment, the dogs. I don't like Pendleton more than I like you. I wish I had Lenore back and I could just keep doing concerts for people. That, at least, makes a little sense to me. The natural world might be collapsing, but isn't there a little bit of salvation in singing a song of beauty as long as possible?"

"Like what we felt together at Wandering Pines and the winery last summer?"

"Exactly," I said. I gave him a hug.

"I need you, Ella."

"Oh, Brandon, I need you too. I just don't know... "

"I don't know either, friend. The world needs our help, though, that's for sure. Let's just see what happens, okay?"

And then I kissed him long and hard, and we went swimming a half-hour afterward.

Chapter Twenty-Five

PENDLETON AND OLAF'S "Plumeria Suite" was tasteful, but if I had the choice between staying there for the night or camping out on the nude beach that was here before this luxury hotel was built, I'd choose the nude beach. Still, the suite had a nice mini-bar, and the icy pog (pineapple, orange, guava) tasted pretty great after our warm swim.

"Ella, if you agree, I think the dogs need to sleep in the pen tonight with the snakes," said Olaf. "They need the bonding time before we release them tomorrow."

"Makes sense to me," I said. Mavis and Sam looked resigned at this announcement. Was I the only one picking up on their burgeoning comprehension skills? I petted Mavis on the head and looked over at Brandon. He narrowed his eyes knowingly.

"Yes, tomorrow's the day," said Pendleton. "But tonight, Bryson has these tapes for you to listen to, mainly you, Brandon, although he said we could all listen to them if we wanted. Some side project he is working on."

"Undoubtedly about microorganisms," said Olaf. "I'm going to pass on that opportunity and catch an early dinner. Join me?"

"Sure," said Pendleton. "You two can stay here and listen. It's all set up with my headphones, or I can blink it to you, if you prefer. There is a tab downstairs open for dinner. See you there tomorrow at 7:00 sharp for breakfast."

"When's our flight back to Brecken?" asked Brandon.

"Whenever we want," said Pendelton. "Let's see how it goes tomorrow."

"I think I want to settle the dogs first and then listen in my room," I said.

"As you wish. Goodnight." Pendelton blinked the tapes to my phoneglasses feed and he and Olaf followed us out of the room and into the elevator. The dogs seemed very happy to get out of their room. Maybe it was the earphones, or the conversation about tapes, I don't know. They've certainly had enough of tapes in the past year, that's for sure.

Brandon and I let the doctors out on the lobby floor and continued to the parking level where the snake cage was stored. The security guard ushered us into the storeroom with no questions asked, and we found blankets and food and water bowls all ready to go next to Sybil and Sheldon's crate. We opened the door to the cage and set up a cozy corner for Mavis and Sam. Sybil and Sheldon eyed our every move from a branch stuck diagonally across their cage. "The masters are here," said Brandon. "Let your education begin." The only response from the snakes was a nervous flicking of their tongues.

"See you tomorrow, Mavis," I said, giving her a hug. She looked up at me concentrating hard. Was that a faint sniff of something different I was smelling in my nose? Yes, but I wasn't sure what.

"And you too, Sam," said Brandon, giving me another one of his looks.

Back in my room, the sun had already set on the ocean, but the clouds on the horizon were still glowing orange and red. Something sweet was blooming outside. Jasmine? No, Pikake. I invited Brandon inside. We put on our phoneglasses and walked out onto the lanai. I blinked open Bryson's sound file and sent Brandon a mirror feed. We optimized the levels, settled back in the lounge chairs, and tuned in.

The hum of the monks was at first Mack Truck-like in its rumbling, then resolved itself into a hypnotic rhythm that settled deeply into my chest and groin. The feeling was so much like playing Lenore that it brought fresh tears to my eyes. My fingers tingled. Now I was deeply gone and mentally rising in the air with Brandon, our bodies dissolving. We were spreading into the night like the scent of the pikake, moving upward and outward over the edge of the railing.

With Brandon next to me, intermingling with me, I felt safe and insecure at the same time. I knew he was an integral part of my experience and yet in important ways outside of it at the same time. Is this what love becomes after the initial rush of mutual and unquestioning flying? I didn't know. The question was too hard to analyze. It belonged back behind us in the hotel room with rationality, logic, and bodies that were hungry for dinner. We were going to float now in a bigger and wiser body beyond those worldly concerns. The beat of the monks' chant was irresistible. I reached for Brandon's misty hand and together we zoomed out over the ocean.

Where do you go when the world is yours to fly anywhere on a whim? Monks can influence electrons from a dif-

ferent time from the other side of the world. Brandon and
I were traveling on those quantum wavelengths now, going
where our hearts had longings. Whose heart was stronger?

Mine was right now, and so it was Wandering Pines we
zipped to with so much momentum in our cosmic bodies
that we threatened to flatten Triangle Mountain. The sweet
breath of a dog stopped us beautifully at the summit. *Jenny.*
Older, wiser, Jenny stood proudly at the front of an army of
golden offspring and lion cubs with birds hovering over her,
protecting her like a queen. I asked her the question burning
in my soul. "Jenny, where is Lenore?" She sent me a scent of
brackish water that turned into this:

I wanted to stay with Jenny and her kingdom, surround
them with the vapors of my love, my body, but Brandon,
sensing his chance to direct us now, pulled me away from the
mountain and back over the ocean again, diving deeply into

it, the blue pelagic expanse, the infinity of salt water that was the lungs and blood and soul of every creature on the planet.

"Over here," he said, weirdly able to speak underwater. "Follow me!" And then we were above the waves again, watching a desperate, fiery woman hacking at the earth with a giant pick, sprouting volcanoes everywhere she struck, surrounding herself with burning mountains to escape the relentless blood of the ocean, the tamer of her passion.

"Hold your breath!" says Brandon, and I flew with him into the woman's fire to the very tip of her gigantic pick. Hot, oh so hot! She struck again furiously and instantly we vaporized into the smallest of small particles. We became her fire, her lava that flowed to the ocean, that spawned the islands, that protected the reefs, that nurtured the fish, that fed the sharks, and the ocean's snakes, the eels that keep the reefs in balance.

"Choose a drop!" demanded Brandon.

"What?" I say.

"Choose your drop of water!"

I pointed and chose and we entered another sea, an ocean of bacteria and viruses, so tiny yet so huge compared to us. We enter one of them together, sliding down its double helixes, and kicking at the proteins like kids kicking dandelion heads into the air on cool summer lawns.

"Ha, look at me!" said Brandon, laughing. He had the proteins dancing with him. A hip thrust to the left and they followed him left, a thrust to the right, and they followed him right. I heard the Rocky Horror Picture Show theme song playing along with the chanting. It's a joke from Brandon's mind, but it was horrifying to me.

"No," I said. "Don't thrust to the right! *Or* the left. Stop it, Brandon! This is not our home. This is not funny. This is not our dance! This is genetics! What are you doing? You can't stop them from dancing now!"

But he was not listening. The genetic particles sensed our discord and trembled in fear. They shot out of the droplet and desperately sought other droplets, to spread the dance, to win in numbers, to infect the ocean. There was no stopping them. Brandon's dance was taking over. The song was getting louder and louder. The ocean vibrated with fear and change. Waves formed, tsunamis.

"Brandon! Stop them! Stop the dancing particles!" But he didn't hear me. He was lost himself in the waves, tossed aside like a now-irrelevant god, a mere catalyst to inevitability. The tsunamis were earthquakes now, spreading everywhere there was water. I reached for Brandon's fading body even though I was drowning along with him, our very particles dissipating together in the chaos.

No! I won't let this happen! I have to be the strong one now! Firmly, I pulled him out of the waves and back into the air where I kissed him on the mouth and breathed just enough motivation into his lungs to fly our souls back to the lanai and the cozy bed that smelled of pikake.

Chapter Twenty-Six

SINCE WE SKIPPED DINNER, I simply inhaled breakfast. The macadamia nut pancakes were just about the best thing I had ever put in my mouth.

"Slow down. You're going to choke," laughed Brandon.

"Maybe you wore me out last night after the tapes," I said.

"You wore *me* out, are you kidding? We need to come to Hawaii more often."

"You honestly don't remember anything from the tapes? *Really?*"

"Nope, other than they did a great job putting us to sleep. Me anyway. I guess you spent the night sucking my face. How'd we end up in the bed, anyway?"

"Please don't use that expression. I really hate it."

"Oh, not my face? Well, what about my...okay, okay, stop kicking me...sorry, you're the master."

"And you're not funny one bit," I said, forcing myself to put down the syrup pitcher that I wanted to dump on his face.

So much for stopping being mad at him. It was not the fact that he felt relaxed enough just now to make a crude joke, but that he said he didn't experience the visions last night that was disturbing me. It was disappointing. The whole time I thought we were together in what we were seeing. It made me wonder about earlier at Wandering Pines when Lenore brought us musically into her world. Was he just faking that he experienced what I experienced back in that garden? Or worse, had Brandon changed, hardened somehow, so that he *couldn't* experience the visions anymore? Or was it just that Lenore was gone and the tapes were no real substitute for the power she had over both of us. Was it maybe like the experience of smoking Enlightenment now? Mildly significant, but no substitute for the full-on effect of music-tripping with Lenore? It was annoying to feel that Brandon would scoff at me if I shared these thoughts with him now.

"Well, the fun's over, in any case," he said. "Here comes Pendleton and Olaf."

I shoveled the last few bites of pancakes into my mouth, washed it down with lukewarm Kona coffee, and gave Brandon one more meaningful and worried frown. The scientists were dressed in expedition shorts and hiking boots. They bypassed the buffet and grabbed their coffee to go. "You guys ready?" said Olaf.

We followed him and Pendleton into the elevator and down to the storage area. Mavis and Sam were ecstatic to see us, mobbing me when Olaf opened the snake cage. Sybil and Sheldon were in their usual places on the branch. I couldn't imagine they were the best conversationalists for the dogs last night. If this crew was going to work out as a wilderness team, Mavis and Sam were going to have to develop their personal relationship to a very high level. Reptiles are not the best conversationalists.

Olaf rounded up some security guards and in a flash the cage was loaded in the van. We piled in and already my thirst had me reaching for a bottle of water from the case at our feet. It couldn't be much past eight in the morning, but it was already hot and humid.

Olaf kept the air conditioning off to keep the snakes happy as we exited the resort and turned onto a winding road heading toward the center of the island. Ahead of us and to the south were two monstrous volcanoes, officially active but quiet at the moment. One, Mauna Loa, contained more mass between its rounded peak and its base than all the mountains of the Sierra Nevada Range put together. The other was dotted with astronomical observatories that looked from here like little golf balls teed up for some gods' morning round.

As we climbed, the temperature dropped significantly. We passed a small town that seemed to think it was located in Wyoming. There were statues of horsemen and cattle in the shopping centers, and even a rodeo corral. One side of the town was bone dry with prickly pear cactus growing here and there, and the other side was lush green and battling the encroachment of the rainforest that occupied the rim of another smaller volcano that loomed over the town.

Olaf consulted his eyeglasses and turned off onto a dirt road leading up into that rain forest, Sybil's new home. Mud path would be a more accurate description of the road. We didn't get very far before the road literally dwindled into a footpath. Olaf managed to get the van turned around in the jungle and parked it under a houseplant the size of a tree, a philodendron, the same type of vine-like plant that my mom has growing all over her art studio back in California.

We got out fighting the sloppy wet leaves to open the back of the van. There were great misty clouds wafting above us between the branches. I watched them swirl and felt the intense heat of the sun when it occasionally broke through. The jungle smelled intensely of rotting fruit. Guavas covered with ants were all over the side of the road and in the ditch.

Pendleton unearthed two backpacks from the back of the van while I located the source of the guavas, a skinny tree next to the philodendron. The fruit were about the size of a lemon with thin yellow skin and pink inside when you broke them apart. I touched my tongue to the flesh and tasted the citrus-y sweetness.

"You young people mind carrying the packs?" said Olaf. "Ella, can you get the dogs to talk the snakes into the packs?"

"Why can't we just carry the cage? Or let them go here?" said Brandon.

"Too risky. We could be seen. Pig hunters use this trail fairly often, and we want to be deep in the jungle before we let them go," said Pendleton.

I looked at Mavis and Sam. They looked about as sad as I had ever seen two dogs look who just stepped out of a car for a walk. "Mavis, time for you and Sam to hide the snakes in the packs," I said. "Then we can go for a walk in this beautiful jungle, your new home." They both rolled their eyes at me and trotted off up the trail.

"What's going on Ella? Stop them!" said Olaf. "We can't muscle these guys into the packs without their help."

"Where are the leashes? I can go get them," said Brandon.

"No! Stay here, Brandon," I said. "This is *not* a time for leashes. You of all people should know that!"

I took off up the trail after my babies. A few hundred feet into the jungle, I found them lapping water from a little stream running next to the trail. Sam turned to me and growled. Mavis won't even turn to acknowledge me.

"I know, Sam, and I don't blame you. This sucks. Just let me come put my feet in the stream with you for a moment. I promise that after we talk, you and Mavis can take off or do whatever you want."

Mavis turned then to look me in the eye. There's rusty red water dripping from her gums. I tried to sit down on a rock and in the process slipped off onto the muddy red ground. I leaned back against the rock to regain my dignity and composure, not caring that I was getting dirty. The dogs came closer.

"Here's the thing, you guys. When my dad rescued Jenny from the Brecken lab and Brandon ended up with Max, those two were just like you, so ready to get out of the lab. And once they were out, phew did they grow! Their intelligence, their powers. It was amazing. Like you guys will grow here. Now I know you don't have the quantum communication thing down pat yet, but I have a feeling it will come, and I'm pretty sure you can understand pretty much everything I am saying. So, here's the deal. This little plan of theirs to get the snakes going and breeding in the jungle, it's going to have an impact. Whether it's a good one or not is going to depend partly on nature and partly on you guys, but

Sybil and Sheldon don't really count as the main thing in my mind. In my mind, Jenny and Max, and now you two, are the main thing. You're the hope for a conscious future because, in case you haven't caught on yet, humans are a few kibbles short of a happy meal when it comes to existing in balance on this planet."

Mavis was listening and pawing at the mud nervously. She paused and looked at me with her head cocked.

"Sorry, I should know better than to speak figuratively to you. I mean humans are stupid, stupid and selfish, and they act before they think things through. This is another example of that, I'm afraid, letting these snakes go. But here's the deal. I love you two. If you refuse to help them now they'll probably release the snakes anyway, and then they will take you back to Bryson's lab and hook you up to all those machines again to see what went wrong. You'll be stuck inside cages the rest of your life with no more freedom than the lab rats. You don't want that, do you? You're not rats. I'm not sure what you are, but I know you're not rats with no more destiny than to add to a data set.

"Look. It's beautiful here, and the jungle is full of fresh food and water. You'll be free, free to run around and become the amazing creatures you are destined to become. Your potential is unlimited because your minds have been opened, touched by enlightenment, ready to cooperate with nature, heal her, and bring intelligent life to a higher plane. I know that about you. I can feel it in my fingers and in my heart. If Lenore were here I would play her for you so you can hear her song, the same one that I think must be playing a little bit in your heads right now. Listen to her song!

You guys, and Jenny and Max, you really *will* be masters, although I don't think quite in the same way as Brandon envisions it. Humans don't deserve that title anymore. The world needs a *new* breed of masters - you guys!"

Suddenly I felt like an ancient monk trying to convince two young kids in an Asian village somewhere that they were the true reincarnation of the Dali Lama, only I have really gone off my rocker because these particular kids are dogs. Oh, to be one of them and just take off with them into nature! Mavis left the stream and licked my face. Sam hesitated a moment and then joined her. I wrapped my arms around them and sobbed.

Back at the van, the dogs took charge without a further word from anyone. Sybil and Sheldon folded themselves into the packs that we had laid open on the ground. We strapped them in. I hauled the pack with Sheldon onto my back and Brandon did the same with Sybil. If he was sad about releasing his lifelong companion into the wild, he didn't show it. His silent treatment of me was back, apparently, but why? Was he scared? Excited? Why was he hiding his emotions from me?

Olaf and Pendleton grabbed walking poles and led the way back up the path. We passed the place where I gave the pep talk to Mavis and Sam and continued following the little stream deeper into the jungle. Birds were singing everywhere, and surprisingly there were almost no mosquitoes despite all the moisture. The pack was heavy on my back but balanced even though I could feel Sheldon slithering around in there.

The stream led us to a series of very old concrete canals carrying rushing red water downhill toward what I presumed must be a reservoir or something. How they ever got enough concrete hauled back here to lay this system was beyond me. Maybe the Greeks did it. Ha! Greeks in Polynesian voyaging canoes, that is. This construction feat seemed no less impressive to me than the Parthenon, and, frankly, far more practical.

We passed no one on the trail, and soon the aqueduct disappeared into a tunnel chiseled out of a rocky lava hillside. Ahead and around a densely foliated corner, Olaf and Pendelton stopped abruptly at a sudden opening. Brandon and I joined them in the clearing and there in front of us was the most gorgeous canyon I had ever seen. It was a quarter mile wide and we emerged on the side of it a thousand feet above the jungle floor. My legs shook a little bit. Two more steps and we'd fall to our deaths. The mist was swirling up from the bottom of the canyon that stretched as far as we could see east to the ocean. To the West the gorge dug into the jungle but was still an integral part of the jungle because the walls of the canyon were covered as thickly in tropical plants as the rest of the landscape.

"Come on, people. No time for gawking like tourists. Our goal is up there at the head of the canyon," said Olaf, pointing.

We followed the narrow trail somehow hacked out of the side of the canyon for a mile or two until we rounded the head of the canyon.

"We leave the trail here," said Olaf. As soon as we stepped off the beaten path, the floor of the jungle became a tangle of weeds and swamp. Wet to our knees, we parted the thick plant life with our hands and pushed onward deeper into the jungle.

"According to our satellite research, only pig hunters come here, and then only if their dogs happen to mistakenly lead them into this mess. We can let them go soon," said Pendleton.

I was glad to hear that. My pack kept catching on low branches, and the mud was threatening to suck my hiking sandals right off my feet. It was hard to believe the ground was so wet here on what was essentially the top of a volcano. It's a rainforest up here and a desert down by the ocean. Go figure.

The dogs found a relatively dry spot and stopped. The mist rolled in thick, and I thought about what the canyon trail was going to be like going back when I couldn't even see my feet because of the fog.

"This is as good a place as any," said Olaf. "Open the packs."

"Anyone want to say anything first?" said Pendleton.

"To a new order!" said Brandon. He placed his pack on the ground and released the straps. Sybil emerged out like a crocodile bursting from a muddy river after its prey. I felt Sheldon thrashing too, so I dumped my pack quickly onto the ground, ripped open the straps, and stepped back horrified. I glanced at Mavis. *Does she have this under control?* The power and speed of Sheldon matched Sybil's in ferocity. If I didn't believe it before, I knew now that these snakes fully have the power to rule this jungle as top predators. If they decided to turn on us and strangle us, they certainly could easily do that. Instead they headed uphill with the dogs and disappeared. Only Mavis turned around briefly to look me one last time in the eye.

Deed accomplished. Predatory snakes were in Hawaii now, for better or for worse. I wiped my eyes and looked at Brandon to see if he was sad to say goodbye to Sybil. For the first time all day he looked me in the eye. There were no tears, and all he did was nod slowly and deliberately.

Chapter Twenty-Seven

ON THE WAY BACK THROUGH the cowboy town we stopped at a run-down shopping center to eat. The place had a bunch of wild house cats running around in the woods behind it. There was a beat up resin statue of a rugged cowboy scratching his navel displayed under the covered walkway between shops that was somehow supposed to motivate people to shop there. I didn't really get its appeal, but it did get my attention. There were a number of restaurants there, all dubious. Olaf was insisting on the Korean place, but Pendleton, like me, clearly had his doubts.

"There is a grass-fed burger joint over there across the road," Pendelton suggests futilely. I nodded vigorously.

"Trust me, you're going to love it," said Olaf, ignoring us.

We followed him reluctantly through the banged-up screen door. It is one of those restaurants where you ordered and paid at the counter, and then someone brought you your food guided by the number given to you on a shiny metal table stand. I made choices blindly. Many of the vegetables in the steam bins I had never heard of. Pipinola? What the heck is that? The atmosphere wasn't exotic or anything special, just a collection of tables and ordinary chairs the primary virtue of which was that they were easy to wipe clean between customers. In an apparent nod to a fern bar, there were a few potted plants struggling to stay alive in the restaurant's darkness. The tables were full of locals, though, a positive sign.

The food came quickly and it was piping hot, fresh and delicious. I don't even bother opening the paper-covered chopstick package. I go right for the fork and down a whole plate of Korean pork in three minutes. Pork. Probably what Mavis and Sam were feeding on too by now. My only complaint about the meal was they portion out only one measly napkin per person. Mine held up for just one swipe across my greasy mouth, but I didn't bother asking for another one. What can I say? I have no inhibitions when it comes to eating.

Thinking back to my "tape dream" last night, I said, "So, now that we accomplished the release, what are the chances we can find a sea turtle around here?"

"Oh, Kiholo Bay, for sure," said Olaf. "We send interns out there from the marine zoology department every semester to help out with the conservation effort. Kiholo is where the majority of the rescued turtles go to rest and breed. It's a protected brackish inlet that the sharks can't get into very often, although they hang out at the mouth of the bay sometimes for a chance at a crunchy morsel."

"Oh, what kind of sharks?" said Brandon.

"Tigers primarily. Sometimes lately great white sharks, but not that often. Black and white tipped sharks are around too, but they're mostly after reef fish, the ones that still remain, that is," said Olaf.

"Do you mean the sharks or the reef fish?" I said.

"Both, unfortunately. The whole ecosystem of the reef is breaking down. Every species except jellyfish has been negatively impacted. Ninety percent of the world's reefs are gone now due to bleaching, you know. Warmer water might be fun to swim in, but it's been hell on the plants and animals."

"But there are still turtles there?" I said.

"Oh, you bet. You'll see them there, for sure. You should go when we get back to the hotel. The shuttle will take you to the beach access to the south and you can walk into Kiholo from there and watch the sunset," said Olaf.

"That sounds like a plan. Are you coming with me, Brandon?" I asked. I nodded slowly at him so he would get the hint.

" Yeah, sure. Sounds like a cool place."

"Hot, really," said Pendelton. "Last time Olaf dragged me there I melted the bottom right off of my flip-flops. You guys have fun. I think I'm going golfing. I could use a break before preparing my report for the board."

Chapter Twenty-Eight

MY RED SWIMSUIT FELT a little tight on me as Brandon and I walked the rocky shoreline from the drop-off point toward Kiholo, but there were a few beach houses there and just enough smattering of people on the sandy spots to stop me from stripping off and hiking naked. Pendelton was right. It's very hot here. I'm glad I brought along a small pack with lots of water.

"So, Brandon. Do you miss Sybil?" Despite too many hours spent in the Brecken lab instead of at the gym or outside working where I know he would rather be, he looked fit in the Calvin Klein swimsuit Olaf picked out for him .

"I'm happy for her. She's in good hands and will make a difference, I think."

"But do you miss her?"

He stopped and turned to me. "Look, Ella, the time for sentimental attachment to things has long passed. The world is dying. The only thing we should be asking ourselves is whether our actions, and that includes having our pets, is helping the world or hurting it. Nothing else matters. Sure, I miss Sybil. She's been my pet since before high school, but how we *feel* doesn't mean jack anymore. Sybil's got a purpose now. I'm happy for her."

He turned and continued trudging through the fist-sized rocks on the beach. I followed him silently until the beach opened up into a shaded sandy area with coconut trees. The mouth of Kiholo Bay yawned in front of us. A few waves from the open ocean crashed into the shallow rocks that poked out here and there as the light blue brackish water met the darker water.

"Wow, what a place!" I said.

"Don't see any shark fins," said Brandon, shading his eyes.

"Let's hope not!" I said. "I need a swim." We kept walking.

The beach petered out into branching paths marked with cairns made of stacked lava rocks. We stuck to the path closest to the water and soon we were climbing over large boulder-like lava shelves overlooking and sometimes dipping into the calm bay. Huge fish periodically leapt from the water and disturbed the silence with their splashes. A gentle breeze started up, but it felt hot to the skin. Only a swim would dispel the heat that was burning us to the bone. Soon we found a perfectly flat rock projecting from the lava field and offering easy access to the water. In a flash we kicked off our Tevas and dived in before the sun-baked black lava could scorch our feet.

The water was very cold, not at all like the ocean water at the resort. My breath came in spurts as I got used to it. "Why is it so cold?" I said.

"Must be underwater springs feeding this bay," said Brandon.

"I get it. But the ocean water coming in is warm."

"Just a minute," said Brandon, and he disappeared under the water. After thirty seconds or so he popped up and said,"Dive down. It's warm!"

I took a deep breath and let myself sink. Sure enough, about ten feet down the water was warm as bathwater. It took me only the time it took to swim back up through the cold water to figure out why.

"Salt water is denser," I sputtered when I surfaced.

"Right, that's why the cold is on top where you wouldn't normally expect it. This place is wild!"

We swam around some more. I tried to see under the water but it was too murky for some reason. Careful not to step on any urchins, we finally climbed back out on the sunny black rock that now felt pretty great after the freezing water. I pulled a couple of beach towels from my pack for us to lie on.

"So, tell me the truth, Brandon. Last night. You must remember something from the experience after hearing the tapes."

"It's better to just leave it alone, Ella."

"What do you mean leave it alone! You just said today that our actions need to be centered on healing the earth. Don't you think these mystical things that keep happening to us need to be discussed?

"Maybe, maybe not. Depends on Mercury,"

"Jenny and Max wouldn't be out there with the lions changing the California ecosystem if we hadn't had *conversations* about our visions, about where Lenore took us. Come on. Are we a team or not? Why are you holding back from me? We have to talk about things when they come up, don't you think?"

"It's not that easy."

I looked at him long and hard. "Yes, I know. It's not that easy. The world is screwed up and human beings are to blame. Don't you think I feel that too? If you think the visions that guided humans to the screwed up place humanity is in right now are the same ones that you and I have been seeing, don't you think *I* wonder about that possibility too? What, if anything, cosmic or otherwise can any of us be sure of anymore? It's just so infinitely sad, the animals dying, the trees, the ocean, the plastic everywhere, the shit that humans have shitted upon the earth. I'll bet if you did an analysis there's twenty tons of plastic floating around in this bay right now. That's probably what those big fish are trying to jump away from for all we know. And the jaunty private jet ride we took to get over here. How many trees in the rainforest are going to die of heat and thirst because of the fuel we burned for our little expedition?"

"There's a good chance we saved this island, Ella. You saw all the damage the pigs had done to the rainforest."

"Yeah, so the theory goes, but we don't *know* that, do we? So there are too many pigs, and rats too from what I hear. A generation ago people around here thought mongoose would solve all the problems. Too bad rats are nocturnal and mongoose like to hunt in the daylight. *That* was a royal screw-up."

"What do you want from me? We've got to *try*, don't we? The lions we freed into the San Rafael Wilderness Area have definitely turned that area around. That never would have happened if we hadn't *acted*, if we hadn't imagined the possibilities."

"I personally think it had more to do with Jenny and Max wanting to live wild and free, and you at a loss for what to do about the lions, but I'll concede your point that it has been a success...so far. How do we know it wasn't just dumb luck, though?"

"We're getting very close to understanding *everything*, Ella. Haven't you been paying attention? We can genetically engineer anything that is needed, and our Brecken AI is so good, there isn't an ecosystem we can't analyze and control if we want to. Problem is we're too stupid politically to get things done. You want to know why we haven't seeded the atmosphere with sulphuric acid yet? Politicians. And humanists too, people second guessing themselves, people too afraid to do what is needed. We'd still have ice in Greenland if we had gone ahead with the seeding program four years ago."

"There's still some ice there ..."

"Not much, and the U.N. is *still* debating the plan in committee. Ridiculous. Someone needs to send the jets and just get it done. I'd do it myself if I had the money and could fly."

"Brecken Research Institute probably has the money. Why don't you just talk to Pendleton?"

"You don't think Bryson already has? They're better than most, but they're still just as mired in bureaucracy as everyone else. Time is running out, Ella. The planet is headed the way of Venus if we don't do something fast."

"I thought that theory was debunked years ago."

"It was when we were looking at only a 2% increase in CO_2. Now that we're staring at 6% it's back on the table. The end of life on earth is coming for sure, unless we can figure out how to breathe scorching hot carbon dioxide."

"In our tape-dream last night I saw a god wielding a fiery pick, heating the world to protect herself from water. I was holding your hand. Did the image come from you?"

"You're not going to let go of this are you?! Okay, you want to know what I saw flying with you last night? I saw the future. The Suit of Wands card. Yes, fire breaks things down to their smallest components, and the essential blueprint of everything that is and will be to come is revealed through its flames. The dance that must be danced follows the stoking of the fires."

I sat up on my towel to read Brandon's body language. He's tight all over and his biceps were twitching. I remembered his dance with the particles in the drop of water and how scared it made me feel, how complicit I felt in the whole thing because he forced *me* to choose the droplet. Was he talking about some kind of End of Days right now?

"Brandon. That dance was a *nightmare*, a bum deal. It did *not* feel right to me. Particles of nature were moving in sync with you, but the Rocky Horror song you were dancing to was a ridiculous joke, and you were taking it so *seriously*. You were messing with something immeasurably potent and unpredictable. You had no business doing that!"

"Somebody's gotta make it his business or we're all lost."

"Maybe our business is to *listen* more, not *do* more crazy things!"

"That's the philosophy of a loser, Ella. This is the era of action. Hey, look there's a tsunami coming. Let's just sit on this beach and talk about it for a while. That's where you're at, you and the rest of humanity. Everything will just stay the same if we just ignore it and keep on doing what we've always been doing. I thought you matured beyond that by now."

"Doing what we've always been doing?! You're saying taking some time to really listen and get some guidance isn't something new? You're a little screwy right now, Brandon. Humans have been acting without thinking ever since Descarte postulated human thought as the final justification for existence. We're *ignorant!* There's more to the world than logic, you know. How many wars have been started because both sides of the conflict were logically sure they were right? Like, *every single one*! Did that stop ignorant humans from acting? Of course not. Acting, that's why we can't get anything done that's truly worthwhile anymore."

"*I'm* screwy? Well at least I didn't get myself shot playing a fiddle that is so caught up in the mystical confusion of the universe that no one even knows what it is doing or why it even has the power it has. That seems a little foolishly on the side of action to me now, wouldn't you agree?"

"You're just twisting words now, Brandon. I can't listen to this anymore. You're talking nonsense!"

"Oh, I am, huh? Well, power rules, Ella, and the sooner you wake up to that fact, the sooner you can get on board with me and Bryson to fix things."

"The way you and Bryson think, you're not going to fix a damn thing."

"You're just jealous that I can keep up with him and you can't."

"I don't want to keep up with him. He's an idiot, and so are you."

"Fine. I'm an idiot. Okay. I get it. Well, this *idiot* is done with this conversation. See you back at the resort. Maybe." He put on his t-shirt and sandals and headed north on the shoreline path.

"The shuttle's the other way, idiot," I said.

"I'm walking. I hope it's really far. I want to be alone until we leave this waste-of-time island."

Chapter Twenty-Nine

I WATCH BRANDON DISAPPEAR up the lava trail. He didn't turn back to look at me once. I supposed I should have cut him some slack. He did just say goodbye to Sybil, a pet that had been with him for years. When Jenny took off with Max for the wilderness last year, I was a mess for weeks. I put the towel back into my pack and hurried to put on my sandals to chase after him and apologize, but then I stopped for a minute and realized that even if those feelings are going on in him, what he said to me about his plans and priorities was pretty darn disturbing. And why did he want to keep his version of the dream a secret from me? What was he afraid of? What's he not telling me? Can I trust him anymore? Do I trust *myself*? He's right. What exactly *are* we doing on this island? I shook my head.

I looked around the lagoon and thought about the beauty of Kiholo Bay compared to my life in Brecken Vista right now. I decided to sit down again and look at the sun sparkling in the blue-green water some more. For all I knew, we might be in the jet heading back to the city before the night was over. I leaned back and rested my head on my pack. The sun was getting low out over the ocean beyond the bay, but it still felt intense on my reddening face. There were tears on my cheeks. From sadness, or anger? I didn't know, probably both.

I noticed the sea turtles that climbed out on the rocks across the bay only after one close to me broke the surface and poked its dynosaur-like head onto my rock. It turned its huge eye directly at me, and my fingers started to tingle. I jumped up and whipped my pack onto my back, instinctively yielding my space to this creature who was kicking and flapping its way fully out of the water. It was monstrously huge, easily three feet in diameter, and thick with prehistoric muscle and shell. Once it was settled, it turned its calm and watery eye on me again, and the tingling in my fingers intensified. I closed my eyes and saw the image of the very same turtle vibrating behind my eyelids as if my eyes were still open. *Jenny?*

I opened my eyes and the vision faded but the real turtle was still there, and now I saw there are dozens more climbing out on every possible resting place around the lagoon. They all turned to stare at me, connecting with my nervous system somehow, like the sun was connecting with my skin. I thought of Sybil and how she and Sheldon were controlled by the thoughts of Mavis and Sam. Are these my masters controlling me? I didn't know, but something told me I must obey them. I *wanted* to obey them, and, strangely enough, I had no questions for them about that at all, just acceptance.

The tingling in my fingers spread until my whole body was as hot as my face. I moved toward the turtles to be closer, to feel their pleasure more intimately, but that direction was painful. I moved back, surprised when the pain stopped and the pleasure got more intense when I did. What was this? I tested it again. Back and to the right, not pleasurable. Back and to the left, ahhh. Amazing. I decided to trust these feelings and this game. I wanted more of it. I followed the guidance of my feelings, seeking bliss. *Okay, I'll play Pavlov's dog, but will I lose the feelings if I break eye contact with the turtles?*

No. The guiding feelings were still there when I looked away, urgent and easy to follow. I walked on lava following the sensations that radiated from my chest and soon I left the turtles and lagoon behind. The game continued. I felt their gaze even though I couldn't see them behind me any longer. Alone, I walked in and around giant waves of frozen black lava. My head was light. The last time I felt like this was right before I got shot playing Lenore at Comey's. I pushed that fearful memory away and stayed with the positive feelings. This time is not like that time. I could sense it in the depths of my body. This guidance had to be from Jenny through the turtles and even from them as well. Jenny would never show me visions that led to bullets. I knew her love was true, like Lenore's, like my grandfather's. I kept scrambling across the lava, well off the beaten path now and far up the ancient black flow.

I paused for a drink of water. Testing, forward left? No, forward and to the right. I kept going, following the feelings in my gut. I rounded a big wave of black rock and startled a herd of goats led by a nasty-smelling male. They scampered off knocking small pieces of lava loose with their hooves. There in front of me where they had been assembled was an opening to a cave, a deep tunnel. I stepped toward it. Yes, go inside the tunnel, the feelings told me. I obeyed.

It's cool and dark inside, and the footing was sketchy, but a hole in the roof lit the cave a hundred feet ahead. The feelings in my body intensified with each step inward, like a building orgasm in fact, but I was seeking the build-up, not the release, and the guidance and *correctness* of the intensifying feeling as the lighted area drew me deeper inside. Out of the sun, I could smell the water of the lagoons on my hair and body masking the stale dryness of the tunnel.

Something hard and white skittered off my left foot. It was the skull of a goat. There were dry bones scattered everywhere glowing softly in the diffused sunlight. Their luminescence drew my eyes down to them, but that direction brought pain. I looked up instead, obeying my moist turtle connection and moving forward again toward bliss.

The light from the hole in the ceiling was just ahead now around a human-like chunk of lava. The closer I got the more I wanted that light. I *knew* that light was mine like it was not just any old light in the darkness, but my deepest inner spirit.

I moved ahead. Only a human-like, sculptural stalagmite was left to stumble around. My feet waded through knee deep, clicking bones now, but I ignored them and held the boulder close to me, hugging its human form as I passed. "Closer," the turtles said, "You're almost there," so I pressed my face against the stalamite's rough chest, and the damp smell of the lagoon in my hair suddenly became the musty expanse of Jenny's fur. Her image flashed across my eyes, Jenny standing tall near Triangle Mountain on a wilderness ridge surrounded by worshiping lions. I laughed to be so close to her again, embracing her, my skin an arcing river of electricity now, competing with the bones for brightness.

I heard music, bluegrass music. Tears came to my eyes and then Jenny was gone and I was naked. The human stalagmite was just a boulder again. So, accepting the direction of my bliss, I let her go and turned inward again, and there beneath that column of shimmering, blissful light inside a secret hidden lava tunnel on the largest active volcanic island in the world was Lenore.

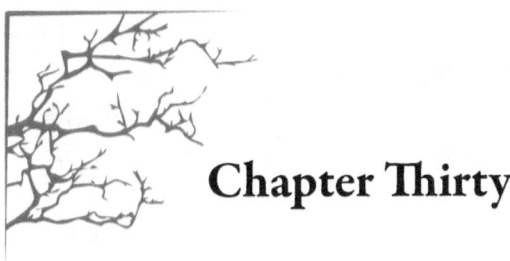

Chapter Thirty

SHE'S PERFECT AS USUAL, not a scratch on her, golden and beautiful, and I scurried forward and found her bow and Granddad's tattered case next to it on the tunnel floor. Afraid of my shaking hands, I quickly zipped everything safely back into her case and waded my way through the goat carcasses back to the tunnel entrance clutching the case safely to my breasts, my breath coming back to me in short gasps.

Emerging in the fading light of the evening on the lava field, all I could think about was sprinting back to the hotel to lock myself and Lenore safely away as soon as possible. I couldn't believe I was holding her again. Then I looked out at the lagoon and the gathering sunset and took some deep breaths. Why not linger a while? I decided to slow down and think about what to tell Brandon, maybe ask the turtles for more advice. A few breaths later I realized I was so overwhelmed with gratitude I could barely walk. I wanted to sink to my knees, but it would be dark soon, so I headed back toward the lagoon, careful not to step in any holes in the lava field.

Eternal gratitude, easy to forget in a stormy world where so much was falling apart, and where there was so much blame to parcel out. Sure these sea turtles have recovered their population on this part of the planet because of the concerted effort of many people to protect them, but that doesn't mean everything is okay for them. Surely they notice the reef fish dying out, the beautiful coral bleaching away to skeletal nothingness. Surely they grieve the beauty of the ocean burning away from acidification, and yet they all somehow heard Jenny's call and climbed out of the safety of the lagoon to help me find Lenore. Why? I don't know. I just know that gratitude was welling up in me like the evening tide that was rushing into the lagoon. The world may be topsy-turvy now, warm waters metaphorically running inexplicably beneath the cold, but still there's beauty, connection, nurturing, and love.

When I got back to the swimming rock, the turtles were still out of the water, their bodies rimming the lagoon like gifts from the ocean, sacks of gold the world had forgotten about. I placed Lenore's case on the flat lava rock, took her out, and put her to my chin. The sun dipped below the horizon just as I touched the horsehair to her strings.

As I expected, her first notes were soft, reverent. I could feel Lenore's joy to be speaking again. Her beautiful notes mixed with my gratitude in a grandparent-like love, that wise love of optimistic acceptance, the feeling you get when you drink tea with them and they let you win at Cribbage because they know deep down in their hearts that the outcome of the game is trivial compared to the loving playing of it.

Lenore and I, we played for the turtles, the wise honus of the ocean, the guides of all life, if only humankind would listen to them. I knew they heard our tune. I could feel their humbleness in the face of the miracle of guiding me to Lenore. "She was there all along. You would have found her eventually," they seemed to be saying to me, but I was not so sure. We don't thank miracle makers enough in this life, I felt.

Lenore played until each note turned every little cloud on the horizon into a fiery explosion of lava-like beauty, and then I zipped Lenore back into her case, put on a thin red Brecken windbreaker from my pack, and started the long trek across the lava trails and beaches back to the dusty access road.

Chapter Thirty-One

ON THE SHUTTLE I MANAGED to discreetly cover Lenore's case with my windbreaker and back at the hotel snuck her into the room and under the bed before Brandon or anyone else saw me. I'm not ready to answer his questions about Lenore right now. I had too many questions myself to think about.

One question was, what now? Go back to the concrete jungle of Brecken Vista, study my tail off, and help Brandon and Bryson torture dogs? No thanks. Maybe if Dr. Vern was in charge, something good might happen, but he's not. It's all Bryson's show, and maybe Pendelton's show too somehow in a James Bond kind of way. I sighed and sat on the bed. One thing's for sure, I couldn't take any more of Bryson being the "master" and my boyfriend reverently kissing the "master's" butt all the time.

Where had Brandon gone to in his mind? My banjo-playing lover? My the-welfare-of-animals comes-before-any-thing-else activist? There's got to be more to this partnership than just sleeping in the same room and having sex every once in a while. Was I wrong to think we were in this life together, equally, thinking and feeling our way forward as a team, freeing lions into the wilderness where they can make a real difference again because we both *knew together deep inside of us* that it was the right thing to do? Where did *that* Brandon go? I thought about Lenore safely hidden now and tears formed. Under what light in what cave might I also find you again Brandon? I felt her presence in the room like the sunshine still tingling on my browning skin. *Lenore! Oh, she's back with me!*

There's no stopping the tears now, and it seemed she was giving me encouragement to shed them from her hiding place under the bed. I lowered my face to my salt-water-weathered hands and sobbed. In my ears I heard my grandfather whispering to me, comforting me, and there was his music, Lenore's music so much inside my crying. Someone hearing me might worry and come in but I didn't care. This weeping was beautifully beyond my control now. I sobbed to honor the music of my Grandfather's love and the love of Lenore that could never be lost, that would be with me forever because of him.

Then, between my fingers I noticed the hiking clothes Brandon changed out of piled on the carpet by my feet, and the towel in the bathroom wet from his shower. Suddenly, I knew what I had to say to him, painful as it might be. I wiped my eyes with the bottom of my t-shirt and gathered my courage to face him downstairs.

Chapter Thirty-Two

ON THE WAY DOWN THE elevator I finger-comb the snarls in my hair leftover from the shower I ended up taking to further delay this confrontation. I was a little ashamed of myself for needing more time to act after making my decision, but at least I felt cleaner. It was tempting to go back even now and delay some more, maybe hide in the closet and play Lenore to ask her for more answers, but I sensed she needed a rest, and that even with her loyal willingness to help she wanted me now to make decisions for myself just like I had to do when she was gone. Did she leave me on purpose for that reason? I stared at the numbers on the elevator buttons. Or could Pendleton maybe have had Lenore all along since the shooting? Kanda could easily have snagged it for him when I was passed out. Did Pendelton then use his agents to hide her in the cave at Kiholo? And why? To somehow screw with my mind? I pushed these crazy thoughts away and forced myself to get back to reality. Lenore's a mystery, that's all. Who can explain her mystical comings and goings? It's better not to try and just be grateful she's on my side.. The elevator opened onto the lobby where the late night diners were enjoying their tiki torch-lit tables and fresh island fish. I saw Brandon at the table closest to the swimming pool. Looks like he and his two bosses were on the dessert course already.

"Ah, the lazy-lagoon-lounger half of the young couple makes it back!" said Pendelton. "Brandon filled us in on your decision to skip the King's Trail Hike back here. Come join us for a little celebratory mud pie. It's supposed to look like a menacing lava flow, but it's more of a caloric disaster instead, I'm afraid. We could use your help."

I moved empty Mai-Tai glasses to make some room at the table and sat down. "Thank you, Dr. Pendleton, but I better not indulge on an empty stomach. It does look good, though." Dr. Olaf nodded his endorsement of that sentiment and spooned himself a huge bite.

"No worries, my dear," said Pendleton. "Your plate of ono awaits you, and there will be plenty of this eruption left-over for you when you're ready for it." He nodded at a wait-er, pointed at me, and stuck his spoon into the mud pie that indeed looked massively endless. My stomach growled. In a flash the waiter returned with a white parachute drink and a steaming wooden plate of fish wrapped in leaves that smelled of roasted sesame oil and soy sauce. I untied the leaves and dug in. The white flaky fish tasted amazing, and the drink was a refreshing mix of coconut water, mango, and vodka.

"So, Ella, you missed our toast," said Olaf. "But here's again to the successful start of Phase One and the return of nature to itself."

"To a better version of itself," corrected Pendelton.

"Yes, indeed. We hope!" said Pendelton.

Brandon raised his glass, but I noticed a moment's hesitation and a quick glance at me.

"We won't know the results for some time, and really the survival of the masters out there is the biggest question," continued Pendelton.

"You mean more than physical survival," said Olaf.

"Oh, I'm not worried about their physical survival at all. They'll eat like kings. Even regular old hounds that get abandoned up there by pig hunters manage to survive without any problem. No, I mean intellectual survival, *connecting* survival, tapping into the wisdom stream that humans opted out of long ago. That's what's going to be interesting to watch."

"How are we going to watch *that*?" said Brandon. I noticed his glass had barely been touched.

"Well, beyond the usual species surveys and satellite imagery analysis, we'll just have to be open and creative about it. Intelligence will out, I always say. For sure we'll bring in some of our psychics, maybe the monks again. Set them up on the perimeter and gauge the vibrations. Of course, you two will be important in that effort too," said Pendleton. "Like any intelligent and sensitive children, Sam and Mavis will most certainly reach out to their early "parental" influencers when their tele-communicative minds develop sufficiently and they feel secure enough to do so."

I thought about the image I received from Jenny and how it led me to the turtles and Lenore, and again I was impressed with Pendleton's uncanny sense of what was going on, with his easy acknowledgement of being-states beyond the conventional, and with his openness to possibility so contrasting to Brandon's default Tarot-card know-it-all stubbornness. Or maybe Pendleton's just talking a good game, I don't know. Listening to him, it's tempting to get sucked into his words, to stick around Brecken and be a conduit for the understanding of the next evolution of intelligent life on earth. Who wouldn't want to do that?

"Isn't this all just window dressing?" said Brandon. "I mean, it's nice and all what we *might* have done on a microlevel to this small little ecosystem on this remote island, and to one little wilderness area in California where things seem to be getting healthier, but aren't we ignoring the larger question here, the one problem no one wants to talk about?"

"Well, clearly Bryson has been talking about it. I hear his very words as you speak. The deep dive into the double-helix!" said Olaf.

"If anything is going to stick in the healing of the planet, it has to be ultimately recorded in the genetic record," said Brandon.

And epigenetics. There's an important distinction between the two," said Pendleton.

"Epigenetic expression ultimately finds its permanence in genetics. Why not put our research energy there first and save precious time? Earth is going to be a second Venus if we don't do something fast," said Brandon.

You *are* becoming a Bryson clone," laughed Olaf. "So, we mess with human genetics now because we can, easily and effectively. To what end, though? What's his plan of action?"

"Well, either to alter humans to better adapt, or give genetic advantages to those who have the best chance to thrive and preserve life on earth," said Brandon.

"Another classic Bryson answer. And so I'll ask you the same question, I ask Bryson all the time. How is that thinking any more justified than the thinking that led to the failed eugenics programs of the past?"

"Because people like Hitler and Mengele were ego-maniacs interested in racial superiority. This is different. Bryson wants to take all of humanity back to our genuine genetic roots," said Brandon.

"Well, he's ignoring a basic problem. *All* of humanity? There are too many people on the planet, no matter how you divide them up racially. So you change people's genetics? People still have to eat, and drive cars, unfortunately," said Olaf.

"What if humans could be engineered to live off a quarter of the food and water that was needed before?" said Brandon. "Wouldn't that have a bigger impact on the planet's resources than introducing top predators in remote areas?"

"Maybe, but he's surely a long way away from that," said Pendleton.

"Maybe or maybe not. And maybe not a long way from other ideas equally compelling. The CRISPR is a powerful tool that we *need* to optimize," said Brandon. "What other choice do we have?" The others did not seem to disagree.

"So, can I ask a practical question, not to change the subject?" I said. "When are we heading back?"

"Tomorrow morning for you guys, I'm afraid," said Pendleton. "Brandon needs his Bryson fix, and you both need to get back to the other soon-to-be masters at the lab. I'll be staying behind to meet with the directors and deliver our report."

I spooned a large slice of mud pie onto my empty salad plate. "I'm not going back to the lab right away," I said. All eyes at the table turned to me. The spoon shook in my hand, but the tingling in my gut urged me to go on.

" Yeah, this has been great, and I'm excited for the changes we probably have made for the better here, but I think I need a little break right now to think some things over, gather a little more energy. I want to go somewhere and be in music for a while." Brandon looked right at me.

"Hmm, that's understandable, Ella, given all that's happened to you lately," said Pendelton. "You could use some more time to heal before you connect with any more breakout lab dogs. Where do you want to go, New York? New Orleans, the part that's still above water, that is? Given all you have done for this project, BRI will pay your expenses. We'll call it research. Are you hoping, perchance, to unearth another Lenore?"

"Something like that, I guess," I said. *Unearthed?* I stared at Brandon. He was looking at his napkin now, his shoulder twitching.

"Well, let's get you off on this adventure fast so you can come back soon. Where do you have in mind? Just don't say Tokyo because we're headed the other way. Anything East is fair game. The jet's all ours for a while."

"Um, can I let you know tomorrow?"

"Of course, my dear. The world is your oyster, for a little while, anyway. None of us can claim more than that these days, I'm afraid, unless, of course, we succeed in stopping the anthropocene. Just let me know in the morning."

The mud pie tasted comforting to me, and I concentrated on its cool chocolateness while the scientists chatted about jets and the growing challenges of turbulent air travel.

I looked pointedly at Brandon and excused myself for a beach stroll beyond the tiki torches.

Chapter Thirty-Three

BRANDON CAUGHT UP TO me a few minutes later by the shoreline. I wanted to get away from the resort lights to see the Milky Way, so I was walking fast and dodging the waves that were pushing their salty foam and plastic bits on-to the beach.

"Look, Brandon. I'm not as ambitious as you are, and I'm not sure I'm really on board with what Brecken is doing right now with Bryson, Vern, Olaf, and Pendleton with their mysterious agendas and elaborate plans for taking over the world. I'm not sure the world needs to be taken over, frankly."

Brandon kept pace with me in the sand. "They're not trying to take over the world. They just want to make it bet-ter."

" Yeah, can you honestly say that's true? How do you know? Is it better that Sybil is now a puppet of eco-warrior dogs attacking wild animals in a forest where they don't be-long? Did you guys even consider asking the native Hawai-ians if this was such a good idea?"

"It's kind of too late to ask their advice, don't you think? The chances of Hawaii ever being the idyllic state it was before Captain Cook came and ruined everything is pretty slim, don't you think?"

"I don't know. Everything just seems so stupidly futile to me right now, so cosmically wrong."

"Are you sure it's not just that you've been stuck in the city and you come here and get a little taste of wild beauty again? I mean this beach compared to Brecken Vista, who wouldn't be tempted to just stay here forever? I know you've been unhappy."

"I told you, I want to immerse myself in music again. I don't know why. It just feels right to me, and the lab feels wrong, dangerously wrong."

"Ella, are you sure about this? Maybe you just miss Lenore."

"No, I'm not sure about anything. But it probably does have something to do with Lenore, and *not* the fact that she's missing. That part you can count on."

"I think about her too, you know, her spirit," said Brandon. "She may be gone, but I love her as much as you do. She's the one who brought us together, gave us the vision and courage to free the lions and give Jenny and Max the life they needed to live. Hell, without her, we'd certainly not be respected students at Brecken. We have a future because of her."

"Well, it's nice to hear you finally say that, but I'm not so sure Lenore cares much about our careers at Brecken, Brandon. I think she has larger issues on her mind."

"Larger issues? Like what? It's not *careers*. I don't care about money and careers, but what could be larger than what we're working on? Nirvana? New-age hippie gardening? The cosmic internet you and Templeton like to chit-chat about? If there *is* a higher power in the universe, and Lenore is connected to that higher power somehow, don't you think *saving the planet* might be the top thing on its mind?"

"I imagine it might be, but what if your lab is screwing things up even worse through all your meddling? What if the answer lies in something other than blindly *doing stuff*?"

"Carbon dioxide levels are not going to come down on their own, Ella, and *doing things* is the only way we're going to avoid mass starvation and the decimation of the planet's species. If scientists hadn't come up with bee drones and hydroponic fish farms, we'd already be starving."

"We killed off bees because *scientists* thought pesticides were a cool way to go. *Scientists* are the ones who got us into this mess in the first place!"

"Not scientists, Ella, greedy masters who used science to line their own pockets."

"And you're so sure Bryson and his cronies are going to be any better?"

"Pendelton is Bryson's master. You like *him* don't you?"

"I don't know... " Brandon stopped and took me by the shoulders. We're far enough down the beach to see the stars now. I stared at them over his shoulder.

"Ella, go immerse yourself in music for a while, if you need to. There will be a place for you when you return. I'll take good notes for you in class, and the dogs will be fine for a while. Just don't stay away too long, okay? I need you. I don't understand you all the time, but I need you."

I knew Brandon wanted me to kiss him. After all, it's a beach in Hawaii and he just said he needs me, but the hotel room was calling me, and *I* had a need to make sure Lenore was still safe under the bed. "I'm going back," I said, turning away from him. "Your stuff will be in the hallway. Don't take this the wrong way, but I need to sleep alone tonight."

Chapter Thirty-Four

THE NEXT MORNING I went to the gift shop and bought a beach bag big enough to hide Lenore. I wrapped her in some beach towels and dirty clothes and stuffed her inside, but not before I removed Lawrence Pinchbeck's holocard from the front compartment where I stuck it after he saw me play at Comey's. Time to see if this guy was serious about representing me or just momentarily entranced by Lenore's music. His hologram picture was just as handsome as I remembered him.

It's all business and serious silence in the van to the airport. I guess Pendleton and Olaf got all the socializing out of their system last night, or maybe they were hung over. I for one slept like a baby and was grateful this morning for the limited conversation.

At the tarmac, I let the ground crew load Lenore into the hold with the other baggage. No need to bring undue attention to her by carrying her on, although I broke a sweat when I put the beach bag on the cart. Pendleton gestured me over to where he was talking to the pilots under the wing.

"So, file the plan for S.F. and then you're taking this young lady to...um, Ella, where are you headed this morning?"

"Nashville, please," I said. "Or as close as I can get to it if there isn't an airport there."

"Oh, there is a big one," said the Captain. "It would be my pleasure, Ma'am. Nashville is my hometown, in fact."

"Well, that's convenient," said Pendelton.

"Oh, I don't live there anymore," said the captain. "Just grew up there, that's all, but this is a lovely excuse to go back. You all can board whenever you are ready, sir."

The flight is a mirror opposite of the one going out, rough as hell over the mid-pacific, and relatively smooth as we approached California. I used the opportunity to spot buildings and beaches from my childhood in the revival season of Big Little Lies. The characters and their convoluted ridiculousness made me think of my mother and the kind of crazy people she attracted to her art studio. I had nothing to say to Brandon, or anyone else for that matter, but I could see them stealing glances at me every once in a while.

We landed. I said my goodbyes simply and without emotion to everyone, watched the unloading of the baggage like a hawk from the window, and in just the time it took to re-fuel and taxi back out onto the runway, the jet was back in the air over Tahoe and heading east. I couldn't help thinking that even Meryl Streep probably doesn't get private jet service like this, and the thought felt good for a moment until severe carbon guilt settled in. Oh well. What are you going to do? At least I didn't own a car. The only car I could afford to buy would be an analog gas-guzzler, and I refused to do that, so I suppose it evened out.

One of the things I am going to do, I tell myself, is to make the most of this opportunity. Lenore came back to me for a reason. No way am I going to let her down. Or Jenny for that matter. I concentrated on remembering the smell of Jenny's fur in the lava tunnel. Was that really just yesterday? Just as I almost conjured it up again in my nostrils, the crazy turbulence began again, and I had to tighten my seatbelt to the point of pain. The tightness across my belly felt somehow right at the moment, though, like a price I had to pay to once again be alone listening to the tunes of Lenore.

Chapter Thirty-Five

THE CAPTAIN WAS RIGHT, Nashville International Airport was no hick place to land. Despite the darkness, the place was lit up like Vegas and seemed as big and as busy as the Strip. The jet taxied toward an empty spot next to its elite brothers on the tarmac and cut its engines. I quickly used the bathroom now that I could without committing turbulence suicide. It had been rough the whole flight. I also grabbed a packaged sandwich from the cabin refrigerator and followed the tired but smiling pilots out the door and down the ramp.

"Would you be needing a taxi, Ma'am?" said the woman in an orange vest pushing the covered cart toward me with my backpack and beach bag. I'm glad I wrapped Lenore's case in plenty of towels and old clothes. Someone could make a lot of money selling turbulence-proof suitcases these days. Maybe they already have. I wouldn't know.

"No, thanks. I'll just blink an Uber," I said, although I had no place in mind yet to go. The attendant smiled and handed me my luggage.

"Very good, Ma'am. You'll need to exit through the terminal, then. You'll see the app lot signs. Just follow them to the main entrance and outside to the south parking lot. Have a pleasant stay in Nashville!"

"Yes," added the captain waiting for me to grab my stuff. I put the sandwich in my backpack and balanced the beach bag on my rolling suitcase. "Enjoy my home town. I hope you get a chance to hear some music while you are here."

"Oh, you can count on that," I said, patting Lenore to make sure she was still in the bag. "Thank you for the lift!"

"Glad to be of service," said the captain.

And just like that I was on my own.

Chapter Thirty-Six

INSIDE THE TERMINAL, I pulled out my phoneglasses, but I didn't blink an Uber. I called my dad instead. It was still a reasonable hour in Humboldt.

"Ella, my dear, how nice of you to call me. You have made my way too healthy dinner salad a genuine pleasure for once!"

"Hi, Dad. Still on your diet, huh? I thought you gave up eating dinner?"

"Oh, the intermittent fasting thing was too much discipline for me, although it did help to lower my blood sugar and LDL's. Now I compromise by eating raw greens and chewing my cud like a cow every night instead. It's so tedious getting old."

"You're not old, Dad."

"Well, it's nice of you to say that, Ells. How's university life treating you? Are Bryson and Vern behaving themselves?"

"Well, that's kind of why I am calling. You ready for a long story?"

"When I'm listening to you, no story is ever long enough. I miss hearing your voice. Sock it to me, baby!"

I tell him about Mavis and Sam and about Sybil and her release with Sheldon in Hawaii. I tell him about Brandon's obsession with Bryson and Bryson's secret CRISPR machine. I tell him about Jenny and the turtles at Kiholo Bay. I ask him to keep Lenore's return a secret.

"Wow, that's just amazing. So Lenore came back to you, huh? Interesting. Can't say I saw that coming, but it makes sense to me, actually, now that I think about it."

"How do you mean, Dad?"

"Well, it's like the quality control work we've been doing lately with Enlightenment. For most people it is a miracle drug, lifting the shade of illusion from their eyes, showing them a way forward that was actually there all along. But for a few it doesn't work, and so they call and complain that Enlightenment's a scam and not any different than other concentrates. At first we just dismissed them as so out of touch that nothing could help them, but their reviews were hurting sales, so my sales manager decided on a different approach."

"Let me guess, they were all racist nationalists, so you outed them?"

"Not quite. Actually, we didn't look into their backgrounds too deeply. Instead, I just holocalled them and encouraged them to try it again while I was on the line."

"So, you've been vaping on-line with your customers. Dad, are you a Tuber star now?"

"No, that's the funny thing. I just puff on an empty cartridge that expels visible vapor. I don't need to smoke Enlightenment As you know, it's kind of a one-time deal, then unnecessary and not even interesting."

"So, you fake them out?"

"Not deliberately. I tell them I'm vaping an inactive substitute, but it doesn't make any difference."

"What do you mean?"

"Just my going through the act of smoking it with them, being with them while they try it, is enough to activate Enlightenment for them."

"That's weird, Dad. So, Enlightenment is just a placebo?"

"No, we know it's not, and we have the brain scans to prove that it significantly repairs and augments important cognitive and emotional connections in the brain. Yet, just my energy somehow in the mix activates it for some customers."

"The power of suggestion?"

"Maybe, but the packaging holograph and the testimonials we send with every order pretty much has that covered. No, I think it has something to do specifically with my individual brain and the drug, maybe because I was there when the monks chanted over it at the lab, I don't know. Just something about my bearing witness, I guess, or my *faith* in it, maybe."

"Like a setting thing. You set the mood, the expectation, and the drug has the space to kick in, I get it," I said. I found an empty table in the airport food court and took out the gourmet duck sandwich from my pack. I didn't open it, though, because the wrapper would make too much noise.

"Partly, but mostly what I've been realizing is that it is more than that. This is going to sound conceited, but I really think Enlightenment would never have become a thing, I mean anything nearly as revolutionary as it is, if I hadn't believed in it so much."

"I can see that. It's pretty much been your baby since you left Brecken."

" Yeah, that's true, but this is more than just a sense of ownership. I don't know. The power of passion, maybe? Belief? A tapping into something powerful that you don't even know you are capable of? Anyway, that's what's been on my mind lately. But back to your situation. Lenore coming back to you. Can you be sure it was entirely *her* decision to return?"

"I don't know, can I?"

"It's just something to think about. So often in life we feel like we understand the parameters, and then with no input from us whatsoever things turn out drastically better, or worse, than we ever imagined they would. It happens so often that it is tempting to throw up your hands and say no effort is ever worth it because there are no guarantees of success. I've felt that way about your mother, sometimes, as you know. And yet, on the other side of that argument are all the times when a sincere belief in something and strenuous work make really beautiful things happen."

"You had a lot of great years with Mom, and I know she feels the same way."

"And she's doing so great with her painting now, I know. I am so proud of her."

"And your Enlightenment product, you are changing the world for the better."

"Well, maybe. I hope so."

"So, Dad, I am in Nashville right now... "

"Really? With Brandon? What, did the semester end early or something?"

" Yeah, it kind of did, for me anyway. I'm here alone, with Lenore, taking a little break."

"Oh, I see. Can't say that's too surprising. That Brecken lab has never been good for nurturing relationships. Too intense. I imagine even more so given what they are messing around with. It's good that you are getting away from it for a little while."

"Thanks for saying that. Yeah, it might not be just for a little while. Dad, what do you do when you love someone and your gut tells you the passion of their life is just plain wrong?" I pulled out a red handkerchief from my pack and wiped my eyes.

"And dangerous, in fact, when CRISPRs are involved."

"*Exactly.*"

"What you do is precisely what you're doing right now, giving yourself and him a little break, a little time to get some perspective. Great choice, Nashville!"

" Yeah, maybe they'll even be a band around here who needs a fiddle player."

"Oh, I'm sure there will be, or else you'll form one yourself, if I know you and Lenore. Do you have a place to stay there?"

"Nope, that service wasn't on the Brecken private jet menu."

"Ooo, fancy. You know how to travel in style. That jet, what a waste of educational resources. Let me guess, Vern flew you out there?"

"Kind of. Pendleton."

"Don't know him, but there are a lot of people in BRI one doesn't get to know, people in very high places."

"Not high enough, if you know what I mean."

" Yeah, you got that right, dear! Listen, there are youth hostels downtown. I never stay anywhere else when I'm there. Great place to meet people, cheap, and close to the music. It's late there, but they're always open. Go have some fun, but keep Lenore locked up when you're there. You'll need your own padlock."

"Thanks for the advice, Dad."

"I love you, Ells. Stay safe, keep in touch, make some great music."

I am too choked up to say goodbye, so I send the heart in hand emoji and blink off.

Chapter Thirty-Seven

THE TWANG DOWNTOWN Youth Hostel was indeed open twenty-four hours and was only a block from the music action on Lower Broadway. It was also close to Lawrence Pinchbeck's office. I checked in and found my single bunk bed in a dorm of snoring millennials. The place was clean and had lockers big enough for Lenore's case, but I took her to bed with me because I didn't have a padlock yet. The sheets were crisp and the pillow adequate. I stripped down to my underwear and was asleep in a nanosecond.

Late the next morning my throat was so itchy I woke up scratching it with the back of my tongue like a dog trying to unswallow a bug. I got about a minute to experience this unpleasant surprise when the itching spread like wildfire to my eyes, and my nose started dripping water like a medieval torturing device. *Allergies.* I recognized them right away. I used to get them just like this in Harbor Vista when I was growing up. It's been a while, though. They went away when I started school at Wandering Pines. I was bummed. For me there's no difference between allergies and having a bad cold, only a cold tends to go away in a week or so and allergies don't.

I reached over Lenore's case to fish my handkerchief from my backpack. I sat up and gave my nose a good blow looking around to see who I might be waking up with this necessary procedure. The room had two bunk beds and four regular cots but was deserted. No wonder. My phone glasses said it was early afternoon already.

I momentarily risked leaving Lenore and wrapped myself in a skimpy white industrial towel and headed for the showers. They're only semi-private, but I didn't care. The hot water was soothing to my sinuses, and I emerged hungry as a horse and slightly less allergic. I got dressed, grabbed Lenore, and headed to the lobby.

There was a different person behind the desk than the one who was there when I stumbled in last night but she seemed equally as friendly. She smiled at me and fiddled with the pearl buttons on her cowgirl shirt.

"Hey, honey. What can I do you for?" she said.

"Breakfast! But first I need to buy a lock somewhere."

"Got you covered. The pharmacy across the street has good locks cheap, and right next door's the E-String Diner. Should of called it the G-String Diner it's so basic and mellow, but they didn't want people to get the wrong impression. Order the Music City omelet. The pancakes are a little starchy in my opinion."

"Okay, thanks. What's your name?"

"Candace, darling, but you can call me Candy. I'm here most every day except when Jerry Jeff is in town. Then you can find me in the *front row*. You here for a gig?"

"Oh, not yet. I mean, yes, I hope." I guess that's a fair question for anybody carrying around a fiddle case here. "Thanks, Candy," I said. She smiled at me sympathetically as I headed for the door.

By the time I found a lock at the pharmacy and got in line to pay, my head was exploding again with allergies. I sneezed a dozen times in line and again when I put my purchase on the pharmacist's counter. Before I could blink my payment, the pharmacist spoke to me over the shoulder of the cashier. "New here?" he said.

"Yep," I said.

"Staying at The Twang?"

"Not too hard to figure that out, I guess," I said, holding up the padlock.

"That and the sneezing. We've got a great doctor behind the next block who specializes in allergies. I send all my sneezing hostelers there for treatment. You're not alone by any stretch. I should get a commission for every person I send to her. My manager doesn't like it when I do, though, because we sell less Zyrtec, but, hey, I'm here to help. She cured my allergies years ago, so I owe her. She's amazing."

"I appreciate it. What's her name?"

"Maria Schnazworthy. Look for her in the next block down, second floor."

"You had me going there for a minute. Schnazworthy? That's funny." I laughed.

"Hey, do you know how many dentists are called Dennis? It's crazy. She's real, all right, and that's her real name. Go see her, unless you enjoy dosing yourself with antihistamines." The pharmacist went back to his computer screen.

I returned to Twangs, waved my new lock at Candy with a smile, and locked up Lenore. Then I went and ordered the biggest omelet on the menu at the E-String. It was greasy and delicious. I soaked up the leftover butter with a piece of sourdough bread and by the time I finished my second cup of coffee my jet-lag was almost under control. Too bad my eyes were so red and inflamed I could barely see. No way am I going to visit Pinchbeck feeling like this. I blinked my payment for the server and went in search of Dr. Schnazworthy.

Sure enough, Schnazworthy was a real allergist, and her office was huge. The Schnazworthy Center occupied the entire second floor of a forgotten backstreet that smells vaguely of urine, probably from late night music revelers wandering over from Broadway to relieve themselves. Might be a good place to grow urban lettuce, I thought, remembering my fertilizing project at Wandering Pines. I pressed a button to get in and climbed the dark industrial stairs leading to an ornate oak door not unlike the ones back at the Brecken Administration Building. I put my shoulder to it and entered, then just stared with my swollen eyes at what unfolded before me.

Intense natural light poured into the massive room from snake-like skylights that somehow articulated from the roof several stories above. The air was fecund with the smell of a country garden, and the reason was simple, there were vegetable plants everywhere. To reach the receptionist, a guy my dad's age with an extraordinarily long silver ponytail, I had to walk between rows of tomatoes and lettuce. When I got there, a big black and white pussy cat was curled up next to his computer.

"Um," I managed. "Do I have the right place, or is this a greenhouse?"

"Are you a volunteer or here to see Dr. Schnazworthy?"

"Well, I don't have an appointment, but I'd like to see her if possible. I'm new in town."

"That's okay. Your swollen face is all the appointment you need. She keeps a pretty open schedule for drop-ins. Let me see." He checked his screen. The cat raised its head, gave me the once over, then went back to sleep. "Can you wait twenty minutes? She can fit you in then. There's tissues over there behind the artichokes. We encourage you to take off your shoes and socks and sit on the floor. It's fully grounded, or you can pull out a canvas chair from back there if you don't like the moss and dirt." He flicked his ponytail off his shoulder and smiled at me.

"Oh, the grounded floor's fine. Um, thanks," I said.

"There's kombucha in the cooler if you're thirsty. I'll call you. The cherry tomatoes and snap peas are delicious right now. Help yourself to as many as you'd like."

If my Dad hadn't bragged about the benefits of going around barefoot all the time, I would never have understood the pride in this guy's voice when he pointed out the floor was fully grounded. I might have thought he meant literally grounded because of the foot of topsoil in the waiting room where crops were growing. This place could be relying on the infrastructure of the building to connect the soil to the surface of the earth, or they could be using metal cables. I looked around and saw a big coil of wires disappearing into the floor in the corner by the kombucha cooler. Pretty cool. We did an experiment about this in the garden at Wandering Pines. Lettuce grown in raised beds where the soil was still connected to the earth always grew better than lettuce in a true raised bed, even if all other factors were the same. New Age organic gardeners say it has to do with magnetic variances, but no one really knows for sure.

I found a sunny spot in the dirt by the peas and marveled at the amount of light coming in through the ceiling tubes. I looked at a green hose. How do they keep the water from leaking into the office space below, I wondered? I picked some sugar peas and popped them whole into my mouth. They were crisp, juicy, and delicious. I saw a few more well-fed black and white cats prowling around. Strange pets to have in an allergist's office! I felt better already just being here, and I couldn't help but laugh to myself what my mother would think of this place. Brandon, I thought, would love it.

A few minutes later a woman my age in overalls and a red flannel shirt appeared in the row next to me. I didn't notice what door she came out of and assumed she was one of the volunteers the receptionist referred to, but then she pushed her way between the peas and tomatoes into my row and offered me her hand.

"Are you Ella?" I nod. "Cool," she says, "Dr. Schnazworthy. You can call me Maria." I shook her hand as I stood up. "Hi," I said.

"Don't bother brushing off the dirt from your pants. It's better if it stays on you. Come into my office, won't you, please? Let's chat."

I followed her back toward the receptionist. "Oh, look at how the carrots are already sprouting!" she said, with open arms not specifically referring to anything that I could see. I believed her, though, and followed her into her office which was filled with one of those multi-leveled indoor cat gymnasiums except this one was for humans and was covered with growing grass and mint plants of every variety. I climbed after her like a school kid onto the main level and we sat under another skylight tube.

"Wow, this place is a trip!" I said.

" Yeah, isn't it something!" said Schnazworthy. "I just love it here. My favorite place to work. Of course, why wouldn't it be? I created it!" She laughed and fell back highly amused with herself, or maybe she was just trying to catch some direct rays from the skylight, I couldn't tell. A moment later she sat up and smiled at me warmly. The top buttons of her flannel shirt had come undone. She adjusted and rebuttoned.

"So, allergies, eh? New or lifelong?"

"New," I said, smiling back at her and sneezing once briefly.

"Live in a sterile environment, by any chance? Urban? Fluorescent lights? Maybe a little too much alcohol and fast food?"

"Brecken University, and yes to all of the above," I said, "But not really the alcohol."

"Ah, California. Let me guess, you vaped some Enlightenment and lost interest in getting drunk? Right? Come on! Did I guess? I guessed, didn't I?" I didn't even have to say anything and she knew the answer. She laughed herself back onto her back again.

"I also try to eat healthy, but it's not easy," I said. "If your place was located in Brecken Vista, I would probably raid your waiting room once a week. Not too many gardens in my life these days."

"And you'd be welcomed. That's why I have it. I like my patients to eat my produce and get down and dirty!"

"But you're an allergist. I don't get it. Don't your patients react to all the compost and plants in here?"

"Oh yes, at first they do, but that's just a phase. It doesn't take long for them to grow up."

"Grow up? You mean to realize that home grown vegetables are what they should be eating?"

"Well, that, but no, their *immune systems* need to grow up. Most people these days are stuck in infancy, disconnected, reactive. Allergies go away when your immune system matures and learns to face the world head on."

"Okay. Still don't get it," I said.

"Come with me. I want to show you something," said Schnazworthy. She crawled across the platform and opened a closet door in the corner. It led to a wrought iron spiral staircase heading downward. The space was illuminated by a small stained glass window. I followed her. Her checkered Vans hardly made a sound on the steps.

At the bottom, the stairs opened up into a large damp room dimly lit with lab lights and red window curtains pulled tight. A young man in a knit Peruvian hat and a white lab coat was emptying a huge bottle of milky liquid into a pan on a stainless steel table right in front of us, and behind him were row upon row of similar bottles stacked on shelves from the floor to the ceiling. The place was warm like the tropics and smells vaguely of spilled milk and mushrooms.

Schnazworthy greeted the young man briefly and disappeared down one of the rows of bottles. I smiled at him and followed her. "Henry there is decanting a new batch of superbugs. He'll encapsulate them once they dehydrate." She stopped and looked back at me. "Not the bad kind of superbugs. I call these superbugs because of their special powers, the power to mature your immune system."

The row opened up into a space with a fancy machine that had generic-looking bottles of pills emerging from its mouth and falling into a catchment bin. "These are all ready." She grabbed a couple of the fist-sized bottles from the bin and handed them to me. "Here you go. Say goodbye to your allergies! Five in the morning and five at night with meals. Takes between one and three days to work, never more than three. While we are waiting for these to kick in, here is a sample of a corticosteroid to sniff to suppress your symptoms in the meantime. One dose a day is all you'll need for that."

"What's in them?" I said juggling the bottles.

"Dirt, germs, probiotics, all the things you needed to be exposed to as a child and probably weren't, or maybe in your case not exposed enough to recently."

"Probiotics? But I eat yogurt."

"Yogurt? You like yogurt! Me too! Yogurt is great, but it's not enough on its own. Here we concoct everything that is in dirt, on fruit, on vegetables, all kinds of things. The superbugs from super planet earth!"

"You are feeding me *germs*?"

"Oh my, yes! Germs are just what you need! And when you say *me*, of course you know you are actually saying *us*. Us because our bodies contain way more genetic material from germs than from our own human cells. We all are a veritable *universe* of diverse germs. I prescribe germs to get your body back into the proportions of interconnected life that your body evolved to thrive in. Don't be afraid of germs, my dear, the bad ones only get you when you don't have enough good ones in your system to be healthy."

"So I take these and my allergies will go away?"

"That's the spirit!" she said. "Your immune system will very soon start to feel at home in your body again with all the education it's going to get from our special probiotics formula. Well, not really *special* unless you happen to think the entire microbial world of our planet is special. Well, I guess it *is* special, and ordinary at the same time! Modern humans have just scrubbed themselves too far away from ordinary, that's all." She beamed at me.

"When I was at boarding school, I did an experiment using urine to fertilize lettuce plants. They were delicious. I can buy into the interconnectedness of life idea," I said.

"Great! Well, there you go, and I hope you'll come back often to visit our little urban garden here whenever you'd like, Enlightenment Girl!"

Chapter Thirty-Eight

BACK IN THE WAITING room/farm I poured myself a mug of kombucha, opened my first bottle of "Schnazworthy's Formula," and swallowed two pills. Already I felt better, if only because of the dose of positive energy from the good doctor who was now courting her next patient in the corn row. The brew fizzed in my nose a little bit and expanded in my tummy on top of my breakfast.

The receptionist flicked his ponytail and waved goodbye to me, and I pushed through the huge door and descended the dark steps back to the dingy street. I walked to Broadway again and checked my phone glasses for directions to the agent's office. I had no idea if he was even in town. I was still a little sneezy, but I was charged up and optimistic now. If I was going to make this adventure work, I needed to take the first steps. I remembered how I felt when Pendelton gave me the assignment to play in public at Comey's. This feels the same, only ten times more scary. A real Nashville agent? Who am I kidding? Even with Lenore on my side, I am at best a mediocre fiddle player.

Undeterred, I followed the blue arrow on my holoscreen and walked the three blocks past bars and music venues to Pinchbeck's office. This time there was no dingy staircase or foul-smelling sidewalks. The Lawrence Pinchbeck Agency was on the top floor of a pristine steel and glass office building. I rode the crisp elevator and tried not to think too much about my jeans and sneakers besmirched with a little souvenir dirt from my doctor's visit.

The elevator doors opened silently onto a white-carpeted waiting area with a huge painting of Dolly Parton looming behind a contrastingly slender but tastefully dressed female receptionist speaking into her Gucci phoneglasses. She pulled them aside and said, "Hi there, welcome. Just a moment please, I'll be right with you."

I smiled at her and looked around for a bathroom. Those probiotics seemed to be riling things up in my lower quarters. I raised my finger and pointed at the restroom. She nodded and I disappeared inside the unisex restroom door that opened automatically. In fact, everything in that shiny and beeping place was ridiculously automatic from the paper seat protector sliding into place to the warm blast of bidet water I wasn't expecting. I'm surprised a mechanical arm didn't emerge from the toilet paper holder to pat me dry. At the sink I used the fingernail buffer twice just because I couldn't believe it actually existed in reality. Country music has come a long way from cowboys cleaning their fingernails with Barlow Knives and brewing coffee in a pot over an open fire, I guess. I enjoyed the painting of that very scene hanging on the wall, though.

She's off the phone when I reemerge from the bathroom buffed and blow-dried. "Hi, how can I help you today?" she said.

"I don't have an appointment, but I'm hoping I can make one to see Mr. Pinchbeck. My name is Ella Bradley, and he saw me play in California at Comey's Coffee Shop a while back and told me to contact him."

"Just a minute, please," she said. "Emma Bradley?"

"No, Ella," I said.

"Okay, please take a seat and I will check with him. There's coffee and tea, so please help yourself."

"Is it cowboy coffee?" I asked, but she pretended she didn't hear me, smiled like she was very busy, and disappeared inside the office door behind her.

I could tell that my visit to the bathroom might not be the only one I'll need before leaving this place, so I skipped the coffee. I willed my bowels to behave and sat in a weird leather chair shaped like a bass fiddle. I noticed all the furniture here had a musical theme. The chair next to me was made out of old welded drums, and the magazine table was an extra large dobro with musical notes for legs. Weirdly, the kitsch doesn't come off as tacky for some reason, just playful and comfortable.

"Ella Bradley!"

I had forgotten what Lawrence Pinchbeck looked like, and seeing him walking from his office caused the whole feeling of Comey's to wash over me again like a wave. By that I mean the good parts of playing there, not the last time when I got shot and lost Lenore. That was a tsunami I would rather forget. This feeling was different. It was right, somehow, a lovely feeling and surprising, kind of like the feeling of coming home a little bit. It took me a moment to find my voice.

"Mr. Pinchbeck. Yeah, I'm here," I said. He smiled and shook my hand firmly.

"Yes, you are. Welcome. I was wondering whether you'd take me up on my invitation. California can be a hard place to leave, especially a nice cool town by the ocean. Come on, let's go sit down."

I followed his gesture and walked with him past the receptionist who was back on her phoneglasses. She smiled at me and sprayed something minty and potent-looking into her mouth.

The corner office was all glass looking out on Broadway. There was a vibro-standing desk with two huge holo-screens, but that's about the only thing normal about this office. It was like a Bluegrass player's dream store. The walls were all filled with musical instruments hanging from a plethora of racks and pegs. Banjos, fiddles, guitars, mandolins, drums, keyboards, vibes, vintage microphones, amplifiers, even washboards and Jews harps. I looked above me and there were a hundred more instruments hanging from the high ceilings with ladders to reach them. All high quality stuff, mostly vintage.

"Wow," I said. "This is quite a collection."

"Yes. My father collected Martin guitars, and when I inherited them and his love for music but not his talent for playing, I settled for adding to his collection."

"As well as collecting musicians, I surmise," I said.

"Yes, you could say that. That's actually quite accurate, in fact. I enjoy supporting great musicians as much as I enjoy taking care of this great collection of magical beauties."

"Do you ever sell them?"

"In a way. I look for love at first sight. If a client falls in love with an instrument in my collection I am happy to make a match. I have a feeling, though, that's not likely to happen in your case."

"It's hard for me to see myself as one of your clients, but you're right, my fiddle and I are pretty close, although I lost her since you saw me last at Comey's."

"I read about that incident. The feed said you were injured but not badly."

"I was, but the worst part was losing Lenore afterward. No one knew what happened to her in the chaos, least of all passed-out me." I flexed my hand and glanced at the scar where the bullet exited near my thumb.

"That sounds horrifying, Ella, and I could tell how much you were in sync with that fiddle of yours. It sucks that it was stolen." He paused and looked at his fiddle collection closest to the door. "Hey, it won't be the same as getting Lenore back, but you're welcome to any fiddle you want in my collection. You've got something special going with your playing. I don't know what it is exactly, but I know it when I hear it."

"That's very nice of you to say. I'm flattered, but Lenore is back with me now, thankfully, although these fiddles all look pretty great."

"Oh, did they catch the person who swiped it?"

"I'm not sure it was stolen. Just kind of mysteriously missing. Let's just say she came back to me undamaged."

"Well, that's nice. That's great! Can you still play her with your injury?"

"Sure, well, I think so. Haven't had much of a chance. This all happened recently."

"And maybe being on stage is a little scary for you right now?"

"Maybe. I don't know."

"Well, look. I wouldn't have asked you out here if I didn't think you had it in you to be something fantastic, and as far as I'm concerned, you are indeed my client, that is if you'll have me as your agent. Your playing at Comey's really affected my heart. We can take it nice and slow. If you're half as good as you were in California when I heard you, I *know* you'll find a very appreciative audience out here. What do you say? Want to stick around Nashville for a while, try playing some gigs?"

"Hey, sure. Why not?"

"Why not, indeed! Okay, then. Great!" He was genuinely beaming. How could I say no? This is what I came out here for, after all. *Then why is my belly in knots?* Oh, right. The probiotics.

"I always start my clients off with a little in-house jam session to celebrate the paperwork we've got to sign. How about you come back here tomorrow night around seven? We'll finalize the agreement and have some fun. Maybe polish up four or five easy tunes, okay? I'll round up some friends who like to jam and some others to listen and share the food. No pressure. Really. I mean that. Think of it as a warm-up, a little party fun, a practice session for what's to come. What do you say? Up for it? Or are you too jet-lagged for tomorrow night?"

"Not jet-lagged at all. I guess I better get used to this, if I'm going to play on stage again."

"That's right, but, hey, listen to me. Seriously, my clients mean everything to me. I'm here to help *you*. The minute it feels like anything other than that, you let me know, because that's how I see my job. Pushed musicians fall off cliffs. I don't push my clients. I give them the opportunity to push themselves to fly, maybe, but it's always up to them. There is no other way to make good music."

"Thanks, Mr. Pinchbeck," I said.

"Call me Lawrence, please, Ella. So, see you and Lenore tomorrow right here at seven. It's going to be great! Can I show you to the elevator?"

"Thanks," I said, "Restroom first, okay?" I shook his outstretched hand.

Chapter Thirty-Nine

THAT WENT WELL, BUT no doubt about it, I needed to do some serious practicing. But where? I headed back to the hostel, waved again at Candy, and removed Lenore from the locker. Most of my dorm companions were up and milling about, but there were still enough sacked out in bed to make playing there problematic. I wasn't too worried about people hearing me. Well, I *was* a little bit, but I know that's what I have to get over, and better now than tomorrow night at Pinchbeck's in front of who knows how many people.

I went back to the front desk. "Candy, I have a gig tomorrow I didn't expect. Got any idea where I could go to practice?"

"Oh, sure, Honey. People bus around here all the time. Just choose any street corner in town. It's early enough for a prime spot on Broadway even, if you're brave enough. Need to borrow a hat?"

"I was thinking about someplace private, but are you sure bussing is allowed?"

"Honey, music is the currency of this town. Ain't nobody going to care, unless, of course, you're playing country-disco tunes, and even those are coming back these days. Not my cup of tea, but who am I to judge? What kind of music do you play, sweetie?"

"Old time and bluegrass mostly. Whatever my fiddle decides it's in the mood for," I said.

"Look, just go for it right outside the hostel. Bussers do great there. Tourists love a free show. I'll keep an eye on you and bring you coffee on my breaks. My squeeze patrols downtown on horseback, and he's never more than a few blocks away if I blink him, so don't you fret about a thing."

"That's really nice of you, Candy. You're giving me courage."

"Life's a river, dearie, and we're all floating in the same direction."

"I'll take you up on that lucky hat of yours, and maybe a stool if you have one?"

"Sure thing, hun. How do you like your coffee?"

"Strong and black, please."

Nervous as I am, it wasn't too hard to match Candy's big smile with one of my own. She brought me a wooden stool and a vaudeville top hat from her luggage room behind the counter. I took a few deep breaths. Something was different in my head, all of a sudden. I could breathe now without sneezing, and my eyes didn't itch anymore. I thought about that saying that nothing feels better than when you stop bashing your head into a wall. Allergies teach you to appreciate your body when you're not allergic, that's for sure. Kind of like how the world appreciates regular old boring weather now after all the extreme events we have to live through all the time, or finally being out of a fluorescent-lit lab where nothing you do ever feels natural or right.

I thought about how at least it wasn't a hundred and ten degrees outside like it had been recently around here according to my weather feed. No tornadoes nearby this week either. My fingers combed through my blond hair, and I took one more hit of energy from Candy's encouraging smile. Then I went outside and set the stool down against the brick wall of the hostel. I'll play for the weather, and for being here I told myself. If people want to listen, I won't let them bother me.

The wound on my hand panged a bit all of a sudden, but there were enough cars and people going by that I could push the pain into the background. People suffer far worse things just to get something to eat than the memory of being shot, I reminded myself. I'm lucky. I still get to make music.

I removed Lenore and her bow from her beautifully beat-up case. I tightened the bow and drew the deeply-grooved resin block across the horse hair a few times. I thought about how my grandfather lovingly did this to Lenore so many times in the past, and how he entrusted her to me. I thought about his beautiful white hair, and then about my ambitious and caring father with hair not yet as white as his dad's trying his best to better people in the world, and finally I thought about Brandon who was trying hard to help too, in his own dark and worried way. I imagined each of them in front of me, asking me with their eyes what *I* was going to do to help the world. I raised Lenore to my chin and started to play.

It was children who first paused in front of me on the dirty sidewalk to listen. "Arkansas Traveler," the classic old-time tune, was the one Lenore decided to start off with. I know this seems strange, but I never know what tune will happen until we start playing. That's always the way it is with Lenore, and I have learned not to fight her. She seems to know which ones I have in mind to play and usually gets around to them, but only after she has taken charge and played *what's right* first.

I looked at a girl dressed like her mom in jeans and cute little touristy cowboy boots and wondered how it would go with Lenore if I formed a band and others wanted input into the playlist. They'd just have to learn who the master is, I guess. Or maybe master is the wrong term to use with her. Lenore's definitely in charge, but in a way that you always wanted to go along with her somehow, like her rewards outweighed the release of control that she gently demanded. Kind of like the slightly annoyed pleasure the mom is getting right now "allowing" her daughter to pause and stomp her boots on the Nashville sidewalk for a few minutes. Like the mom had any choice! She didn't. Other children stopped their parents to listen too, and soon there was a crowd of them clapping and stomping.

Lenore moved on to "Bill Cheatum," another old-time classic that's relatively easy to play. I'm relieved that I could still follow tunes to the end without making too many mistakes. I cringed at every slip up, of course, but the kids didn't care if I flubbed a note every once in a while and neither did their parents. That relaxed me. Candy was right. Playing out here in the open air was perfect for my self-confidence. When "Bill Cheatum" ended I expected the parents to grab children's hands and move along, and so did the kids. They looked ready to resist, but it was actually the adults who decided to stick around. A few coins clinked into the hat. I saw a dollar bill parachute in there too. The gathering grew. It was getting hard to get by on the sidewalk.

By the time Lenore and I ran through several versions of "Liberty," "Cherokee Shuffle," "Sally Ann," and "Whiskey Before Breakfast," Candy had brought me two cups of coffee that I barely had time to chug down, and people were buying lawn chairs from the pharmacy to sit along the sidewalk like it was a parade or something. I couldn't have asked for this to go any better, as long as I didn't get arrested for blocking the sidewalk. People were dropping business cards into the hat, asking me to put them on my email list (like I even had one), and inquired about CD's for sale. I decided to play until my arms got tired.

That happened sooner than I wanted it to, but perhaps not soon enough for the traffic on Broadway that was naturally stopping to see what the fuss was all about. This may be perfectly legal, but the last time at Comey's when I attracted a big crowd things didn't end well, so I finally decided to quit. When I stood up to put Lenore back into her case, however, the happy crowd chanted, "Encore! Encore!" so I demurred. Lenore chose "Jerusalem's Ridge," a Bill Monroe tune in three rocking parts. Now everyone, even the peace officers who arrived frowning were smiling and stomping their feet.

I was fully present through the first two parts of the tune. Then, right at the end, a film formed over my eyes and the familiar smell of lion dung hit my nostrils. The sight of the crowd and the fumes of idling cars disappeared. *Jenny?* That smell! I barely had time to remember Lyca and Siam's cage at Renegade's vanity zoo when this image appeared on my eyeballs:

LENORE AND I PLAYED on, and the image cleared at the end of the song replaced by the sounds of more clapping. Tears sprung into my eyes. The audience probably thought I was crying because of gratitude for their applause, but wasn't that. *Jenny was communicating with me again!* Did Lenore's music reach her somehow back in California? I sat very still savoring what just happened despite the raucous cheers and whistles that also made me smile. My whole body shivered with the same feeling that enveloped me when Lenore came back to me in the cave. Somehow, more than the applause, more than the cash overflowing the hat that Candy let me borrow, this sensation convinced me that for the first time in the last year and a half I was truly on the right track, that miles from anywhere I had ever lived before, away from everyone I had ever loved, I had discovered something to do that was worth all the sacrifices, something that was powerful enough that it just might be the genuine purpose of my life.

Chapter Forty

THE E-STRING DINER seemed to be as popular for dinner as it was for breakfast. There was a huge line of couples and families waiting for tables, but the hostess seated me at the counter right away. Another advantage of flying solo, I guess. The counter hostess, who looked like she might be Candy's younger sister, suggested a Yazoo beer on tap, so I didn't argue with her, although I chuckled at where it might be brewed. She slapped it down, spilling some foam and then told me in no uncertain terms to order the pulled pork sandwich, a house specialty. Again, what's the point in arguing? But I added a fresh garden salad in honor of Schnazworthy and the happily fading memory of my allergies.

"You know I had tickets for a matinee at the Grand Ole Opry and we never made it this afternoon because of you," a male voice behind me said. I turned in my seat to look at him. He seemed friendly enough with striking red hair, and I saw a middle aged woman smiling behind him with a couple of red-headed offspring in tow.

"Oh, I'm sorry," I said.

"Hey, don't apologize. We loved it. Reminded me of the time we were going to the New York Metropolitan Museum of Art and ended up instead sitting on the steps all afternoon watching an actor mimic people walking by. So funny! He was worth that whole trip to the Big Apple as far as I am concerned. The hell with the Mona Lisa."

"I think the Mona Lisa is actually in the Louvre, isn't it?" I said.

"Whatever," he said. "The point is your playing was captivating." Then he lowered his voice and whispered, "You saved my marriage. I don't know how, but you did. That's what I really want to thank you for."

"Wow. Really? Uhm...why?"

"Well, I can't go into that because it's personal. Let's just say Sally there and I listened to your fiddling and came to an understanding about our lives with the kids that we've been working up to for a long time. I'll let you get back to your dinner, but I'm glad I saw you here to say thanks. I'll never forget you." He smiled and walked back to join his family. Sally and the kids waved at me. They left the restaurant with their arms around each other.

I chewed through my sandwich and salad and Candy Two asked me if I wanted another beer. I declined politely, thinking I needed to get a good night's sleep tonight before tomorrow's gig at Pinchbeck's. She brought me a piece of chocolate cake instead because I guess no one ever refused dessert at the E-String.

My phoneglasses rang. It was Brandon. Right away my glow of new-found independence and success dimmed a little bit, but I blinked him on anyway. "Hey," I said.

"Hey, Ella. Good time to talk?"

" Yeah, sure. Just grabbing a bite before turning in. How are my babies?"

"Oh, they're fine. A little bored. Bryson didn't do much with them while we were gone. No sessions. I took them for a long walk around campus and beyond today."

"Did you tell them if they behave themselves they can get a gig like Maven's in Hawaii?"

" Yeah, something like that. I think you might have to get back here before Bryson does anything more with them."

"Oh, really. Why? Not convinced of the success of the release?"

"Well, he said all the right things when Pendleton and Olaf filled him and Vern in on it. Then he took them all into his office lab."

"So the secret lab is out of the bag, eh?"

"I'm not sure what they talked about. They didn't invite me, but I am sure Bryson will let me in on it on an as-needed basis."

"That's what bosses do."

" Yeah. I'm not the boss, so I do what I can to help. This is big, Ella. Bryson's research is important. I want to make you proud of me."

"You're doing this for *me*?"

"What do you want me to do? Both of us can't go running off."

"Look, Brandon. I'm not *running off*. Some important things are happening here for me, for my independence, for who I *am* in the world, or at least who I will be."

"So what is happening?"

"I don't know. Important things. I can feel it."

"Important things you can't put your finger on... "

"Why do I have to?"

"You don't, I guess, for a while. Just can you respect that *I* can put my finger on important things we're doing here together right now. Things that can change the world. Things that feel like destiny, a hero's destiny."

"Oh, you're a hero now?"

"It's not the right word, but, yes, I am doing something important that I want you to be proud of. I'm not proud of it yet, because it's not finished, but I can tell it's going to be big. Bryson can tell it's going to be big, and the same with Pendleton. We're *all* part of this big thing, whether we want to be or not."

I stuffed a big forkful of cake into my mouth just to stop me from saying what I was thinking next. I let the pause linger, then decided to say it anyway. "What we're all part of, Brandon, the big thing that we're all part of, is the *world*, and the world is falling apart primarily because of science and technological "advancements" and people thinking they are heroes when they are really just greedy and egotistical and short-sighted."

"You're still worried that we did the wrong thing with Sybil and Hawaii? Is that where this is coming from? It's too early to tell, you know."

"That's part of it. What *you* did, primarily, by the way. I don't know, Brandon. My gut's been in knots about this whole Brecken thing ever since we showed up there, and not just the Hawaii release. All I know is that the knots are loosening since I flew away from California."

"Well, that's good, I guess. As long as you come back. I need you, you know."

"You like to think that, but I'm not so sure. Who needs someone around who doubts you all the time. Just go for it, Brandon. Change the world with Bryson. Lenore and I need a little more time to figure out if that's my thing or not."

"Lenore?" Immediately I regretted letting the cat out of the bag. Alcohol does that to my judgment sometimes. I took another bite of cake to give me time to think.

" Yeah, Lenore. Long story. I'll tell you about it next time. I have to go."

"Wow, Lenore. Okay. I'll be interested in *that* one."

"Me too. Let's just say she has to do with the important things I can't put my finger on."

"I understand, I guess. Well, Lenore's a master. What choice do you have?"

"Right. What choice do I have? She's the *master.* You got it."

"Um, Ella. Are you mad at me?"

"No, Brandon. Just tired. I need to go. Keep walking those babies of mine, okay?"

"I love you, Ella."

"I know that, Brandon. Thanks." I blinked off. I know I should have said I love you back, but doppleganger Candy brought the bill, and I wanted to finish the cake and get back to the excitement of my single cot in the real Candy's commune of adventuring transients.

Chapter Forty-One

AFTER A WEIRD NIGHT of dreaming in which I was desperately pacing up and down the rows of Schnazworthy's waiting room searching for severed hog's noses to pick from the twisty green vines to feed to a snake in my backpack, and a contrastingly normal day of walking up and down Broadway taking in the Nashville sights like any other tourist, I put on clean bluejeans and a flannel shirt, grabbed Lenore from her locker in the common area, waved to the real Candy, and headed to Pinchbeck's.

When I walked in, there were about a dozen older people and a scattering of musician types my age milling around the instrument chairs. Someone had transformed the receptionist's desk into a bar, and a sharp-looking fellow, the only one in the room with a manbun and no receding hairline, was back there mixing potent-looking drinks. Pinchbeck saw me as soon as I stepped out of the elevator. "Ella, welcome!" he said. I shook his hand, not quite ready to give him a hug yet, although I could tell he wanted to give me one. Later, maybe, I thought, when I knew I could trust him. *Oh, what the hell.* I went ahead and gave him the hug, bumping his knees with Lenore's case. It was a short hug and not uncomfortable at all. He was excited to see me, and after my little concert on the sidewalk, I was ready to play for anybody.

"You can put your stuff over here next to the bar. When you're ready, you can play wherever you feel like. In the meantime, want something to drink?"

"Oh, just water, maybe a little lemon in it?"

"Timothy, set our honored guest up with agua con limon, por favor."

"Coming right up, Ms. Bradley," said the barkeep. He looked to me like he had stepped right out of an Armani hola-ad.

"Thank you, Timothy," I said. He flashed a row of straight white teeth at me. "De nada."

I put Lenore and my backpack down on the far end of the bar and Pinchbeck politely steered me among the guests introducing me to names I promptly forgot. They all had the same polite questions for me, though. Who have I played with in the past? Who are my favorite musicians? Where am I from? Pinchbeck let each one ask me one or two questions and then told me a little bit about them so that they started talking about themselves instead of me. I could tell he did this on purpose after sensing that questions made me nervous. I was grateful to him for this.

How weird it was that when people first meet you and talk mostly about themselves they tend to really like you, whereas the people who want to hear you talk instead are less easy to impress. That's the way it was with me, anyway. Maybe because I sucked at chit-chat. In any case, with Pinchbeck at my side I managed to not make a fool of myself with anybody. I admit it's tempting to exaggerate my musical capabilities with these people, seeing as how I am now a "signed" musician, but I sucked at that game too. I can lie to my mom sometimes, but these guys remind me of my father too much, and I have always been honest with him. The few women there who are there in a professional capacity–and why weren't there more of them, I wondered?–I wanted to like immediately, but I felt a distance with them that was more than just initial get-to-know-you social awkwardness. That was a familiar pattern for me. The only woman I have ever really gotten along with in my life so far has been Lenore, and that's probably because she's really my grandfather, I think.

Pinchbeck kept me moving until I needed a refill on my lemon water. My initial impression of the gathering was correct. The older members of the gathering were music producers, owners of theaters, recording studio executives. The younger folks were mostly musicians and their partners. I noticed that many of them had their banjos, mandolins, and guitars with them, although I didn't know why they bothered with so many available instruments hanging in Pinchbeck's office. Maybe Pinchbeck was just really picky about who he allowed to touch his collection. I couldn't blame him if he was. I know I would never let just anyone play Lenore.

"Hey everyone," Pinchbeck announced. "Can we get a few of you to jam a little bit now? Give Ella a taste of our musical inclusivity so she can feel comfortable joining in when she feels like it? I think you're really going to like her fiddle playing."

"Sure thing, Lawrence," said a woman with blue hair. She unpacked a mandolin and started tuning it. That immediately relaxed me. Mandolin players are always tuning their instruments. It's the bane of their musical existence. Tuning a

mandolin was like trying to get the two presidents and con-
gress to agree on anything, an endless process.

A young guy with cowboy boots picked up his guitar,
and another guy about as skinny as I have ever seen unpacked
a banjo. They gathered in front of the bar where Timothy
handed me another drink. I stood to the side next to
Lenore's case and marveled at the unself-conscious way these
guys navigated the creative dance of playing with each other
on demand. It didn't seem like they were a group, but they
probably grew up jamming with other musicians. It was like
breathing to them. They were relaxed and laughing, while I
was taking huge deep breaths and trying to merge with their
mood. Remembering the applause yesterday on the street
helped a lot to quell my nervousness.

"So, what are you guys in the mood for?" said the guitar
player.

"Let's do something really easy to warm up," said the
mandolin woman, still adjusting her strings and looking at a
tuner app on her phoneglasses.

"You mean really easy like "Angeline the Baker"?

"Ha, Yeah, that sounds easy enough to me!" said the
skinny banjo dude, and he immediately started picking the
melody at a rapid pace. He didn't play it simple, though.
The embellishments were phenomenal, and he wasn't even
warmed up!

They all joined in with equal skill and enthusiasm, and to
be present for such skill and mastery was humbling. "Angeline the Baker" was such a simple little tune, but in the hands
of these pros, it became so much more. My ears loved the
rightness of the sounds reaching them, like they had been in

a desert and finally here was an oasis of pure succulent music. I forgot where I was and their music flowed over me like honey causing the same overload of sensation in the back of my throat that amazing honey's sweetness sometimes caused. It was a comfortable feeling, but also one of urgency. I heard Lenore calling me from her case under my tapping hand.

The mandolin woman bobbed her head to the music and smiled at me when I pulled out Lenore. She's probably jealously thought it was normal that I didn't have to tune her up. Violins stay in tune pretty easily when the strings are broken in, but truth be told Lenore has never needed any tuning, or any maintenance whatsoever, in fact. She could even return to me when she gets stolen! If she had that much faith in me, I said to myself, the least I could do was play her when she was in the mood. Besides, that was what this whole gathering was about, to hear us play.

I joined in just as the song was winding down, which gave everyone a little boost to keep it going. I couldn't say Lenore and I were as good at embellishing as the other musicians, but we held our own surprisingly well, and everyone was smiling when the tune finally wound down.

"What do you want to play next, Ella?" asked the guitar player.

"I don't know. Let me see... " I put my bow back onto Lenore's strings, and she launched into "Salt Creek," a slightly more complicated tune with plenty of opportunities for everyone to riff off it. I could tell Lenore was really going for it, and I doubt whether she was responding only to the pressure of the situation. Probably, like me, she was beyond that now and was playing for her own mysterious purposes.

"Salt Creek" went great, and so did "Back Step," "Big Sciota," and "Sally Ann," some of my personal favorites. Lenore kept me rooted where I was near the desk, but I could feel her spirit reaching out to the room and drawing the audience toward her, like a vortex of love. It was pure fun, and more than just fun at the same time. Again, the feeling that I had found my calling washed over me like a universal sweetness again. The musicians were cool as they took a break, but I could tell from their eyes that they were feeling some of the same sensations, especially the guitar player. The small audience didn't want us to stop, but Pinchbeck says, "I know, aren't they great? But you know how these office welcome concerts go, we don't want to wear out our new client. We'll let you know what gigs Ella gets going forward, and you can say you heard her here first!"

"Thanks for coming to Nashville, Ella," said one of the recording studio guys from the back. " Yeah, thanks to all of you for playing tonight. It was great," said another person. People smiled at Lenore and me and gradually drifted back into their party conversations.

"That's some powerful playing," said the mandolin woman approaching me. Up close her blue hair seemed to glow like it was radioactive.

"Oh, thanks," I said. "It's mostly coming from the fiddle itself. She has an interesting personality."

"Yeah, she sounds great. Nice bluegrass tone to her, not too chamber orchestra-y."

"You sound pretty great yourself. What's your name?"

"I'm Mae."

"Nice to meet you, Mae."

"But, you know, it's more than just the tone of your instrument. I found it hard to play tonight because I got sucked in so deeply by your playing."

"Oh, well is that a good thing? Sorry!"

"No, it's a good thing. Like I said, powerful. It took me back."

"You were alive in the eighteen hundreds?"

"Funny. No, I mean back home. It took me back home."

"Oh, where's that?"

"I grew up in Kentucky. A farm outside of Bowling Green. It's beautiful, peaceful and quiet."

"Sounds nice."

"It is. You can hear the music of the butterflies there, if you know what I mean."

"I'm not sure I do, but that sounds pretty great."

"I didn't think so when I was growing up, but tonight for some reason I feel different about it, like I miss it. Deeply, I think."

"Oh, well. Maybe it's time for a visit!"

" Yeah, I think you're right. Maybe even more than a visit. I can't make nearly as much money as I can here, but I'm not sure that's really so important anymore, if you know what I mean. My parents are getting older. They would never ask me to come home, but I know they could use some fresh hands to dig in the soil."

"You're lucky."

"Yeah, I really am. I actually really am! Thank you!" She wiped her watery eyes with her sleeve, and I looked behind her and saw a few other people waiting to speak to me with similar expressions.

"Well, Mae. Let me know how it goes. I loved playing with you. Maybe we can play again sometime, okay?" She nodded silently and walked away to put her instrument back into its case.

"You were great, Ella." It's the skinny banjo player.

"Well, thanks. I just met Mae. What's your name?"

"I'm Danny. I've got anorexia."

"I wouldn't have noticed," I said.

"Well, I've been in denial. Anorexia is mostly a girls' problem, or so I have been saying to myself. How could I have anorexia? I'm a guy. What a lot of horseshit, huh?"

"I guess."

"Well, I want to thank you for coming tonight. Somewhere in the middle of Sally Anne it hit me. I needed to get some help. Get my act together, you know? I've thought about it before, but something about tonight made it all come home to me, you know? Well, I don't expect you to know because you're not me, but I'm telling you my resolve was different tonight. More real. Like I could really see myself clearly for once and what I needed to do. I love music, but I love writing more. I'm going to get myself cured and write about it, you know, to help other people with what I've got, like you helped me."

"I didn't realize I helped you, but I'm glad I did, if you think I did. That makes me feel good, Danny."

"Sorry to lay this on you, but I thought you'd want to know. Now I'm going to go get me a grass-fed cheeseburger!"

"You go, Dude!" I said. "And good luck with your writing!" I wanted to give him a hug except I was afraid I might break him. It was weird that he shared this extremely personal thing with me, but I was glad he felt I helped somehow. It's part of being a musician to be open to people's weird confessions like that sometimes, I guess. That's probably why we are musicians and not stock brokers.

"I couldn't help overhearing your last two conversations." It's the guitar player wearing shit-kickers standing behind me. I turned to face him, still holding onto Lenore. "Do you always have this effect on people?" he asked.

"I don't know. It seems to be happening more and more lately, but what do you mean, effect?" I said.

"Like a drug trip. Psychedelic. Like people hear your music and trip out and have big life revelations."

"Did that happen to you?"

"That happened to me a long time ago, but I will say tonight felt a lot like the first time I vaped Enlightenment."

"Funny. Enlightenment is my dad's company. He discovered it."

"Well now, ain't that interesting? I'm going to have to ponder that, after I come down from tonight's concert, that is." His smile reminded me of Brandon's. They shared a similar physique, powerful, well-proportioned. Brandon plays the banjo, though, not the guitar.

"You got high tonight, huh?"

"Yep."

"I found after I did Enlightenment, without my dad's permission, by the way, that I didn't need to do drugs any more."

"Oh, I'm the same way. I got high tonight on your *music*, Ella." He let that sink in for a moment. His eyes were deep blue just like Brandon's, only gentler in a more open way.

"My name is Charlie. This might be pushing it a little bit, and I don't want to make you uncomfortable, but I'm between gigs right now, and I was wondering if you just might need some guitar picking to go along with that interesting fiddling of yours?"

# Chapter Forty-Two

IT TOOK PINCHBECK A week to get back to me after the office concert. While I'm waiting to see what happened with him, Charlie joined me for a few sidewalk concerts in front of the hostel. He was easy to play with, and his technical mastery made my occasional goofs less obvious. After bussing the first time we had to get another hat from Candy to accommodate all the cash thrown at us. Turned out she knew Charlie from some solo concerts he's had at the Opry. There wasn't anybody Candy didn't know in town, it seemed. When I asked Charlie why she didn't parlay her connections into a better job, he said she could but really liked being there at the hostel helping young people find their way.

After the second traffic-snarling bussing gig, Candy's husband reserved a spot for us at a local park. It had a pagoda and a mini stage that was perfect. I Googled Charlie on my phoneglasses. He's had a successful country western career, and even an album or two. Why he wanted to start over at the bottom with me was a mystery, except that we were having tons of fun together playing outside, and at the end of each mini-concert, so many people were grateful for his down-to-earth humbleness and for the mysterious magic of Lenore.

My phoneglasses buzzed while I was having my usual burger at my booth in the E String. "Ella. Lawrence Pinchbeck here. I would have gotten back to you sooner, but my life has been in turmoil ever since your office concert."

"Hi. That's okay, I mean about you not calling, not the turmoil thng."

" Yeah, well, it's not okay, and it's taken me until now to get some perspective on it. I've had three employees quit. Want to hear why?"

"I guess ..."

"My receptionist told me she was going to go work for her cosmetic surgeon because she wanted to help him help people find their true inner beauty. Do you remember her? Her date was the part owner of The Stage House Theater. He books more acts for me than all my other venues combined. He listened to your concert and decided to sell his interest in the theater and move to Fiji to raise some new type of bananas. Something about wanting to stop some disease that is decimating them there. I guess it's a real thing since I haven't seen bananas in Krogers in ages. I wished him luck, but that's kind of weird, don't you think? And Danny canceled his contract in order to go work for Krogers. Equally weird, not to mention ironic since I've never seen him eat even one morsel of food. Oh, and remember Mae? The mandolin player who can fill a venue no matter who she plays with? She called me up after the concert to tell me she was going to help her parents grow maize and raise goats."

"Wow. Interesting."

"Yes, very interesting. It's been a challenging week."

"So, I guess that means you probably don't want me to play any gigs for you,"

"Well, I've got a little theory about that. Yes, it's been a sucky week. I'm going to miss those people. My life will not be the same without them, and it took me a little while to get over how much I tried to support them over the years. It felt a little bit like betrayal, except for what happened yesterday."

"They changed their minds?"

"No. They're definitely gone, but I don't mind anymore because the new majority shareholder of The Stage House just left my office. He's apparently a big fan of mine and wants to offer me exclusive booking rights. Plus I just signed three bands I have been wanting for years. Apparently they saw the light too, and my new receptionist is a luthier who is pumped to help me restore my antique string instrument collection."

"Wow, well that's lucky. Congratulations. You sound excited."

"I am excited. Are you sure you didn't know about this?"

"Know about what?"

"That these things were going to happen?"

"Um, no. How would I know *that?*"

"Well, all this bad luck turning into good luck, and your playing, and all these players were in the audience and such ..."

"So?"

"Well, remember when I gave you my card at that coffee shop near Brecken?"

"Yes?"

"I didn't give it to you because your playing was particularly good. I mean it was decent, don't get me wrong, but not wildly impressive technically, if you know what I mean. I gave it to you because of what your music made me think about and feel."

"Hmm... "

"I sign a lot of musicians, and I've been in this business for a long time, but before I heard you play I was a little discouraged about the amount of money I was making. I was on that trip to California, in fact, because I felt I should be doing something else in my life, something more lucrative, a big change, you know? My brother works in the Silicon Valley, and he got me an interview with a music streaming startup that he's invested in. The interview went well, but then some voice in my head told me to stop at your coffee shop, so I did. While I was listening to you I realized that I didn't want a Silicon Valley job that made a ton of money. I knew if I took that job it would be a mistake. I started really missing what I was doing, and I hadn't even really decided to leave yet. I realized that I loved booking musicians in my cozy little Nashville office with my instrument collection and impromptu concerts."

"Oh boy ..."

"Maybe you know what's coming?"

"I don't, but this isn't new, frankly. I got into a little bit of trouble with the Brecken administration over something similar to this, but go on."

"*That's* interesting. Hmm. Anyway, thinking about this made me get on the phone with all these people again."

"You mean Mae and Charlie and everybody?"

"No, the new ones who signed with me who weren't at your office gig. It took me a while to put two and two together, but then it all clicked. Guess what they all had in common?"

"I think I might already know... "

"Yep, they all recently heard you and Charlie playing in the park. Well, one saw you on the sidewalk on Broadway before you came to the office gig, and the rest saw you at the park afterward."

"Lawrence, can I call Charlie so we can meet this morning? I'm finishing up breakfast here at the E String. Maybe it's time we all had a little chat about Lenore."

Chapter Forty-Three

I WAS LOOKING UP AT all the instruments hanging from Lawrence's office ceiling and trying to tell the story of Lenore in a way my agent and stage partner could accept and understand without thinking I was a nutcase. Lenore has been such an important and secret part of my life that actually talking about her to anyone but my dad and Brandon felt like a betrayal. What if she got mad at me for this and quit being my friend? I took a few deep breaths. She wouldn't have come back to me and led me here to Nashville if that were the case. Still, when I put who she was and what she has done in actual words to people I was just getting to know, it made me nervous, like I was playing with forces that were best left alone. Not for the first time in my life did I wish my grandfather had left me a holo-manual for Lenore, or at least a list of dos and don'ts.

I rapidly discovered, however, that I didn't have to worry about being judged. Lawrence was in awe of Lenore's seeming power to clarify thinking and priorities, and Charlie genuinely wanted to know more about her powers of telepathy.

"So you actually summoned your talking golden retriever and the pack of escaped zoo lions by playing Lenore in the California mountains?" Charlie asked again.

"Yes, it was the afternoon of graduation from Wandering Pines, and my boyfriend and I were headed for a winery for summer employment when I got a strong feeling to drive up into the mountains to say goodbye to Jenny. I hadn't seen her for months, but I knew she was okay, somehow."

"And then you played Lenore up there?"

"Again, it was a message from Lenore, to play her in the open like that. I don't know if it was just happiness about graduating or maybe about having my family there with Brandon. I was feeling joy that Jenny, Max, and the zoo lions that Brandon cared so much for were having a real life, a life they wanted, a life that was good for them and for the ecology of their new home. I played, and Jenny heard Lenore and came to say goodbye."

"They came from far away?" said Charlie.

"Yes, from behind a ridge far out of earshot, even for a fiddle with Lenore's bright and loud tone."

"Amazing. But you said this happened before with Jenny? Has it happened with anyone else? I mean, how do you know it's Lenore sending telepathic signals and not just Jenny perceiving things telepathically?"

"Well, I guess I don't really, except Lenore somehow knew where I was when she came back to me after I was shot."

"You were shot?! What do you mean she came back to you?" asked Lawrence.

I took a long sip of the Keurig Lawrence handed me when we arrived. I filled them in about Pendleton, Comey's, Kanda, and the horrifying nightmarish trance I fell into before fainting on stage and waking up to chaos and the missing bullet that pierced my hand and shoulder. Then about not finding Lenore, and the trip to Hawaii, Jenny's nasal message about the turtles, Kiholo Bay, the cave. Each story came spilling out of me like a confessional, like a therapy session where I could finally air things out like I've been wanting to do with Brandon. I didn't tell them about how Brandon has been too distant, too obsessed with Bryson and the lab and proving his worth to everyone to listen to me.

It was both easy and painful to revisit it all, and by the end I was gripping the handle of my mug so hard that I was surprised it didn't snap off. I was crying, and pissed that I was crying because I knew the tears were mostly because I was missing Brandon. I mean these guys were great, but they will never know what Brandon and I had together, the feeling of rightness being in his arms, playing music with him. Is this the way life is? You get little glimpses of real love, real connectedness, and then, boom, the universe cuts you off like you've had your fun and now you can suffer the rest of your life?

"Wow, Ella. I had no idea. How did you ever have the energy, not to mention the courage to just take off and come here like you did?" said Lawrence.

"I don't know. After Hawaii, I just couldn't go back to Brecken Vista. I kept your card, of course. Coming here seemed like an opportunity to reconnect with myself, with Lenore, to do something different, get out of the city. I mean I understand Nashville is a city too and all that, but it's a city where I get to call the shots for once and see what it's like to just be me. Plus I had a private jet at my beck and call."

"And a fiddle guiding you," said Charlie.

"Yes, exactly," I said.

"Or maybe a golden retriever?" said Lawrence.

" Yeah, hard to say which, I know. I feel like both are keeping an eye on me, holding me up. Maybe they are two arms of the same loving spirit working together."

"Like angels, you mean?"

"Maybe, or my grandfather. But the angel framework for thinking about this seems so limited to me. It's like this Sam Shepard movie I saw with my dad one time about a woman who has a car accident and almost dies. She carries the white light back with her and finds that she can heal people with it. She's just all love and in awe at her channeling power, not at all conceited about it, just humbled by it, you know? And awed by helping people get better, the ones who don't need their sickness more than health, that is. She discovers she can't help anyone who doesn't want help deep down inside. She's learning as she's going along. Anyway, the local bible-thumping evangelicals start questioning her powers and accuse her of selling her soul to the devil, and her life turns to crap because of them. Angels and God and Christianity, it *may* be a framework large enough to contain this mystery of Lenore, but not the way most people in our country approach it. Religion for them *reduces* the sense of awe. It provides simple lame answers to complex questions. Lenore and Jenny are about something greater and more mysterious than that, I think, something we're not going to wrap our brains around using prescriptive words and logic."

" Yeah, I hear you. I studied Shakespeare in college," said Charlie. "The more he wrote about truths in love, the more complex and mysterious love became for him. For every step he took toward understanding it, he watched love retreat two steps deeper into mystery."

"I think there is another point to be made here too," said Lawrence. "Most world leaders have no real clue how the awesome physics of a nuclear bomb really works, but they are more than happy to use that technology for their own purposes. We have to be careful."

"But bombs can't think. Somehow I think Lenore and Jenny are immune to abuse like that. As Brandon likes to say, 'They are masters.'"

"Masters, huh? Interesting. So, if this collaborative power between Jenny, Lenore and your grandfather is real, and I do think it is real because I know how it affected *me*, then we probably need to cooperate with it, not force it into things," said Lawrence.

"Let it emerge for the good of the world," said Charlie. "Be its agents, its nurturers."

"Like Schnazworthy bringing nature back into a sterile office building, or raising lettuce with your own urine," I said. The reference was lost on Lawrence, but Charlie nodded because I had told him about Schnazworthy and my high school garden project one time after a gig in the park. Suddenly I missed my early mornings picking lettuce in the Wandering Pines organic garden. But that feeling of longing was wrapped up in a new feeling, a feeling I never had at Brecken despite Brandon desperately wanting me to feel it. I looked around at all the instruments here. There's a difference between just being a part of something and really being on a team. What is this new feeling fluttering in my heart like a long-delayed chick finally hatching? When I saw

Lawrence and Charlie looking at me with real respect in this successful but funky office, I realized what was emerging was a feeling of truly belonging, a feeling of higher *purpose*. Did my Dad have this feeling when he left everything behind, including his marriage to Mom, to go to Humboldt and create his Enlightenment business? Did Jenny feel it when she chose a life in the wilderness over a cushy life with me? Such brave beautiful beings!

"Or maybe our agency is just listening for once to the music of the universe," said Lawrence.

For a moment his words were lost on my dreaming mind, but then I clicked back into the conversation and knew exactly what I wanted to say. In fact, from this moment on, I felt that no matter how distracted I may get by whatever happens in my meditations and in my body, I would always know exactly what to say with these new partners of mine by my side.

" Yeah, while the human race is still alive with functioning ears on their heads to hear it," I said.

Charlie and Lawrence nodded. My fingers tingle. The sensation of needing to play Lenore brought my attention back to my fiery chest, but this time it's more than just a phenomenon to be in awe of, it's a burning sensation of *calling*, a sensation of *rightness*, a recognition that for once *I* am the master of what clearly and irrefutably has to be done with the gifts that have come my way.

"Friends," I said. "Together, we will make music that will change everything for the better. It's time to play the tunes of Lenore to the whole world!"

Chapter Forty-Three

LAWRENCE FELT THAT our successful formula would breed further success and that there was value in being discovered on the street, especially if our gigs continued to attract large crowds. While he had the connections to book us pretty much wherever he wanted, he thought it would be best to let things continue to develop slowly. We agreed and decided to keep playing at the pagoda in the park for a while to see what would happen. Of course, it didn't hurt our growing popularity that Charlie had played before at the Grand Ole Opry. More than that, he was just so talented he made my rudimentary playing seem better than it really was. With each park gig I did improve my technique, but a Dixie Chick I ain't and probably never will be.

Frankly, my lack of talent didn't seem to make any difference to those walking by and heard us in the park. Anyone with kids always stopped to listen, and the kids attracted other kids as the families danced on the grass and listened to Lenore until she was finished for the day. There was always a line of folks afterward waiting to tell us how profoundly the music affected them.

Interestingly, we never seemed to see people more than once. They listened, told us they loved the music, and that was the last time they came. Even the homeless people in the park only came once, and we noticed that there seemed to be fewer and fewer homeless around town each time we played. Charlie felt Lenore was helping the down and out see possible solutions to their problems that they were unable to recognize before. I hoped that was the case and we were not somehow chasing them away to an even more crowded encampment somewhere. I hated to think that Lenore could be dissolving a community instead of building it.

A few weeks passed, and Lawrence decided the next step was to book us at a local school gymnasium that hosted inexpensive concerts. His idea was to hand out flyers to people at the park gigs to advertise a five-dollar admission charge. After we played, people eagerly took the flyers to give to others but expressed no interest in coming themselves. In a way this was good. It meant Lenore was doing her thing, but we worried about getting an audience. Turned out we filled the gym easily like it was a fall homecoming rally.

"I hope you don't have your heart set on establishing a gang of groupies," Lawrence said to me after the concert. People whooped and cheered at the end. It took over two hours to hear all the stories afterward of the new decisions they had made about improving their lives.

"What do you mean?" I said. "They seemed to love it." My hands were sore from playing and signing autographs.

"True, but when I ask these people waiting in line to see you if they would come back for another concert in a month, no one seemed interested. They said they had too much work they wanted to get done instead. They grabbed lots of handouts for their friends, though."

"We're like the Blue Man Group in Vegas," said Charlie. "A must-see ... once. An act you love to recommend to others."

" Yeah, this has never happened to me before, promoting a band people are crazy about but have no desire to listen to again. It's an eye-opener."

"Lenore wants them to get on with their lives," I said, signing another autograph.

We played several more gym concerts, each time handing out low-cost vouchers for the next concert. Still, it continued to be just new people every time. Lawrence ultimately decided that was okay as long as they kept passing on the word. To that end, Lawrence set up Insta and Hologram pages for us. They get tons of hits but few people bother to follow us. Instead people just post heart-felt grams about their newfound plans and ambitions. Clearly we're influencers, but not the kind that can brag about having more followers than others. I suspect we're also getting buzz from people sharing phoneglass videos they take at the concerts.

More important than all that, each time I played Lenore, the feeling that I was doing something right and making a difference grew stronger in my chest. Maybe grew is the wrong word because once it hatched, sharing the feeling that remained in my heart made it as large as a sunrise, as constant and as expanding as the love I felt as a child from my Grandfather even though he passed away almost a decade ago.

Chapter Forty-Four

NOT THAT THE SUCCESS of breaking Lenore out upon the world meant my life was all rainbows and unicorns. Far from it. My cozy little cot at the hostel rapidly became too public a place for me to sleep and Candy nicely suggested I look for a "homestead" of my own. "You're getting too hot with that fiddle, honey. I'm just not sure we have the building or the personnel to keep you and your instrument safe anymore. Besides, a girl with your talent and good looks is going to need a little privacy one of these days, don't you think?" She was right, although I often felt I was somehow extending my daredevil adventure by returning each night to the first place I crashed in Nashville after my break from Brandon and the lab. The public nature of it and the energetic company of young people on similar adventures gave me solidarity with others I hadn't yet experienced in college. How could I, living with Brandon and spending all of our free time in the lab?

Lawrence owned his own condo near his office, and Charlie's building on the edge of town had no openings, so I blinked through a bunch of depressing apartment ads all the time imagining that the worldwide uptick in bedbug infestations was sure to catch up to me given the sad choices popping up on my holoscreen. My Dad set me up with some savings that I had been dipping into lately, but I would prefer to spend that on schooling or travel rather than on a lease for a place I wasn't even sure I would stay in very long. I was about to give up and spend the money on something I couldn't afford when this scrolled up on my glasses feed: "Urban Allergy Farm needs night resident to babysit crops and feed cats. Grazing privileges. Stargazing possible on moonless nights. Price negotiable for the right person." I looked at the address. Schnazworthy! I blinked the number right away.

"Oh hi, Ella!" said Scnazworthy when she came on the line. "Of course I remember you. You're interested in my rental, huh? It might just be perfect for you, provided your allergies are gone?"

I told her how they miraculously disappeared overnight.

"No miracle, Ella, just good old common wisdom. Well, the place is still available. Most people don't like straw mattresses. Why don't you come on over here, and we'll just see if you like it?"

I dashed over there. You know those cat yoga places that were briefly popular a few years ago? Well Schnazworthy's rental looks like it could be the holoset for one of them. It's a small two story apartment connected to the waiting room but opening to the front of the building, the part overlooking Broadway. Like the waiting room, the space had a dirt floor full of vegetable plants, and it, indeed, had a straw mattress partitioned off from the living room with Mexican blankets. Downstairs there were two straw bales in the living room/kitchen with an old door thrown over them for a table, three curiously asymmetrical cat towers covered in

Berber, and a couple of old Ethan Allen rocking chairs, perfect for playing Lenore. Upstairs was the bedroom/hay loft and it had a cute bathroom with a functioning sink and toilet and a wooden door with a kitschy moon cut out of it like for an outhouse.

"It's perfect. I'll take it!" I said before she even mentioned the reasonable rent. The cost turned out to be less than the youth hostel, well within my budget. As she handed me the keys, I learned my only duty was to make sure the place didn't flood or burn down during the night, and to feed the cats on the weekends. I didn't have many clothes, so the wooden wine boxes stacked up along the bedroom walls had more than sufficient space for my needs. It took me two walking trips from the hostel to move in. I could have done it in only one, but the goodbye hugs from Candy felt so good I wanted to go back for another round of them. After I unpacked, a process that took me all of a half an hour, the Brecken swimsuit that Olaf brought for me to wear in Hawaii was the lone blotch of red among the earth tones and the literal earth of my new digs.

It took me a few nights to get comfortable, though. The old building had a symphony of mysterious moaning and clicking sounds when the daytime bustle of human voices no longer masked them. It felt like being in the hold of an old sailing cargo ship rather than in an organic garden. The lack of moonlight indoors added to the feeling of being swallowed completely. After the first night, I bought a soft night light for the bathroom and an even softer foam topper for the mattress. Sleeping on straw had its romantic allure, but getting violated by tiny straw pricks every time I rolled over was something I couldn't get used to. Jenny might not be proud of me for that considering she sleeps on the ground in the wilderness every night, but I'm not a dog, and I don't have thick fur.

I did, however, acquire a new family of three furry friends who were not shy at all about sharing my bed with me. Schnazworthy, or Maria as she preferred I call her, introduced them as Wynken, Blynken and Nod. Nod was the mother of this tuxedo family. When they sat next to each other they reminded me of Vermont cows on a carton of Ben and Jerry's ice cream. They were all females. "The dad jumped from the window and took off when Wynken and Blynken were born," said Schnazworthy. "Why he needed a larger world to live in than this paradise is beyond me. Or maybe not. The call of the wild can be compelling, no matter how comfortable your family circumstances are, I guess," she said.

The Saturday morning of my first-week anniversary there I woke up to Nod who was sharing my pillow with me. Wynken and Blynken were draped over my legs purring loudly, and Nod's sweeping black-tipped tail was a car wiper set on intermittent speed with my face as her windshield. I gently shoved them away and got up to pee, ignoring their dirty looks. Even the cutest cats can seem so offended sometimes, even if they are the ones who are being invasively obnoxious, but fortunately only for a moment or two. Sleep with three of them for a week and you learn they are more accepting, affectionate, and resilient than you might give them credit for. Or maybe the small measure of relaxed affection

I got from this particular group relationship was more than everything I was getting lately from Brandon.

Brandon. So handsome. I splashed water on my face and wondered why I still missed him so much. Despite caring deeply about the big cats in Renegade's vanity zoo, he's definitely more of a dog person than a cat person. I was too, but without his concurrent obsession with snakes. I thought about Jenny sleeping with her new lion family in the wilderness and wondered how they were getting along. Was she becoming a cat person? Ha! That would be ironic. I thought about blinking Brandon to ask him if he thought a dog could become a cat person and find out how he was doing, but then I remembered Lawrence booked a huge outdoor gig at a football stadium for this afternoon, and I needed to get a move on to fuel up with Charlie at the E-String.

# Chapter Forty-Five

BRANDON COULD LEARN a few things from Charlie. Charlie's the most talented guitarist I know, really one of the best in the world, but does that mean he feels he has to boss everyone around? No. He lets me, or really Lenore, take the lead and then just adds ninety percent of the artistic flavor and texture to the mix. It's the same at brunch today, I noticed. I decided on the buffet, and so did he. I piled food on my plate willy-nilly, my eyes bigger than my stomach, as usual. He followed my lead but applied food artistically to his plate like Banksy applying spray paint on a warehouse wall. When we sat down my plate was a mish-mash, and his was so beautiful that it seemed like a sin that he was going to eat it, until, that is, you actually see him eat it. Each bite he takes makes beautiful deliberate artistic sense. The masterpiece remains a masterpiece on his plate even as it gets smaller and smaller until it is gone.

"I've been getting some weird holograms," he said. I'm trying to learn from him by taking bites from the same side of my plate as he is taking them from his, but it was a waste of effort because my original placement of food was a hopeless mess to begin with.

"Oh?"

"Yeah, about our concerts. Weird thing is that they are from people who haven't seen us play."

"Do they want tickets or something?"

"Some do, but most don't. These aren't very nice holograms, Ella. One is from a wife whose husband left him after coming home from Nashville. She's got three kids to support, but he drained their savings to go join some weird commune in Africa."

"Hmm," I said.

"Another one is from a manager of a gift store, saying his boss fired him after hearing us play saying that he decided employing him was the reason the store was losing money."

"Uh, oh"

"Nah, it's no problem. These are obviously coincidences. People make all kinds of decisions when they go on vacation and have time to think about things."

"I know, but still, they blame us? I wonder... How many holograms?"

"About a dozen. I can forward them to you. All the feedback from those in the audience is gushing."

We finished our plates, thanked Candy 2, and Ubered to the football stadium. It's at a popular community college, but the stadium was not much bigger than the one we had at my original high school in Harbor Vista. The place reminded me of that time when I was wondering if I had the looks and inclination to be a cheerleader type chasing after football players. Not for the last time do I mutter a tiny prayer of gratitude to my parents for sending me to Wandering Pines.

Lawrence, as usual, played roadie for us and had everything ready. This time there was even a little stage set up on the track in front of the home stands which were substantially larger than the visitor bleachers on the other side. Again, we were lucky with the weather. No tornadoes or heavy thunderstorms had rolled through the area since my arrival. Not that Tennessee hasn't been suffering from them. It has. Everywhere the weather has been terrible. Missouri has had sixty straight days of rain, and Wisconsin has had seventy. The storms just happened to be missing us, that's all.

So far, Lawrence's theory of the arithmetic compounding of our attendance numbers has proven accurate. It doesn't seem to have any top-end limits to it, even when he decided to start raising prices for tickets to cover growing expenses. The pattern was the same, new people, no repeat customers. Charlie and the low price of tickets really attracted the family crowd, although today all kinds of people were coming through the turnstiles. To see an act in Nashville for ten dollars was an irresistible bargain for anyone, I guess. So far the crowds had been quietly appreciative, and we haven't needed to hire any security.

Our concerts were usually short in length, and people didn't seem to mind that at all. A tune or two of Lenore's music was usually enough to work her mysterious magic. After that, it was all frosting on the cake with Charlie and me having a good time and the crowd accepting whatever tunes came their way. It was like Maslow's hierarchy of needs related to aesthetic enjoyment, I figured out. Lower order listening needs got satisfied first, allowing the higher order experiences to be rich and satisfying like Belgium dark chocolate after a healthy salad. Again, the Belgium chocolate was mostly due to Charlie's talent, and the salad, of course, to Lenore.

Although I am driven to get her tunes out there, I am completely humbled as a musician to be playing them, especially next to Charlie.

Remembering to be humble, but also knowing that I had a duty to give Lenore to the world is how I gather the courage to stand in front of these ever-growing crowds. Today was no different. I was here on a mission, and Charlie was here to do that too but also to have a good time playing some kick-ass tunes. We're a good combination, I think, as I put Lenore to my chin to start things off. Charlie's finding a new purpose uplifting his surfer boy attitude toward music, and I was finding that his laughter helped take the pressing edge off my drive to impact the world.

Tonight, Lenore started off with a simple tune, as she usually does. "Arkansas Traveler" was catchy, recognizable, and got people on their feet right away. I saw Lawrence at the soundboard smiling and slapping his hands on the console. He always wore a cowboy hat and boots to our outdoor gigs. Charlie took about ten go-rounds at the melody, offering all kinds of variations, and when I warmed up enough I took a few myself. I could feel Lenore was playing with rough strength today. Maybe all the testosterone-fueled football energy of the surrounding stadium was affecting her.

We acknowledged the applause, and Lenore moved on to a really difficult tune called "Glasgow Reel." I was nervous to tackle it, but there's no arguing with her, especially when she was in this rowdy mood. Charlie raised his eyebrows at me when he heard the introduction but soon started cranking along with Lenore. The tune hits the crowd like a bolt of lightning. Never had I played a tune this well or this fast, especially early on in a gig.

I've lost control before while playing Lenore. In fact, I've come to believe she's always in control when I play her, only sometimes she allows me to revel in the *illusion* that I am playing her instead of the other way around. This time she was spending no time or energy indulging my misperceptions. The tune had a momentum all its own. My arms and fingers moved like well-oiled pistons, and the music sounded incredible. While I loved this feeling of commitment and newfound talent, I also recalled the time at Comey's when similar feelings came over me and I ended up being shot. Was this my time again for something bad to happen? I worried about that, and then I worried that my worrying about that might make it happen. I forced myself to let it go and concentrated on the tune.

As I said, the tune has a momentum of its own. I played on and looked up at the crowd sitting in the bleachers with the blue sky above them. The sun was resting in the highest branches of the stately oak trees growing behind the stadium. I saw three crows sitting in the nearest branch. Were they enjoying the music? Probably they were just here for food the audience spills in the bleachers. As if to contradict this, the highest and biggest one unfolded its wings and swooped directly toward me over the crowd. I held its gaze. Weirdly, it slowed down, even as the pace of Lenore's music increased. It started getting larger, its wings expanding. Blackness spread over the crowd like the opening of a misshapen umbrella. How was that crow doing that?

I looked back at Charlie to see if he was seeing the same thing, but turning my body caused a sharp ripping pain in the nerves of my feet. I tore my gaze from the spreading blackness to look down. Sure enough, my sneakers were floating just inches above the stage and a warm liquid feeling of numbness had replaced the pain and was spreading up my legs. What was happening to me? How could I play like this?

Charlie took a turn at the melody and started a long riff, but Lenore somehow kept up even as the deepening numbness traveled across my hips and up into my chest and arms. I looked up at the crow. It's wings were incredibly large now and very still, like a frozen parachute casting a menacing deep shadow on the swaying crowd.

And then I was flying upward toward the crow and it wasn't menacing at all. Lenore's music was pulling me into its warm shadow. I was worried about the audience. Will I fall on them? Hurt them? But they were focussed on Charlie and not paying me any mind at all.

As soon as I merged with the hovering wings of the crow, the feeling of warm tingling expansion released the numbness in my body. The feeling was one of belonging, of ownership, of *communion* with those listening to me still playing with Charlie on the stage below. Each separate feather in the blackness of the crow's wings gave me a special connection to a person in the crowd, a warm, loving connection. I felt each person's soulful love as a mother might feel a feathery baby tickle at her breast, but also I felt the whole crowd as one, as a whole moving entity with its destiny intertwined fully across my variegated wings.

The music built. Lenore kicked up the pace to an impossible level. From above I calmly watched myself playing on the stage. How could I keep up with that tune, I wondered? And yet I did. And also I hovered and flew.

With the music's faster rhythm came a new evolution of feeling. The feathers lost their warm breast-like comfort. The warmth was there still, but new sensations were layering on top of the old. The new ones started as quick little shocks of ripping pain like what I felt earlier in my feet, followed by a disturbing tartness, like a quick sharp blast of lemon pulp you never expected to travel up that straw of your otherwise refreshing summer drink. The invasion of these new disturbing sensations jolted the darkness into movement, making my wings flap upward slowly, powerfully, purposefully. Pressure pulled downward upon each individual feather of the flapping wings. It was the weight of people rising below me, each one connected to a different feather, each one ripping away from the bleachers below. The warmth of the wing as a whole and the pain of the people below were connected, moving as one, moving with the music. But where are we going?

Upward my wings pulled the people until they hung below me like marionettes, like floating clouds gathering power. It was too much weight. A dizziness overcame me. Don't let them drop! The music was spinning and so was I. The people entwined below me were forming a hurricane. It gathered momentum, driven by the repeating melody. It twisted and turned bouncing off the beams of the stadium then crashing toward the turnstiles.

A huge sadness overcame me. Turnstiles? Leaving the concert? Why are you leaving? Why am I *making* you leave? Is it my music? Do you not like my music? Do you like my music too much? In my dizziness and pain I asked the hurricane questions, but I *was* the questions. And there are no answers. Only the questions.

The twisting crowd approaches the turnstiles, powerless to cut the cords that held the storm together. The turnstiles felt their approach and started spinning with anticipation, their blades sharp and eager. Below them, a flowing culvert of sewage flowing like pus in the burst vein of a gigantic gangrenous limb.

Where was their fear? Why was there no screaming? No other sounds but the tunes of Lenore. All of humanity was below me, connected to my body, part of my music. I was part of the all. I was the all, holding them, feeding them into the turnstile.

I flapped and tilted them even closer toward the nightmare blades because I had to, because we all had to listen and tilt that way. The tunes of Lenore. The nightmare tunes of death. There was a jolting zipper of pressure on my farthest feathers from the outer bands of people sliding into the buzzing turnstiles. The pulverized flesh of people flew off the blades and splashed into the oozing sewage like a nightmarish sprinkler. More people entered feet first, ignoring the carnage, eager to beat the odds, and a few do jump over safely, shedding their strings. They cheer the others on, "You can do it! Jump! You can escape like we did!" But very few do. They can't hear the survivors' shouts above the meat grinding and horrific dismemberment of the people.

The center mass of the crowd spun into the blades, a full-fledged storm overwhelming the gates. A few made it through, shot over the blades by the momentum of those sucked through below. As cords are cut, I felt a new lightness in my wings and a sense of rightness, a horrible sense of obligatory rightness, like taking drunken pleasure in ripping wings off flies or roasting live frogs to death in a campfire. When it was over, only a handful of survivors stood in terrible sunshine outside the stadium.

What was next? Numbness returned. The tune was winding down. I noticed a few strings from my wings were caught in the turnstiles. They would me toward the spinning blades. I fought their pull, flapping furiously, unwilling to let go, but I knew what was coming, what was *inevitable*.

I was pulled feet first into the spinning blades. I felt no pain, just deepening numbness. It was the end of me and the tunes of Lenore. I watched my body grind to nothingness until my severed head plunged like a boulder into the crowded current of death. Eyes open, I flowed among the gore from red to black, to not-black, to just not.

Chapter Forty-Six

"NO, YOU WERE AMAZING. Your playing was spot-on. We cranked out about a dozen tunes and the crowd left happy, snapping up vouchers for their friends."

I am not believing a word Charlie and Lawrence are telling me. They say I invited them to my place for dinner after the concert, which I guess explains why they were in my living room digging into a big salad from Schnazworthy's waiting room. A delivered pizza that apparently I insisted on ordering rested amid a flurry of bamboo napkins on the straw bale door table. None of this made any sense to me. All I remembered was coming to consciousness with a chewed piece of tofu pepperoni in my mouth and Charlie laughing and asking me to repeat myself.

"How the f*** did I get here?" was what I had said after spitting out the tofu. They've been trying to answer my questions and clarify reality for me ever since.

Once they convinced me that I was not in some kind of afterlife, that this was indeed my apartment and that the kitties brushing up against our legs were indeed Wynken, Blynken, and Nod, I told them about my music-dream. I may not remember reality, but every detail of controlling the human hurricane of horrifying turnstile death was crystal clear.

"But it sounds like you weren't really in control," said Lawrence. "If you were, why sacrifice yourself at the end?"

"It felt like *everyone* was in control," I said. "Everyone had a hand in it. Mine was just the starring role."

"So everyone died, including you, except for a few lucky chosen ones. Was there anything special about the survivors?" asked Charlie.

"You mean were they carrying bibles with crosses hanging from their necks? No. There was nothing special about them at all as far as I could tell. They weren't celebrating having survived, nor were they horrified at what had happened to the others. They accepted that it was just a matter of luck. They entered the turnstiles with as much willingness as anyone else in the storm. *Everyone* thought they would make it. No one resisted and most of them died. They were the only lucky ones who didn't. They were just standing there nonchalantly on the other side of the turnstiles safely away from the open culvert that swallowed the crowd and me up. I didn't see what they were doing as I was fighting to not get pulled in, but I imagine they watched me get chewed up too."

"So weird," said Charlie.

"And no sense of guilt on your part?" said Lawrence.

"No. As I said, the whole thing felt fated, inevitable, even as I fought it at the end. Like who feels guilty about a hurricane?"

"Well, you *might* if you were the one swinging the clouds around."

"I know, but no, no sense of guilt at all. Just a sense of starting a tune and having to play it through to the end," I said.

"No matter how challenging and painful," said Lawrence.

"Exactly," I said.

There was a happy rhythmic knock at my door. That could only be Marie. I got up and let her in.

"Oh, you have guests! How nice!" she said, coming in with a big bouquet of goldenrod. Charlie and Lawrence, both gentleman, smiled and got to their feet.

"This is my landlord, Dr. Schnazworthy," I said. "These are my partners, Lawrence and Charlie."

"Oh, delighted! Look, the first goldenrod of the season! It usually blooms in August, but, you know, everything's changing now. I used to get depressed about it, but now I just revel in differences. Don't you? So much of life is attitude, don't you agree?"

I could see that Lawrence was trying to reconcile Marie's stethoscope with her mannerisms, but Charlie wasn't puzzled at all. He's smiling at her like he's seen a vision of Madonna. (Not the singer Madonna, the saint, well, I guess it could be the singer since she's still pretty hot.)

"I used to be allergic to goldenrod," said Charlie, "but I saw a holovid about

allergies and started putting little pieces of it in my bathwater. Now, no more sneezing."

"That's impressive. So you like goldenrod? I have a collection of goldenrod jumping larvae in my lab. You should come and see them sometime."

"I'd love to. I love goldenrod. Ragweed too. They have power that most people want to fight. I decided to get them on my side. It's better that way."

"Well, now aren't you a breath of fresh air! Ella, you've been holding out on me. Your friends rock! Well, I shouldn't be surprised. You rock, too, from what I hear. I've had ten new patients come to me saying they heard about me at one of your concerts in the park. It's all I can do to not blow your cover where you live, they are so effusive. Anyway, thanks for that!"

I could see that Schnazworthy was looking mostly at Charlie even as she was talking to me, so I said, "Hey, Marie, why don't you show Charlie around your amazing office. I think he might like to see it."

"Hey, you *all* can come!" she said.

"No thanks," I said. "You go on, Charlie. I think I'll have last piece

of pizza here with Lawrence and then kick him out. I think I could use an early night tonight."

Marie took Charlie by the arm and waltzed him out the door. I found a ball jar for the goldenrod in the kitchen and placed it on the door table next to the pizza box. It did have a strange beauty, I had to admit.

"Look, Ella," said Lawrence, splitting the last piece of pizza with me. "I think this dream, or break with reality, or whatever it was that you experienced, is a warning. Maybe you want to quit this Lenore business?"

"Yeah, *maybe* ..." I checked in with my body about this idea. Nope, not resonating. "But I love Lenore, Lawrence, and love isn't always supposed to be easy. Maybe I have been wrong about her all along. Maybe she's not the all-knowing God I have made her out to be. She came back to me. Why would she do that if she didn't want to be played?"

Lawrence looked about to say something but instead took a bite of pizza.

"Yes, I have been in awe of her. Yes, she has worked miracles, but isn't she entitled to a bad day every once in a while? What if *she* is still learning who she is? What if *she* is also just flexing her muscles, coming into her own, *testing* things out? I'm going to give up on her just because of a little amnesia? A little nightmare? A little personal discomfort? No one got really hurt, right? I played okay, even though I don't remember doing so, right?"

"You sure did, Ella, better than okay. The phoneglass vids are trending."

"Well, there you go. Power wouldn't be truly powerful unless there was some mystery involved. I say let the discoveries continue."

"No matter what might happen next?"

"There are a lot of bad things that are going to happen next whether we want them to or not. That's just the world we live in these days. We humans screwed things up big time. At least Lenore, to her credit, has mostly done good, by me and by everyone. The only one sort-of bad thing she's done so far was my dream."

"As far as we know," he said.

"Yeah, as far as we know."

Chapter Forty-Seven

SUNDAY MORNING I WAS lying in bed blinking through my feed and realized Lawrence wasn't kidding about our concert recordings going viral. Apparently yesterday's stadium gig was memorable enough for almost everyone in the audience to go back through their perma-vids and post highlights. Of course my feed was loaded with uploads since I was tagged. Some were just, "Hey, saw a great concert last night, you should check it out," but so many others linked our music to sincere announcements about new plans and dreams. Again, my playing was okay, but Charlie's was outstanding. People didn't seem to care. It also didn't seem to matter to them that our band didn't have an official name yet. Lawrence wants to call us the Charlie Ella Band, but Charlie just wants to call us Lenore. It doesn't matter to me. What matters right now is that none of the vids had crows in them or flowing rivers of gore and death. Would people have been as inspired to share the concert if they knew what had been going on inside my head the whole time?

Nod was kneading the blankets and about to curl up with Wynken and Blynken on my belly when banjo music started up and Brandon's face flashed on my screen. Sending the cats flying off the bed, I sat up immediately and quickly wiped the sleep from my eyes.

"Hey," I said, blinking him on.

"Hey, stranger," he said. His voice was subdued, tired.

"You're calling me," I said.

" Yeah, I came home to nap for a few hours. Bryson is installing an alarm system in the lab and the only time they could do it is now, so we're going to make up the time tonight."

"Sounds like not much has changed," I said.

"Yes and no. Actually, a lot has changed, Ella. That's why I'm calling."

"You quit the lab and are coming to play banjo with my band?"

"Ha! Don't I wish. No, I'm not sure I even remember how to play anymore. I haven't touched my 'jo for months. It's all the time in the lab as usual for me. That much hasn't changed, I'm afraid."

"So what's going on?"

"Bryson and I got called into President Mitchell's office."

"Oh, interesting. Was Pendleton there too?"

"Of course. I thought they were going to shut us down, but instead they just wanted to talk about you."

"About me?!"

"Yep. They want you back. Big time. And your new fiddle."

"What new fiddle? Oh, right. Why?"

"Well, Mitchell wanted us to see some new satisfaction survey data, and it seems Brecken now has a one hundred percent approval rating among all its students, and a significant uptick in grades and research accomplishments. No other university in the country can brag of that. He says at first he attributed a dip in ratings to your concerts at Comey's, but now he realizes you actually helped the school retain people who truly wanted to be there. He wants you back playing on campus again."

"Brandon, how could my playing there have had such an effect? Only a small fraction of the school's students ever heard me at Comey's."

"Well, they've seen the vids, I guess. Word of mouth. You're having a huge impact, apparently."

"So, he doesn't need me there. People can just watch the vids. No big whoop."

"Bryson thinks Mitchell wants you on campus and directly associated with Brecken, so, you know, they can say they were responsible for you, that Brecken inspired you to help others. It's good P.R. Or maybe they want to study you somehow. That's what I think is going on."

I didn't know what to say for a minute.

"Brandon. It's not me. It's Lenore."

"Lenore? No, it's definitely you. You thought it was Lenore, that's all, but the power's in you. Besides, how could it be Lenore? She's gone, although Mitchell says the fiddle you found to replace her is very similar according to a spectral study."

"They're spectral-studying my fiddle?!" Somehow a tough piece of straw had worked its way through the foam on my bed and was sticking me in the thigh. I pulled it out angrily and flung it on the floor.

"Look, don't get mad at *me*. I'm just telling you what went on. Pendleton asked me to call you and try to get you to come back, so that's what I'm doing. I also miss you, by the way."

"Yeah, and I miss you too. Look, I don't know if I can come back. My fiddle kind of needs me right now, and I haven't exactly told you everything that's going on. You got the brain power for this conversation? I know you need a nap."

"I live on Jolt these days, like Bryson, so go ahead. There are fifteen hundred petri dishes to inoculate tonight. It never ends, so if you have bad news, now's as good a time as any."

"No bad news, Brandon."

"That Charlie guy hasn't replaced me?"

"No, Charlie likes my allergist. You'd like Charlie, and Lawrence, my agent. I'm serious about wanting you in the band."

"It would be fun, I admit, but the world needs saving, El-la. It's bad out there. So many people, so much suffering, so many animals going extinct because of us." He sounded exhausted again.

"I know, and carbon dioxide levels are not leveling off at all. The tornadoes. It sucks. I'm glad you and Bryson want to save the world. We all need to work toward that end. I just hope you understand that I am trying to do that too, in my own way."

"I do, really. So, what's going on?"

I took a deep breath and told him about Hawaii and Jenny's message that came to me like the old days, and about what happened with Lenore appearing in the cave after he left me alone at Kiholo Bay. I told him about what had been going on with the concerts in Nashville, and finally about the dark visions I had yesterday while playing at the stadium. There was a long silence when I finished.

"So you didn't want to tell me about Lenore being back because why?"

"I don't know, Brandon. I was mad at you maybe. I mean I *was* mad at you, but it wasn't like I didn't trust you. It was like I felt Lenore maybe didn't trust you or at least not at that moment. I had just gotten her back. I didn't know what was going on. What if Pendleton had somehow taken her away in the first place? I just wanted her safely for myself again for a while."

"It doesn't seem to me that Pendleton, or anyone else, could have known you would walk into some random cave in the middle of a bunch of lava, not to mention slipping into it ahead of you to plant her there, so I doubt if they had Lenore. Besides, what good would it have done them to keep Lenore from you in the first place?"

"I don't know. To study her? Spectral analysis? Quantum analysis?"

"They couldn't have known about the cave."

" Yeah, I'm sure you're right. That's the conclusion I came to, of course. So, Lenore is like a god, or a spirit. I mean I already suspected that but ..."

"Look. I don't know what to conclude, but I will think more about this. I've got to go back to the lab now, though."

"Sorry. I spoiled your nap."

"That's okay. By the way, if you get any more famous, the drone-reporters are going to be buzzing me at nap time for

interviews when they learn we live together. Or did live together."

"Maybe we'll live together again soon," I said, softly.

" Yeah, maybe again soon, if it's okay with your fiddle!"

"If it's okay with your *Bryson*."

"I guess we are just not in charge."

"Nope, we sure aren't, even though it *feels* like we might
be sometimes."

"Life was a lot simpler in high school." Brandon sighed
and ran his hand through his long hair. This was one of those
moments when I wished the phoneglasses people had the
scent-transmission thing out of beta. I'd love to give him a
hug and smell his skin again, even if it was only virtually.

"We got better sleep then, anyway!" I said.

"Well, when we weren't out midnight cruising we did."

I laughed. "Bye, Brandon. Tell the lab boys hello for me."

"I'll tell them that you're thinking things over."

"Okay, that's truthful, but don't tell them that it really
isn't up to me."

"Your secret love life with Lenore is safe with me, although I think the world might put two and two together
pretty soon."

"Well, when the world figures her out, have them tell me
what they know because she's still a friggin' huge mystery to
me."

"Okay," he said. He smiled and blinked off.

Chapter Forty-Eight

WELL, IT TURNED OUT the math problem of Lenore was way more complicated than two plus two, but within a year people still caught on anyway. You know that Kevin Bacon game where you name a different actor and within six steps you connect her to Kevin Bacon? It was like that, only the feed reporters with their AI were able to connect the policy changes and remarkable about-faces people in power were making all around the world to holo-vids and attendance at our concerts. Maybe they got the hint about where to investigate from the Brecken admissions office, I don't know. Once the word spread, however, the feeds started drone-dropping the admin building with each new development. Red and blue network drones were also buzzing Brandon and barking out questions at him so often that this winter he had to move into the secured lab building with Bryson just to avoid the hullabalu. I couldn't imagine how much that sucked, but he seemed to be really into it. I still missed him, but at least he had some cute dogs with him in there to keep him company. He said Bryson was close to a breakthrough with his CRISPR machine, but what that breakthrough was he didn't know or wouldn't say.

In *my* life I have cats, but Lenore's popularity has also had an impact on my urban garden getaway. I offered to move out when the place started getting mobbed and dive-bombed by drones, but Marie wouldn't hear of it. She and Charlie talked Lawrence into buying the building and hiring some kick-ass security. It's kind of a hassle now having to go to and from concerts in limos and putting up with guards and such just to sleep in my straw bed, but such was the price one pays for notoriety in Nashville, I guess. It's nice to have Charlie in the same building, though. When he was with Marie, the two of them were so cute together that they always made me feel relaxed and at home. The attention our band had brought into Marie's life had also really upped her clientele. Schnazworthy Probiotics now occupied the two top floors of the building as well as the basement. Even one of the two presidents, the liberal one, had come for a consultation with her. Marie advised her to put an herb garden on the roof of her half of the white house.

Lawrence, bless his heart, had stayed true to his passion for music, only charging what was needed to cover expenses, even though those had been rising astronomically because of security. He still didn't want to book big venues because he felt the coffee shop/family vibe was a key part of Lenore's allure. I didn't disagree with him there, not to mention that a huge concert would intimidate the crap out of me. Since the stadium nightmare, we've pretty much stuck to parks when the weather didn't suck and to small clubs when it did, so it's gotten more routine to perform, and Charlie's talent inspired me to practice daily and improve my technique. I don't practice because it makes any difference to the effect Lenore's music has on people. I practice for me, for my own artistic development. It's something I can work on and see results from that are directly related to my deliberate effort. This other stuff that was happening, the changes and all, while powerful and consequential and directly related to my playing Lenore, didn't feel in my control one single bit. I don't feel *used*, exactly, but when reporters asked me what my overall plan was, I have to admit I had no clue. "The music is helping people be true to themselves," I say. But what that really means scientifically was too hard for me to say. It's kind of like trying to figure out why Schnazworthy's Probiotics are so effective. There are thousands of strains of microorganisms in each drop. It would take an infinite amount of time to test each one individually, not to mention in combination, to nail down why the drink made people feel healthy and cured their allergies. The music was just doing its thing as guided by Lenore, whoever, or whatever she is. Since that little problem at the stadium, she hasn't taken me on any more "bad trips." Instead it just felt familiarly good to play her, like getting a nice long massage or being held by someone you truly loved, like my grandfather, or my Dad.

Dad must have known I was thinking about him because he called me while I was sitting in my favorite rocker blinking through my newsfeed. His face popped up on my holoscreen replacing disturbing images of starving Somalian farmers facing their unprecedented third year of drought.

"Hey Ells," he said.

"Hey Dad! What's going on?"

"Well, I was wondering if the new Joni Mitchell would have a few minutes to spare for her poor lonely dad."

"Oh, Dad, I am hardly Joni Mitchell."

"Do you remember when you had no clue who Joni Mitchell was? Or Crosby, Still, and Nash for that matter?"

"I do, Dad, you've told me this story a hundred times, how I stood on stage at a fundraiser with them and everyone from my school to sing "Teach Your Children" and all I could say afterward was that their teeth needed fixing."

"Ha, ha! Yes! Those were the days. What a pleasure it would be to go back to those days when the Vietnam War was the only thing people got riled up about."

"Well, that and inequality," I said.

"Yes, we've never been able to get it all straightened out, have we? So sad, the human race."

"But Dad, you're making it better with Enlightenment."

"And you with your music. And, by the way, we're including holo-vids of your concerts free now in every new package we send out. I hope you don't mind."

"Why would I mind? But really, Dad, they are all over the feeds now."

"I know. Maybe I just want to brag a little bit. You *are* my daughter, after all."

"Oh, Dad. That's sweet, but I'm not so sure about this whole thing anymore."

"What do you mean, Ells?"

"I mean, sure, the CEO of Ford hears my music and decides point blank to ditch making internal combustion engines, including parts for old cars. So, that's great, but there's lots of people who can't afford an electric vehicle who are now without transportation. Not to mention the oil companies that have quit pumping and fracking cold turkey. It's killing the economy and turning people into beggars."

"I know. It's bad up here too. Not everyone knows how to harness oxen or plant without tilling. They're learning, though. Small farmers markets are thriving, at least for growers who can get their produce out of the fields."

"And it's not just that. *Families* are breaking up. We think it's good that everyone is following their dream, but are we just helping them to be more selfish? What if dreaming is a luxury humanity can't afford anymore?"

"Especially in your field."

"Right, musicians. They're starving. So are actors and artists. They're following their dreams right into oblivion!"

"Except for you, of course."

"Me. Right. I suck, but I happen to have Lenore. There are so many more talented fiddle players than me in the world. It's not fair."

"So, you are feeling responsible. I hear you. I felt that way too when the North Korean leadership smoked Enlightenment and gave up on nuclear weapons. I mean, that's a good thing, I guess, except that no one cares about their pathetic country now and North Koreans are dying right and left from illness and starvation."

"Do you wish you had never invented Enlightenment?"

"Yeah, sometimes, although I didn't invent it, you know. I just spread it around a lot."

"Like me and Lenore." I looked at her safe in her tattered case leaning up against my door table.

"I suppose we could say that if it hadn't been us it would have been someone else," Dad said.

"Like the way scientific discoveries historically seem to happen at the same time in completely different places?"

"Yeah, something like that. It's like, you know, I had a passion for Enlightenment ever since the monks at Brecken infused it with their meditative energy. I *needed* to bring it to the world. Or, rather, something working inside me needed me to do that. I'm just not sure which it was, or whether it makes any difference."

"Well, that's the point, right? Is it self-fulfillment, or the fulfillment of some other kind of destiny? I *need* to play Lenore. Is that coming from me, or is it some force in Lenore that is using me as a vehicle for its own expression? How can I be sure that what has taken hold of me is really doing good in the world?"

"Well, I guess you don't get to know that for sure. No one does. It's a matter of perspective, this doing-good thing. The deer gets taken down by a lion in the woods and the lion is happy but the deer isn't. Maybe it's not good or bad. Maybe it's just the way of the world."

"You make me think of Jenny."

"I know. What a great dog! Have you had any messages from her lately?"

"Not since the one that guided me to the cave. I feel she is keeping an eye on me, though."

"No doubt she is. Her powers are probably pretty incredible by now, and her part of the wilderness she's prowling around in hasn't been so healthy in decades."

"I'm not so sure about our little experiment in Hawaii, though. Won't pythons just mess things up more than help? They can attack humans, you know."

"Well, maybe humans need to leave the jungle alone for a while, I don't know. It's probably like all the changes, there are positives and negatives. Olaf and the Brecken scientists had a passion for that experiment. That's as good a guide as anything considering the other vibes around those labs."

"You mean because of the influence of the monks?"

"And because of Jenny being there, yes. And you and Lenore."

"Pendelton probably heard her music. I don't know, though, about Bryson and the others."

"Oh, yeah. Pendleton is a *big* Enlightenment fan, and I'm sure all of them have heard recordings of you playing Lenore. They're nothing if not thorough down there at BRI."

"When I think about them I get scared, though."

"As well you should. Those people have their hands in *everything*, believe me. I don't think they're evil, just maybe a little too enthusiastic."

"More than you or me?"

"Good point. No. But maybe not as introspective."

"Still, it would be nice to know."

"What would, dear?"

"Well all these changes and disruptions we're causing. It would be nice to know if they were good or not."

"Maybe good or bad is binary thinking. Maybe changes just *are*."

"Then what are *feelings*, Dad? *Nothing*? Brandon and I felt that releasing her and Max into the wilderness was the right thing to do. Did those feelings come from Lenore? Or Jenny? I think they came at least in part from Jenny. So we followed those feelings and things got better in that part of the world. So what else can we follow if not feelings? Science can't wrap its knowledge around enough variables to be trusted, can it?"

"No, the best scientists use facts and logic to follow up on intuitions and feelings. Sometimes there is time for pure logic and sometimes there isn't. Like when we wasted four years chasing proofs before ramping up carbon-trapping technology. Waiting for proofs could easily delay humans into extinction."

"So we follow feelings, I get it. Even scientists. But how do we know if the feelings are good ones or not?"

"I don't know, Ells. Maybe if the feelings come from love?"

"No one can define love, Dad, other than it is a feeling too. So, we have to live with feelings justifying feelings?"

"And giving it our best analysis, yes."

"In love."

"Right, within the parameters of love."

"And what are those parameters, then?"

"I don't know, dear. You expect me to know that?"

"Dad, *you're* the Enlightenment parent. Help me out here. I'm changing the world and I don't know why or how. If it's love, how do I know it's true? How do I *know* something is right when I just have a *feeling* it is right?"

"The only thing I can say is what the head monk who came to Brecken told me before we flew them all back to Tibet. He said, 'love is a feeling of balance from the future that emanates from animals, plants, rocks, air and water. When we act in accordance with that feeling we experience love, and when we don't, we feel alone.'"

I looked once again at Lenore, balanced against my table and thought about Jenny receiving those meditations of love long ago in the lab I have abandoned where Brandon works his butt off. "Love's not easy, is it Dad?"

"No it certainly isn't Ells, but what else do we have that's as worthwhile in this life of ours?

"What else, indeed, Dad ..."

"I love *you*, Ells."

"I love you too, Dad."

Chapter Forty-Nine

LIKE MOST PEOPLE THESE days, I spent a lot of time scrolling through my phoneglasses feed amazed at the disasters and stupidity of the world. Today was no different. Since Dad's call a week ago, I've spent so much time holo-screening in my bed that the restaurant mattress lumps looked like a wavy roller coaster of an outdoor Christo installation. I thought about taking a picture of them and sending it to my artist mom, but then I decided not to. I knew I needed to call her one of these days, but she could call me, couldn't she? I did get one text from her a few days ago that I haven't returned. It was a half-hearted congratulations and a complaint about the security she needed at her studio now. Probably she's jealous. If she were smart, she'd leverage being my mother to sell more paintings. I'm worried she was having second thoughts about what she wants to do with her life. That would probably be my fault, or Lenore's. She gave up a lot, including Dad for her studio.

I didn't have a lot of options about this vegetative bedroom activity, by the way. Our gigs were packed and people mobbed us mercilessly before and afterward. I can do yoga, pick produce in Marie's waiting room, practice Lenore, but forget going out for a spontaneous walk by myself. Forget going to the E-String too, or anywhere else for food and fun. There were just too many news drones and angry people out there now. For every person who heard the tunes of Lenore and made the break to follow his or her dream, there was another person, or two or three, whose lives got way worse because of that, and the word was out that Lenore and I might be the ones to blame.

I knew that a lot of good was happening because people were learning to be their authentic selves, but I couldn't help feeling every political riot and every mass shooting was also somehow due to me and Lenore. I know that's irrational, but that's how I felt a lot of the time. I felt elitist and snobby because the ones suffering the most out there were those who hadn't had anywhere near the economic advantages I've had. Maybe my fame was forcing me into an elitist jail that I deserved, like being stuck on my mattress scrolling was what I deserved for egotistically thinking that Lenore and I could help people we had no real connection with at all. I mean, it was one thing to be a person with a trust fund who decided to blow off a college education to play the fiddle, and it was another to be a dirt-poor laborer whom others depended upon for their survival to decide to do a similar thing.

This morning my feed was full of design holo-vids about the latest advancements in survivalist bunkers. For sale are add-on living pods with fifty years of dehydrated nutrition packets, entertainment consoles with every movie and feed digitized and equipped with its own power source backup. Holo-sunrooms with 100% equivalent solar rays powered by pedal bike generators with batteries. Super security sensors, military-grade weapons, lasers, trip alarms, etc. Do these people really think their quality of life will actually be any good in these bunkers? Wouldn't it be better to just stop raping the planet? Fix the bigger bunker, if you know what I mean. Besides there are plenty of islands in the Pacific that are way better paradises than a well-equipped coffin, except for the fact that storm surges were washing them away.

I whipped my phoneglasses off and reached down to pet the cats. They've listened to the tunes of Lenore almost daily and as far as I can tell haven't changed a bit. Eat a little food, prowl in the garden, play with each other, sleep most of the time. They've got life figured out. Self-fulfillment isn't a huge issue for these three, that's for sure. Nob loved to be scratched under her chin. The others preferred their backs petted. They purred and cuddled up close to me all black and white and shedding copiously. I've forgiven them for that. That's what you do when you love, right? You forgive faults, sweep up hair, focus on the good. Have I done that enough in my life, or have I been too judgmental? So what if Brandon was a little simplistic in his hierarchical thinking? Why was I not supporting him better in his goals? What was I doing sleeping in a bed a thousand miles away from him washing sheets that smell only of me and a few spoiled cats?

I put my phoneglasses back on and started shooting a vid of Nob's face. I blinked in for a closeup and just held the lens there recording her micromovements as she purred. What was she thinking? Does she worry about the thousands of her stray cousins in Tennessee who suffer in the crazy weather and die of starvation because there are just too many of them? Does she worry about the decline of songbirds and mice that are not meal options anymore because they have all been poisoned by glysophates and nicotinimides? As if to answer my silent question she rolled over, stretched a paw toward me and pulled her whiskered mouth into a smile. She's a cute one, that's for sure. I'm jealous of her mindless elitism even as I am tortured by my own. I reached out to scratch her chin and noticed my shoulders were rock tight.

I blinked off the recording, and freed my head from the device before it sucked me into more endless hours of holo-feeds and TicTok videos. I dislodged the cats and stumbled to the bathroom for a hot shower. Afterward, toweling my hair, I felt better. At least I was awake now and could move my arms. I put on my usual torn jeans and sleeveless blouse for the coffeeshop concert this afternoon and pulled Lenore gently out of her threadbare case. My fingers tingle.

Sometimes I have my best practice sessions with Lenore in the morning before I have anything to eat, but this was the first time in a while that my fingers tingle like they used to when the idea to play Lenore had an urgency to it, when it felt like she was violently shaking me to help her wake up and express herself. To feel this begin again in my fingers this morning was exciting, and a little scary.

I rosened up her bow and touched the horsehair to her strings, her amazing strings that have never once needed adjusting or replacing to stay in tune. Immediately, a terrifying and surprising shock. The current from Lenore sparked on my fingers and traveled up my right arm like thousands of needles pricking violently across my neck and spreading like fire to each corner of my body. My eyes go blind immediately with the pain. Lightning flashed in my ocular nerves, and it was all I could do to make sure Lenore dropped onto the bed instead of onto the hard dirt floor.

My eyesight returned slowly, but my skin felt like it had been torn from my flesh and slapped back onto my bones again as an afterthought. What was the message here? I looked at my phoneglasses on the bed next to Lenore and her bow. Should I pick it up and call someone? Charlie? Lawrence? I needed to tell Lawrence about this! What if this happened at the concert? I decided to take a few deep breaths and focus on my body.

What was happening deep inside right now? I was in pain, yes, but it was lessening. I could still see with my eyes, and that was good. My heart rate was a little high but not outrageous. I scanned my body. The shoulders! They were still so tight. Loosen the shoulders? I pulled my shoulders backwards, opened my chest toward my mattress and Lenore. A new feeling arose as I did this. It was a message. She was trying to tell me something with that shock. Some new energy. Powerful. A message, yes. But what was it?

I closed my eyes and let my body guide me back over the sensations. Pick her up again, my shoulders said. I obeyed. I bent over the bed where I dropped Lenore and grabbed her neck with my left hand lifting her. With my right hand I gently picked up her bow. No shocks. What did my body want? There was no clarity, but that wasn't new, there never had been before with Lenore. Her music would come whether I was ready for it or not. The tune could be a skin-ripping eye-blinding shock, or music that moved the world. The essential question was, was it *right*? Does it *feel* right? I used to know that automatically. Now I didn't know anymore, but I bravely put the bow to the strings again anyway.

As if the first shock blasted away a built-up dam, the flow of needle sensation was freer in me now, gentler, still powerful, but not shocking enough to make me have to let go of Lenore. The feeling traveled up my right arm and spread throughout my body. It settled in my eyes, taking them over, but this time with a gentler sense of love. My nose picked up a distinctive smell of mouse poop and then, like the old messages from Jenny, this image appeared in my eyes:

Oh, Jenny! You are reaching out to me again! My heart glowed, but wait, these were not dogs I recognized. They were not Jenny and Max, nor were they Mavis and Sam whom we left behind in Hawaii to guide Sybil and Sheldon.

But they were definitely a golden retriever and a Bernese mountain dog. Were they the ones ending the message? Or was the message *about* them somehow? They were not doing anything in the vision, just sitting there. Who then was communicating with me? And why?

The vision was so overwhelming it took me a minute for my mind to focus back onto my nose. When it did, the scent intensified as if to underscore a point, as if to convey an urgency to the message. The mouse smell ... Oh, right! It's rat! It's the smell of the lab! This was a pair from the next group of Brecken lab animals who have gotten older. This must be Walt and Toni, I thought, at least that's what I called them. This was a message from the lab! They've broken through to me and Jenny. But what was their message? They seemed so calm and yet the energy was frantic. My whole body was shaking from the initial shock and from this vision. Then slowly the shaking stopped and the vision faded. *Wait! I don't understand!* But the connection was gone, and all I was left with was a sensation of wetness and heat everywhere as if I had stepped back into my hot shower again with my clothes on.

The heat had melted the stiffness from my shoulders, and so it felt even more right to play Lenore. I wanted to hear her, maybe learn more. The tune she chose for us to play ws a modal tune from centuries past, sad and pleading, almost illogical in its progression, yet stunningly beautiful, nevertheless. As Lenore guided my fingers, the new heat in my body relaxed my eyes, opened my heart. I listened for the answers I needed, the tune coming from Lenore's place deep within me.

The tune rose and fell taking its time, convincing me of its wisdom and its mysteriously caring love. I saw the face of Jenny before me, then my grandfather, then Dad, Mom,

Charlie, Lawrence, Candys One and Two, Schnazworthy, even Bearman from long ago. They rose and fell in my mind and flew outward, like I was the one sending pictures now to Jenny and not the other way around.

It felt good to be a sender finally. It felt right. Afterward, when the images had all shimmered and traveled off on the loving waves of music, Jenny appeared, reversing the flow. My heart longed for her, and she beamed at me with her golden smile. She took me back to the garden at Wandering Pines. Here was the bench where Brandon and I first joined our bodies in love. The bruised naked body of a man lay seemingly lifeless across the bench now. It was Brandon. Jenny whined and nuzzled him, gently pawing at his blood-encrusted head until he sat up a bit and looked painfully over his shoulder at me. I felt with every part of my body how much he needed me, but I was afraid to say his name. There were broken petri dishes embedded in his head and on the side of his mouth. He held my stare for a moment chewing on glass, pleading with his eyes, and then the tune ended and Jenny disappeared. Only then could I shout his name. Brandon! I hugged him and laid back gingerly with him onto the bench, hoping that my weight would revive him and not cut him further.

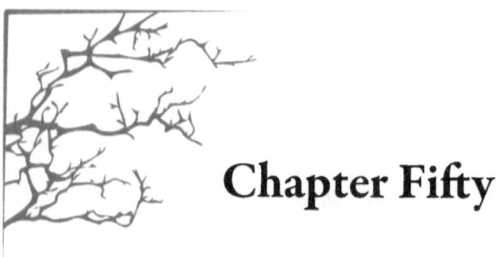

Chapter Fifty

THERE WEREN'T MANY musicians in the world who could get away with telling their agents they needed to miss a show because of a weird dream, but Lawrence not only accepted my panicked insistence, he bumped my credit to unlimited on the band's spending account and blinked the number to book me a first-class ticket on the next direct flight to Brecken. I didn't have a whole lot of time to tell him everything Lenore had shown me, but he'd heard enough stories from audience members, and had enough Lenore experiences himself to know that this was important. When I got to the part where Brandon was seriously hurt and had not answered my calls or texts all morning, that was more than enough for him. While I packed, he finished booking the flight and then drove me to the airport himself in his Tesla pickup. He called Charlie from the car and told him he was on his own for the afternoon concert.

No one recognized me at the airport, and once I was in my seat at the front of the plane, I accepted the hot towel from the attendant but waved off the warm nuts. They looked delicious, but I didn't want to choke while I was trying to connect with someone, anyone at the Brecken lab who could check on Brandon. If one thing from my dream was clear, he wasn't doing very well. So far all I've gotten back from them is, "We're sorry, but this is a secure area that is not accepting any outside calls at this time." It didn't matter to them that my name should still be on the authorized security roster. I called the main number and asked them to connect me with Brecken Security. When they came on I asked them why I couldn't call the lab. "I'm sorry, Ms. Bradley, but you were deauthorized last winter."

"Deauthorized?! No way! Look, I think there might have been an accident over there in Dr. Bryson's area," I said. No response. "Dr. Bryson and Dr. Olaf. The biology lab, where the dogs are?"

"Yes, that part of campus is a secure area now. What is the nature of the problem you want to report?"

"I can't really say specifically, but I'm pretty sure there's an emergency going on there, possibly with injuries."

"This call indicates that you are not in the area."

"Right, I am Ella Bradley. I've been taking a leave from the lab for the past year, but the experiments are with quantum communications, and I am telling you I got a communication saying something very bad is happening."

"I see. Do you know who sent you the message? There have been no emergency communications from any of our secure areas in the last twenty-four hours."

"It's a *quantum* message. The sender could be a number of entities. It's hard to explain."

"I see. Well, Ms. Bradley. Thank you for letting us know. We will look into it, but you're not an authorized lab member or communicant, and there has been no official communication from that particular secured area, so unless we can verify who sent you this emergency message and what exactly the message said, and unless we have an authorization for you to act on their behalf, there's not much we can do. Extraneous communication is strictly against security protocols. But as I said, we will look into it."

"Look, I'm not a reporter trying to scam my way into an interview. I'm Ella Bradley. Just get somebody over there to check it out, please! I'm telling you, something is not right!"

"We know who you are, Ms. Bradley, from your voice print. Security regulations forbid unauthorized communication into the secure area, but your message has been noted and recorded, and we will keep a close eye on things as we always do. We pride ourselves on safety around here, you know, especially in the labs. And even more especially in the *secure* labs. Perhaps your quantum communications network can patch you through. We have no knowledge or control over that at this time. Thank you, Ms. Bradley, for calling Brecken security."

I blinked that bitch off and blinked on the number for the President's Office. They picked up on the sixth ring, just enough time for me to realize that if I had any hope of getting through to Brandon it would be through Olaf or Dr. Pendleton. Dr. Vern would help me too, but he was probably locked in the lab with Bryson and Brandon. I was about to blink off when I got an inspiration.

"President Mitchell's office. How can I help you?" I recognized the efficient voice, and miraculously his name, Franken. For some reason I thought about members of the Brecken board using the President's office as a workout room. I shook off the thought.

"Hi Franken. It's Ella Bradley here calling from Nashville."

"Oh, hi Ella. How's the music business treating you?"

"It's been great, but I'm headed back to town. Any possibility President Mitchell might be available?"

"Well, his schedule is pretty full this week, but I could possibly fit you in next Wednesday, if you'd like."

"Franken, this is kind of really urgent."

"Well, he's in a board meeting right now."

"He is not going to be happy if I don't get to talk to him right away. Some music executives heard me play recently. They are flying in with me just for tonight and are dying to see the research Dr. Bryson and Dr. Vern are doing with the dogs. They are very excited about possibly underwriting the effort. The connection between music and quantum communication, you know ..."

"Let me just see if I can slip him a note, Ella. Can you hold?"

The jet finished taxiing and started down the runway. "Ella! President Mitchell here. So nice of you to call. You're coming back to Brecken I hear?" I blinked up the volume on my glasses.

"Yes," I shouted. "I'm on the plane right now with some new friends of mine from Sony/Virgin. They are insisting they want to see our lab first hand because they have a deadline for their portfolio. I want to bring them by when we land."

"Of course. What time do you land? I can send a car. I'd be happy to personally take them over to the facility myself, of course."

"Well, that's a great offer, but no need. You're busy, and they want to stay anonymous for the moment. They heard me play a few days ago, and this idea kind of centers around me and my music, if you know what I mean?"

"Yes, I certainly do, Ella, and I must offer you my apologies for our earlier misunderstanding of your, uh, talents. Your music has sure made a difference to our campus. It didn't seem like we could be doing anything better than we already were, and then all of a sudden we are. That's due to you. I hope your visit will be more than just a brief one?"

"Actually, I am glad you brought that up. I would like to do more for Brecken, kind of as a payback for all the lab has done for me. I'm thinking I could help out in the admissions department for a while, maybe do some promotional concerts?"

"Of course! We can work something out. It would be an honor to have you back."

"Okay, we can talk tonight after I show these guys around. Their return flight is a red eye. In the meantime, do I need a security clearance upgrade or something? For some reason, the switchboard won't let me communicate with anyone over there anymore."

"Oh, maybe. Dr. Pendleton said Dr. Bryson was getting drone-bombed and invaded by reporters lately, so things have gotten tighter. I'll take care of it. Do you still have your old ID code on your glasses?"

"I sure do."

"Okay, no problem. But what about the airport pickup? What time?"

"We get in at 2:00. Whether these guys want to use private transportation, I don't know. They have their own security concerns, as you can imagine."

"So you'll go with them?"

"Yes, probably, but can you have a car for me there just in case, please? This is all very last minute, and I don't want anything to go wrong."

"I will have Franken make the arrangements for you, Ella. 2:00 P.M. from Nashville. No problem. Do you want us to let the lab know you are coming?"

"Right away, please. That would be great, thanks, and especially please contact Brandon. He handles the dogs now. He will clean up the poop and will make sure the subjects are looking good by the time we get there. These country guys are all about the pups, you know."

"Okay, Ella, Consider it done. It will be nice to have you home again."

"Thanks, President Mitchell. Looking forward to working with you again."

The jet leveled off and I asked the attendant to bring the nuts I missed out on with lunch. Blatant lying must be an appetite stimulant, I decided. I might even have a chance to eat them before the inevitable turbulence kicked in.

Chapter Fifty-One

I SUPPOSE I SHOULDN'T have been surprised that Pendleton met me at the Brecken Vista airport. The wind and rain was so bad I was impressed that they even let us touch down. A few of my fellow passengers clapped in relief when the reverse thrust finished and gentle vibrations from wheels on the tarmac replaced the jolts from the flight. At the gate I asked for a plastic bag to cover Lenore's inadequate case since we had to deplane outside in the rain. Pendleton was just inside the terminal.

"Welcome back to sunny California," he said. "Enjoying the accommodations of our modern airport?"

"Frankly, I'm just glad to be alive. Why do people still fly anymore? It's a death wish." I let him give me a hug. It's been a long time since we parted in Hawaii, but I was still grateful to him for supporting my decision to go to Nashville. He looked about the same, a little older, a little more disheveled.

"I assume you didn't check anything?" he said.

"Correct. Can you take me to the lab, please. It's urgent."

"That's why I am here. Mitchell said you sounded very upset."

"I'll tell you about it in the car."

I expected a limo with a driver, but Pendelton came in his own car, one of those new hydrogen-powered Porches with electric backup. It looked like it was ready to go out on the runway and take off instead of demeaning itself by putting up with a mere road. Knowing Pendelton he probably had stoplight control, and considering that we didn't hit one red light navigating the crazy intersections at the airport I'm pretty sure that was the case.

"Do you have something in particular that is worrying you about the lab, or is it just a more personal result of the general swath of dire destruction your music has caused in the world that is bringing you back?" he said once he opened it up on the highway to the University. My body pressed into the passenger seat like I was still on the plane. The car must have radar immunity too, I guess.

"Dire destruction?"

"How else would you describe it, Ella? But I suppose you don't really realize what's really happening to the world since you're primarily focused on your band."

"Well, first of all, Dr. Pendleton, *you* are the one who encouraged me to play Lenore in public, and I do look at my feed pretty regularly. I don't have a lot else I can do since I get mobbed so much these days."

" Yeah, Olaf has been giving me hell for that too lately. Since you got popular, he's had to do most of the care and feeding of his lab animals now because so many interns have quit, many to become musicians, by the way. I admit it might have been a mistake to let you and Lenore loose on the world considering all that has happened, although in my defense I do think it was good for you personally."

"What do you mean, all that has happened? There's something wrong with people doing what they were meant to do, doing what gives them fulfillment?"

"Obviously you haven't been paying attention. Everything is shutting down, Ella, evolving too quickly. It's chaos. People are quitting jobs right and left, families are breaking up over disagreements about where to live and how to make a living, trade organizations are crumbling, banks and the military are in free-fall. There's general disregard for authority, and even those whose dreams are to be leaders can't find enough people willing to follow them. The disruption to hospital services alone is going to cost us millions of lives in the next few months."

"And you and Olaf blame all this on me?"

"And your father. There is no doubt that the combination of Enlightenment, the tunes of Lenore, and whatever other force is empowering the rise of cognizant animal species like Jenny and the lions, has really put it to humans, at least human civilization as we know it. Things will never be the same again, I'm afraid."

"You're making me feel horrible, Dr. Pendleton. "Do you know how many people thank me for my concerts? Maybe this disruption is just civilization figuring out a way for people to follow their hearts, to do what is right for them, instead of what the system wants them to do? What's wrong with that?"

"What's wrong is that it's an elitist's dream, Ella. *You* can follow your dream, sure. You're rich. Doors are open for you, and there aren't that many consequences for you if things don't work out, but most of the world's not like that, you know. When most people get passionate and try to follow their dreams, as they are foolishly getting the courage to do now that you and Lenore are a viral sensation, people suffer and die. It's economics 101 Ella. There are too many people, not enough opportunities."

Our car zoomed up to the north gates at Brecken and the guard waved us through. Pendelton steered past the cactus garden toward the lab buildings. I should focus on what I needed to say to Brandon in a few moments, but I forgot to pee when I got off the plane, and now I really had to go. Also, I was having a hard time accepting what Pendelton was saying. What right has he to criticize me? Hasn't he had every opportunity in life handed to him too? What's wrong with sharing the wealth with others, so to speak?

"Isn't this America, Dr. Pendelton? You know, follow your dreams, be successful? You've heard of that, right?"

"That's just a masterful piece of propaganda to keep the masses of oppressed people hoping for a better life. You know better, Ella, or at least you should by now. America is run by an elite class of powerful people strategically distributing just enough crumbs to keep the rest of the population under control. The power structure is less hidden in Russia and China, but it's essentially the same. There are the masters and the followers. And we're one of the masters."

"*Masters*. You sound like Brandon."

"And now that you have gotten everyone thinking *they* can be masters, we've got a hell of a power struggle on our hands, not to mention the wholesale breakdown of the present structure of the civilized world."

"Well, maybe the civilized world needed a little shaking up before it destroys the planet."

"We were on a good track to help ecosystems recover with the implanting of smart predators thanks to you. Olaf had high hopes. The initial results from Hawaii have been promising. Sybil and the dogs have basically purged that area of wild pigs and the native birds are recovering. Now, who knows what will happen. No one wants to work the cargo ships to Hawaii anymore. The people are going to suffer there, the ones who can't live off the land, anyway."

"The people could have hunted pigs, you know."

"They still can in most places, if they hoarded enough bullets, that is."

"Or they can garden. Hawaii is great for raising vegetables."

"People will never want to just be hippie gardeners, Ella. The hunger for power and accumulated wealth is too ingrained in our nature."

I looked out at the stately buildings of Brecken going by and remembered my early morning moments of peace picking the lettuce I raised with my own urine in the Wandering Pines organic garden. And then the strident arguments with my mother and others about that project and how much I wanted recognition for being right about my ideas. Was I after power too? Did I design that weird toilet because I wanted to get rich off of it, or to really help humanity? Did my Dad create Enlightenment because he really cared about people's personal destinies, or because he wanted fame and power? Have I been ignoring the bad things my concerts have caused in the world because I dearly needed to be praised for the good I thought I was doing?

We pulled up in front of Bryson's lab building, and now that we're finally here, I was frozen in my seat. Pendelton opened his door to get out, but I stopped him with my hand. "Did you have Lenore all the time?"

"What do you mean?" he said.

"Lenore. After I got shot at Comey's. Did you have her? Bring her to Hawaii and somehow let me find her there? You and Kanda? Did you have Kanda take her from me?"

"We didn't feel it was safe for you to have her again considering what happened. There was no shooter, Ella. Somehow you got shot, though. We needed to figure out why. I don't know how she came back to you, although we have done tonal analysis to determine that she's the same instrument you were playing before the shooting."

"So you studied her."

"Yes. We didn't waste any time. Full tonal and psychic analysis, including a series of other musicians playing her at different coffee shops. Nothing. No effect. We were at a standstill. Then she just disappeared from my office, presumably to come back to you, although we didn't know she had done so until we analyzed the vids of you playing in Nashville."

"Your agents followed me there. I hope they quit after they heard me play. So you let me go to Nashville on the jet to see if my playing without Lenore would have the effect."

"Yes."

"And I did, but then you figured out Lenore had come back to me."

"Yes, and we'd really like for you to tell us how she managed that."

"Well, you can chalk it up to magic. I did. So the Lenore effect, as you call it, is really an Ella *and* Lenore effect."

"That seems to be the case, Ella. You're an essential element behind whatever is going on."

"Or my grandfather."

"Possibly. It was his fiddle, after all, but right now you are the present catalyst, for lack of a better word."

"So, I'm responsible for the mess the world is in right now."

"Well, no one thinks you did it on purpose, but yes, it would not have happened without you playing Lenore. There are those who want you killed and Lenore destroyed. I've convinced them it's too late for that with the vids having the same effect and all."

"Well, that's considerate of you, I guess. Dr. Pendleton, I didn't tell President Mitchell about this on the phone, but I'm here because Lenore sent me a dream of Brandon cutting his mouth by chewing on broken petri dishes. Do you know exactly what they are working on now?" I looked out at the lab.

"Bryson's reports are about CRISPR alterations to our top predators to augment and solidify their human-like learning capabilities."

"I think that's a lie. I feel it in my gut, and you should too. Bryson didn't support Olaf's vision. He's up to something much more serious. We need to get in there right away and find Brandon. The only problem is I really have to pee."

Pendleton hit a button and the doors folded open. I grabbed Lenore and ran.

# Chapter Fifty-Two

PENDELTON WAS IN BETTER shape than me, so he beat me through the rain to the door and scanned us through. I ducked into the john but I took Lenore with me. I'm never going to let her out of my sight again, especially with Pendleton around, the thief. The back of my spine tingled with anger at him for not telling me Lenore was safe after my shooting. Weirdly, as I pushed my belly to relieve myself as quickly as possible, I wondered how Charlie and Lawrence were doing with today's concert. Do they realize how serious the negative effects were that we were causing in the world and just decided not to talk to me about it? Was our playing like a few years ago when the subject of climate change was so serious no one wanted to face up to it and everyone just kept burning coal and driving fossil fueled cars? And how could something as seemingly harmless as a little fiddle music cause so much trouble anyway? The power of the force of habit was amazing to me. Here I was panicked to find Brandon, and I still efficiently doubled over a single piece of toilet paper to wipe myself dry.

Out in the hallway, though, I sprinted to catch up with Pendleton, and found him stuck in the hallway outside the lab arguing with a security guard.

"I'm sorry, Sir. Section Five, Paragraph Three: 'When a lab procedure is vulnerable to unacceptable variables due to intrusion, the head scientist can order a complete quarantine for up to twenty-four hours. This one has been in effect since this morning, sir.'"

"Authorized by Dr. Bryson?" said Pendleton.

"That's correct, sir. I can't let you in. I'm sorry, sir."

"Get Dr. Bryson on the 'com."

"That I can do, sir. There's no regulation against verbal or holo-communications, if anybody will pick up, that is, sir."

"Try holo first."

We stood away from the feed screen and waited while the guard blinked the code on his glasses. We couldn't see into the lab until someone answered, but when the transmission light turned green, Pendelton said, "Bryson, what the hell are you doing calling a section five? That wasn't on the schedule, was it? Pick up and talk to us. Ella Bradley's here with her fiddle, and she wants to speak with Brandon."

No answer. We waited. "Hit the emergency alarm in there. Just for ten seconds to get their attention," said Pendelton.

The guard hit the alarm. I could hear it faintly whining behind the steel doors. A moment later Bryson appears on the holo. He looked tired and skinny, like he'd been on an old-fashioned regimen of chemotherapy or something. Holos always do that to people's images, but this was way more than just repro-glare. "Sorry, I had to wash my hands," he said.

"Bryson. Ella's here to talk to Brandon. What's going on? Why the Section Five?"

"Brandon's getting the subjects ready. We're doing an inoculation study this morning. It's quantum-augmented, so we don't want anybody else coming in who hasn't been acclimated to the tapes like we are now. We should all be finished by this afternoon."

"Finished by this afternoon? You mean you're ready to let the next group of predators go? Olaf hasn't even identified the next target area!"

"Yes, that's a problem, but no one's quitting in this lab, so we're pushing ahead. We'll be ready, even if he won't be."

I watched Bryson and strained to try to see Brandon in the background, but I didn't see him or any of the dogs. That didn't surprise me. The background resolution of these campus security holo-coms was notoriously awful.

"Okay, well, can you give Brandon a break to talk with Ella? She's standing right here."

"Hi Ella. You've come back to us?" said Bryson.

"Hi Dr. Bryson. Yes," I said, stepping into the beam with Pendleton. "It's really important that I talk with him. I know you are busy and all, but I just need a few minutes alone with him."

"I can't let you in, Ella. I mean, maybe you've been around the tapes long enough, but I don't think we should take the chance. This is touchy stuff, as you know, and we've progressed significantly since you left after your Hawaii vacation."

"Holo's fine for the moment. Just five minutes, okay?"

"He's putting the dogs into the sound room. I'll tell him you're here." He stepped out of the beam.

"Do you want me around, Ella?" said Pendleton.

I gestured for him to follow me out of earshot of the guard.

"Did you see what Bryson looked like in there? He's not in his right mind. Something *terrible* is about to happen. I know it."

"Look. You talk to Brandon when he comes on, and I'll go get some reinforcements from security and the override master code for this. I could try ordering Bryson to stop whatever he is doing and let me in, but I don't think he'll comply."

"Maybe kill the power to the building?"

"Maybe, but that might put them in danger. Let's see what we learn when you talk to Brandon, if he comes to the com-beam, that is."

"If he doesn't, I'll blink you," I said.

"I should be back in ten or fifteen minutes tops."

Pendelton sprinted back to his car, and I returned to the com beam.

"If my boyfriend comes on, do you mind?" I asked sweetly to the guard.

"I have to stay by this door, Miss, but I can redirect the beam to the front entrance com, if you'd like. You'll have privacy other than people coming in and out for the other labs."

"Thank you. Please do that." He nodded militarily and blinked into his control glasses.

I sprinted back to the entrance to the building just as the snowfall of the building's greeting com beam resolved into Brandon. He looked about as beat up as Bryson did earlier. His hair was down and greasy, and it looked like he hadn't shaved for weeks. Even his eyes, usually so hard to read on these machines, looked dark and menacing.

"Brandon, my God! What is going on in there? You look horrible."

"Ella, you shouldn't have come back here. Go! Now. Far away. Back to Hawaii if you can."

"Tell me what's going on. Lenore sent me a frightening dream about you, but I don't know if the dream is more scary than this. When was the last time you ate something? Took a shower?"

"Doesn't matter. Just leave us. Important work. Got to get it done," he mumbled.

"You're talking like a madman, Brandon. Get *what* done? What are you and Bryson *doing* in there?"

The question seemed to jar him into remembering himself a little better. He met my gaze, wavering as it must be through the transmitter. "We both used the tapes on ourselves. It opened our eyes, showed us the path forward. We're upping the immune system of the dogs, I mean upping the frontal cortex *through* the immune system. It's complicated, but necessary for their release."

"What do you mean? We weren't working with the immune system. Bryson said something about *inoculation*?"

"It's complicated, Ella, and it's happening right now, finally. You really want me to bring you up to speed on a whole year of what you've missed? Yes, it's immune related, a pathway for augmentation of the cognitive ability of the subjects in relation to microbial exposure. They're getting their doses as soon as I get back."

"So, you're making them smarter with microbes some-how? Okay, I get it, I guess, but why do I have to go away? You said just now I should go away, go to Hawaii."

"I'd like to think of you resting in Hawaii. I know we argued there, but you were so beautiful by that bay. Go there, Ella. Go there for me."

"Brandon! You're rambling, talking nonsense. *Hawaii?* Focus. You're not telling me everything. I know when you are holding something back from me. Lenore sent me a dream of you eating petri dishes. You were bleeding and desperate. Why would she do that? Don't lie to me!"

"I'm not lying to you, Ella. We're helping the subjects get smarter, that's all. Yes, go to Hawaii. Ask Pendelton for the jet again. Enjoy a day or two at the beach. What else is life for, huh? Enjoy *everything* before it goes away, Ella. You can do that better than I can. You are so beautiful. I love you, Babe. I've got to get back. Get it done. We don't have much time ..."

"No, don't step off! Stay here. Talk to me more. What about the petri dishes? What's in the petri dishes exactly?"

"Nothing. Don't worry about petri dishes. How can Jenny know anything? She's not here. We're just tired because we have been working so hard, you know? Remember what that's like? We're getting it done! We're doing what *has* to be done."

"Brandon. Hold on. Jenny is sending me a message!" My nose filled with the smell of rotting flesh, like dead animals sometimes smell on the side of the road. Then this image appeared before my eyes:

"Do you see that, Brandon? What's going on in there? Who are you murdering?"

"I see it too, Ella, but that's not me. That's you and your grandfather."

Could he be right? It *is* a woman wielding the sword. But then what was Jenny trying to tell me? And why now? No! I'm not a deliberate murderer, even if I have caused serious problems. Jenny's warning me about something. "Brandon, Jenny's not a literalist. I'm not a murderer, and neither was my grandfather. This is a warning that you're in danger, that something really heartless is about to happen."

"We're all in danger, Ella, haven't you been paying attention? I've got to go. This is what I am called to do. Today's the day we save the world. You're beautiful, you know that, don't you? I miss you so much. Thank you for being who you are." He backed away from the beam.

"Brandon, stop! Don't do what you are about to do, whatever it is! Brandon! Sweetie. Let me in! We can talk about it. There's time to talk this over. There's always time. Bryson is always in a hurry, but that doesn't mean you have to be. I know I have been gone, but we're *partners* in all this.

We're stronger when we work together. Like at Wandering Pines. We made a difference working *together*. Jenny's on our side. We need to heed her warning."

"I'm sorry, Ella. You've been gone too long. We've moved on without you. Bryson's the master now." He took another step back and faded from the beam.

"No, Brandon! I'm the Master! Listen to me. Stop! I'm telling you. *I'm the Master!* Open the doors. Let's go home for a while. That's an order! Grab something to eat. You need a shower. We'll talk it over, and then come back and help Bryson later."

Through the static I heard, "No, Ella. Hawaii. Go there. Work to do. Time is of the essence. Saving the world. Good-bye, Ella." And then his voice was gone, and there was just static and snow.

Chapter Fifty-Three

PENDELTON MAY HAVE a lot of power around here, but he sure was taking his time getting back with reinforcements and the security codes. A group of graduate students with rain jackets on over lab coats pushed past me by the entrance.

"Hey, do any of you have access to Dr. Bryson's dog lab?" I asked urgently.

"No, sorry," one of them deigned to answer me. The others just ignored me, lost in break time chatter. Outside the rain storm intensified, and the humid air they let in swirled around me like confusion. In my lungs the wind felt like a slightly cooler version of the air in the rainforest where we let Brandon's snake loose on the ecosystem.

The urgency to play Lenore arose in my belly like an amber alert on my phoneglasses. Where was she? I put her down when I was talking to the guard! He was still standing there dutifully when I dashed around the corner back to him and picked up her case. It was a desperate ploy, but maybe if he'd never heard a tune from Lenore it might make him decide to let me in. I opened her case right there on the linoleum floor and slapped some rosin on her bow. "Pendleton is coming back with the head of security. Mind if I play a little tune while we wait?" He kept his arms crossed in front of his chest but shrugged.

The thing about the Orange Blossom Special was that most of the song was just messing around with sound effects on the strings, but the mood of a locomotive chugging head-long who knew where was a perfect choice for the circum-stances, both mine and Brandon's. Lenore directed my fin-gers over the simple notes to keep the tune going but didn't let my mind stay in that sterile laboratory hallway very long. At first I saw the locomotive smoke chugging from Lenore's strings in time with each quarter note sawed by the bow. Then, I *was* the smoke and I realized Lenore was not able to hypnotize the guard into quitting. Like most people he'd probably had already seen a vid of us playing and since he was here, loved his job. He was one of the steady ones with limit-ed imagination. No, she knew to bypass him and just let him stand there stupidly and importantly.

Being smoke, Lenore and I knew our openings, our many pathways through buildings and trees. We wafted up-ward into the hall vent and through the ducts over the door to the screened opening into the lab. There it all was before us, the blue glow of the computers at the control console, the indoor play area for the subjects, their cages, the audio labs, and Bryson's private lab down the hallway.

Immediately my heart was pulled toward the puppies, now grown dogs that I had abandoned. Some of our smoke wafted purposefully onward toward Bryson's CRISPR lab, but some followed my heart to swirl around and hug the sub-jects running loose in the hallway. We were in both places at once.

The smoke of me that was longing to find Brandon curled under the plastic barrier and expanded into the tiny hidden lab. Like two starving corpses, Bryson and Brandon were there working side by side over a lab table with uncovered petri dishes. Brandon sniffed and turned to look at me. He met my eye and heard the tune of Lenore.

"The Master has arrived," he said. Bryson glanced at him annoyed at being distracted, then ignored him and stared back at the petri dishes spread out across the table.

"Bring the subjects in now," he commanded.

But Bryson froze. He couldn't hear the music. Brandon, who did, turned into smoke like me and entered the tune with me. He rose and we swirled together above the table. We danced in rhythm but couldn't merge.

"You are not all here," he said.

"No, I am also with the dogs."

"And the dogs are also with Jenny. You love them more than me?"

"I love them because they should be free, like we should be free."

"To have a healthy life in nature?"

"Yes, an aware, healthy life, like Jenny and Max have."

"And Mavis and Sam?"

"Yes, and Sybil and Sheldon, like all the animals we've seen on our flights with Lenore. A life like they don't have in this lab."

"Or anywhere, lab or otherwise. Their world is dying, El-la. Our world is dying. Because of *us*."

"I didn't mean to destroy it, Brandon. Really I didn't. I needed to play Lenore, and then people just did what they had to do. At first it was beautiful, people following their true hearts and dreams, and then it all got screwed up! It's terrible now. I'm sorry!"

"Not your fault. Her tunes are very compelling. We're in one now, aren't we? Maybe we've always been in one, who knows? But it's not just you. It's all of us. The too-many of all of us, whether we hear Lenore's music or not."

"Animals don't have a choice over what we've done. We've taken their songs away from them."

"They'll hear their tunes again soon. Jenny and Max will make sure of that. They are not afraid of the human world falling apart. They are the world's hope, and we must help them. Just one more step is needed." A wisp of Brandon's smoke gestured down at the table, and suddenly Lenore let me know what the petri dishes held.

"It's not an inoculation is it, Brandon? Those are swords, aren't they? Swords in the petri dishes."

"Yes, Master."

"Why am *I* the master?"

"Obviously you were chosen by Lenore to play her tunes to the world."

"But why?"

"Education. The convicted deserve to know the reasons for their punishment, don't they?"

"Is this what you and Bryson are doing? Punishing people by *killing* them?"

"Humans are killing *themselves*. It's inevitable. We're just speeding up the process so that innocent life has a chance to live on and heal under new masters like Jenny and Max."

"It's not your *place* to do this, Brandon! *You are not God!* Bryson is not the Master!"

"I told you. *You're* the master, and it's not punishment. It's enlightenment. You're the master because you gave everyone a glimpse of why this had to happen."

"*I* did? How?"

"In a world of love where all actions are in line with the future health of everything, chaos and death are not tragedies. Death is a needed action of balance, of loving ongoingness, the ultimate action of the world aware of itself. It is neither evil nor good, just a note played along the way, the note played at the end of a tune before the start of the next tune in the endless concert of the universe. Lenore chose you to understand this, to help others understand this. That is why you are the Master."

"Brandon, if you release these microbes, you are evil."

"Evil is a concept born from the refusal to see love operating within necessary chaos and death. Death is the Grim Reaper, the closing of one door to open another, a very misunderstood card."

"But you are choosing death for others, for all humanity! How can *that* be okay, Brandon?"

"I heard Lenore's tune. So has Bryson. And here we are, doing what we are driven to do, what we *know* is the right thing for us to do. We are following our destiny. If that's not a guide for genuine living, what else is, Ella? You don't think a CRISPR machine can't be a lyric in one of Lenore's tunes?"

"No! It's too much power, Brandon! No one has the right ..."

"Humans have not had the right to do *anything* they have done to screw up life on earth. Did humans have the right to unleash the industrial revolution on the world? No! A CRISPR machine is *nothing* compared to the destruction of coal and the internal combustion engine. When the planet gets out of whack, nature brings things back in balance. Like with Jenny and Max. You, me and Bryson, we're also just instruments in that, that's all. It's all love, every bit of it."

"But you *know* better!"

"Maybe. But to a certain extent, all creatures know better when there gets to be too many of them and they suffer and starve. We're just deluded enough to think we're doing it in some special anointed way, that's all. We're not anointed. Jenny and Max know that. Nature *herself* is the anointed. They're the new masters now, but they are also *guardians*."

"But I love you! I love music! I love Lenore! People deserve to be fulfilled!"

"I'm just doing what I have to do, Ella. There is no fulfillment for anyone, or animals, or plants, or *anything* when there's *too many* of anything, including people. Too many people playing tunes just creates noise, very dark and unbalanced noise. But play your tune, Ella. I'm playing mine. That's all we can do. You're the Master, but like everyone else, all you can do is play your tune."

The smoke that was Brandon swirled from my embrace and descended back into his body. Bryson unfroze and Brandon ripped back the plastic barrier from the doorway, letting the dogs into the CRISPR lab. They stood at attention like troops controlled by a distant general. Bryson and Brandon scooped out the petri dishes with their gloved hands and spread the gooey and deadly contents onto the thick coats of the subjects. The dogs waited but danced in place anxiously. They knew what the reward was that came next – their freedom, the freedom to roam the outside world, the freedom to spread the fatal microbes and join Jenny and Mavis who will train them how to survive.

Pendelton arrived too late. He led his haz-mat security crew past my dreaming body still playing Lenore in the hallway. They forced the loyal guard to stand down and blinked their way into the lab, but all they succeeded in doing was startling the exhausted Bryson enough to stop his heart. They found Brandon outside supporting himself against the opened back gate of the dog enclosure. He was watching the dogs howling and scampering toward the cactus garden and the chaotic city beyond where they would rub themselves on every man-made object they could find until they eventually made their way to Jenny in the labyrinthine forests of the Sierras.

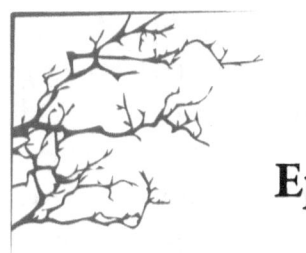

Epilogue

IT WAS EARLY MORNING in the Wandering Pines garden, and the lettuce I was trying to pick was lush and healthy. It's not easy to bend over with my belly as big as it was, but I wanted my hands in dirt every day for the health of my baby. It was nice to have Brandon out here with me. He figured the only reason he survived was because I had left the dog pen cleaning duties up to him when I bailed on the Brecken lab. That, and working so much he hardly had a chance to shower. Why I survived, I could only guess. Probably it was because of living at Schnazworthy's and swallowing her probiotics every morning for breakfast. There were no definitive answers because there were no more people around with the ability or luxury to do the research to find out. Humanity was decimated. Everyone still alive had questions, of course, but no one had answers or time to investigate theories. Somehow technology was involved. Only people who worked directly on the earth were still breathing, and the handful of us survivors were way too busy just trying to raise enough food to eat to ask too many questions.

Brandon was up early with me feeding the chickens and checking the traps. I don't like traps. Too technological, I think, but the neighbors down the way use them and haven't gotten sick. Brandon argued that I needed more protein in

my diet than just pigs and chickens. His theory is that tech
illness has to do with concrete, not metal, so I reluctantly go
along with him when he traps and roasts a deer. After all,
he was part of the team that brought the microbe into existence. He probably knows more about it than anyone alive.

Brandon insists that that part, the sensitivity-to-technol-
ogy part, had to do with quantum alteration for a better
world not with the CRISPR. He thinks it came from either
from the monk's chants, or from Jenny's communication
with the subjects, or maybe even from that last time I played
Lenore outside the lab when I tried to stop the release. No
one really knows. It could even just be electricity that activates the microbial pathology, although the lightning storms
so common these days don't seem to make people die. Whatever the relationship is between the microbes and humans in
the modern world, it spared no one whose lives were spent in
cars and buildings. All the computer watchers, stock traders,
truck drivers, oil field workers, sailors, teachers, store owners perished. The engines of planetary destruction shut down
completely in the two months it took for the microbes to
spread by touch and air to every corner of the world. Only
the poorest of the poor, subsistence farmers living on the
fringes, the ones scratching out a meager living from the
undamaged soil too inconvenient for the corporate tractors
managed to survive. Then the second wave of deaths hit. The
smart ones, the survivors who noticed that their neighbors
who fell to the temptation of living in the abandoned buildings and driving the abandoned cars were the ones who kept
on dying, just hunkered down and kept going, kept their
hands in the earth and gave humble thanks for being alive.

The memory of Schnazworthy makes me hope that she and Charlie survived. It's likely, although I'm pretty sure Lawrence didn't have a chance, surrounded as he was by his computers and sterile lifestyle. I hope they are smart enough to move their garden outside. There's no way to know for sure, of course. Electronic communication existed as only a memory now, and it's a long horse ride to Tennessee. When I play Lenore, sometimes I think I hear Charlie's guitar strumming in the background, but it could just be my imagination. Was it my imagination that I once flew a private jet to Hawaii and to Tennessee? Seems so unreal to me now.

I stretched my sore back and looked up at the blue sky devoid of contrails. Soon I will give birth in our cabin, and the population of Wandering Pines will grow by five percent. It's not formally a school anymore, of course, although we all learn from each other and there was a decent library. There were still a few young people, ones who were allowed to play in the mud all the time, so there would be a future for humans here, we hoped. The serious horse people and the garden people, of course, survived. No one could ever get their hands unhealthfully clean doing those activities. Everyone else here caught the twenty-four hour death. There were too many to bury. The survivors designated a canyon for the remains and used horses to drag the corpses there for the turkey vultures. We visited the mounds each Sunday like Buddhist monks to pay our respects and remind ourselves of the fleetingness of life.

We're the only ones at Wandering Pines now who came from the outside. We arrived on horseback six months after the culling, so they knew we were immune and let us in. Besides, we're legends here. It feels like home to live here again. We celebrated our first year back last weekend with a bluegrass hoedown in the dining hall like old times. There were a few new bluegrass players coming on strong besides Brandon and me. We played informally almost every night since there are no holovids to watch on phoneglasses anymore. Lenore lets me be just a plain old intermediate fiddler when I play now, at least most of the time.

I've picked enough lettuce for the day, but I didn't call for Brandon quite yet. I wanted to just look at him working for a while. He's still trying to put on weight since the beating he took at Brecken and all the physical effort it took to get here and just to live. I was mad at him for a long while, and he got pretty sick after the culling, but he survived, maybe because of exposure to the microbes before they got CRISPERed, and I'm glad I stuck with him because we never would have managed the horses and the long ride down here if it hadn't been for his understanding of big animals. I still remember the stench of rotting bodies in Brecken Vista and the gratitude of the horses for helping them find a way out of there. They were thoroughbreds from a Brecken mansion. The surviving stable hand was happy to let us have them since he had way too many to take care of after everybody around him died.

Brandon and I had a lot of time to talk things through on our journey south. Maybe I still thought he and Bryson could have acted differently, but he argued that if they hadn't done it, somebody else was bound to, and he's probably right. In any case, there's no going back now. It's Jenny's world now, and we're just lucky to be in the first generation to witness the healing. And it's a world with a person I deeply love still in it, so I count my blessings. He's gathering eggs now. I took a deep breath and decided I could wash the lettuce now and then walk back to the kitchen with him.

As I opened the valve to let the stream water flow over my harvest, I wondered if my Dad was still alive way up north. I think there's a good chance he was, although I'm almost certain my mom must have perished. Maybe someday the population will grow enough that a safe way to deliver mail by horses will develop. I hope so, and I hope that someday he can join us here and be a grandfather to my baby. Grandparents are really important, I think. I still feel my grandfather's love when I play Lenore.

Brandon probably knows I sometimes sneak out at night when the moon is full to play Lenore alone near the canyon of corpses. What he doesn't know is that Jenny's pups, now full grown, come to me there sometimes to listen. They give me scents and glimpses of their lives, their love for nature, their guardianship over everything my species so sorely neglected. At least I hope they are the ones guarding things. Brandon and I don't really know who the masters are anymore. Things evolve and change. All we know is that it is not us anymore, and that's really just fine. We humans had our chance.

When I play there by the skulls and bones in the moonlight, Jenny's pups don't get too close, and I can't blame them considering what she and Max must have told them about the human species, but I hope she also told them the good things, how we loved them and helped them find their destiny and freedom. I imagine with fondness that I am a bit of a grandparent figure to them, and that Lenore and I might enter into their family lore like my grandfather entered into mine. I don't know why Jenny herself doesn't come to visit. I keep hoping. Maybe she's getting too old and tired. Death catches up with all of us eventually, but I still know, as I'm sure Jenny must know, that if we live in tune with nature's laws and rhythms, we sometimes get the chance to fly high enough with the tunes of Lenore to feel a bit of paradise.

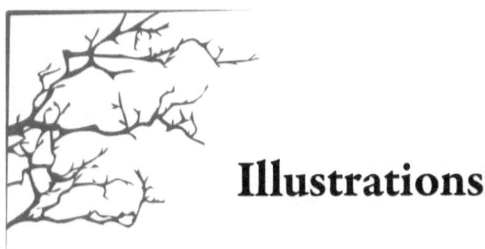

Illustrations

ALL THE ILLUSTRATIONS in this novel were suggested by my late golden retriever, Jenny, by my daughter's kitty, Lyca, and by Google's Advanced Search Engine filtered by "free to use or share, even commercially." Much heartfelt gratitude is extended to the artists and photographers for generously sharing their work in this manner.

Acknowledgments

I WOULD LIKE TO GRATEFULLY acknowledge my spouse and partner, Kate Mulligan, whose support in innumerable ways has made this novel possible.

Other books by J.T. Blossom

THE TUNES OF LENORE (2019), *Trespassing* (2018), *Horse Boys* (2017), *The Last Football Player* (2023), *Mahina Rises* (Coming 2023 - 2024), and *To Be Or Not To Be* (Coming 2024) Visit **JTBlossom.com** for more information and other works.

About the Author

Mr. Blossom holds a BA degree in English from Carleton College and an MAT degree from Colorado College. Teacher and artist, Mr. Blossom concerns himself deeply with technology and environmental issues and feels there is hope to create a better world through the power of stories to change hearts and minds. He presently lives on an organic farm on the Big Island of Hawaii where he gives away fruits and vegetables and maintains an active free library at the end of his driveway.

Read more at https://www.jtblossom.com.